THE BRATVA'S BABY: A DARK MAFIA ROMANCE

(Wicked Doms)

JANE HENRY

Copyright 2019 by Jane Henry

Cover design by PopKitty

Photography by Paul Henry Serres

Chapter One

Kazimir

The wrought iron park bench I sit on is ice cold, but I hardly feel it. I'm too intent on waiting for the girl to arrive. The Americans think this weather is freezing, but I grew up in the bitter cold of northern Russia. The cold doesn't touch me. The ill-prepared people around me pull their coats tighter around their bodies and tighten their scarves around their necks. For a minute, I wonder if they're shielding themselves from me, and not the icy wind.

If they knew what I've done... what I'm capable of... what I'm planning to do... they'd do more than cover their necks with scarves.

I scowl into the wind. I hate cowardice.

But this girl... this girl I've been commissioned to

take as mine. Despite outward appearances, she's no coward. And that intrigues me.

Sadie Ann Warren. Twenty-one years old. Fine brown hair, plain and mousy but fetching in the way it hangs in haphazard waves around her round face. Light brown eyes, pink cheeks, and full lips.

I wonder what she looks like when she cries. When she smiles. I've never seen her smile.

She's five-foot-one and curvy, though you wouldn't know it from the way she dresses in thick, bulky, black and gray muted clothing. I know her dress size, her shoe size, her bra size, and I've already ordered the type of clothing she'll wear for me. I smile to myself, and a woman passing by catches the smile. It must look predatory, for her step quickens.

Sadie's nondescript appearance makes her easily meld into the masses as a nobody, which is perhaps exactly what she wants.

She has no friends. No relatives. And she has no idea that she's worth millions.

Her boss, the ancient and somewhat senile head librarian of the small-town library where she works won't even realize she hasn't shown up for work for several days. My men will make sure her boss is well distracted yet unharmed. Sadie's abduction, unlike the ones I've orchestrated in the past, will be an easy one. If trouble arises eventually, we'll fake her death.

It's almost as if it was meant to be. No one will know she's gone. No one will miss her. She's the perfect target.

I sip my bitter, steaming black coffee and watch as she makes her way up to the entrance of the library. It's eight-thirty a.m. precisely, as it is every other day she goes to work. She arrives half an hour early, prepares for the day, then opens the doors at nine. Sadie is predictable and routinized, and I like that. The trademark of a woman who responds well to structure and expectations. She'll easily conform to my standards... eventually.

To my left, a small cluster of girls giggles but quiets when they draw closer to me. They're college-aged, or so. I normally like women much younger than I am. They're more easily influenced, less jaded to the ways of men. These women, though, are barely women. Compared to Sadie's maturity, they're barely more than girls. I look away, but can feel their eyes taking me in, as if they think I'm stupid enough to not know they're staring. I'm wearing a tan work jacket, worn jeans, and boots, the ones I let stay scuffed and marked as if I'm a construction worker taking a break. With my large stature, I attract attention of the female variety wherever I go. It's better I look like a worker, an easy role to assume. No one would ever suspect what my real work entails.

The girls pass me and it grates on my nerves how they resume their giggling. Brats. Their fathers shouldn't let them out of the house dressed the way they are, especially with the likes of me and my brothers prowling the streets. It's freezing cold and yet they're dressed in thin skirts, their legs bare, open jackets revealing cleavage and tight little nipples showing straight through the thin fabric of their slutty tops. My palm itches to spank some sense into their little asses. I flex my hand.

It's been way, way too long since I've had a woman to punish.

Control.

Master.

These girls are too young and silly for a man like me.

Sadie is perfect.

My cock hardens with anticipation, and I shift on my seat.

I know everything about her. She pays her meager bills on time, and despite her paltry wage, contributes to the local food pantry with items bought with coupons she clips and sale items she purchases. Money will never be a concern for her again, but I like that she's fastidious. She reads books during every free moment of time she has, some non-fiction, but most historical romance books. That amuses me about her. She dresses like an amateur nun, but her heroines dress in swaths of silk and jewels. She carries a hard-covered book with her in the bag she holds by her side, and guards it with her life. During her break time, before bed, and when she first wakes up in the morning, she writes in it. I don't know yet what she writes, but I will. She does something with needles and yarn, knitting or something. I enjoy watching her weave fabric with the vibrant threads.

She fidgets when she's near a man, especially attractive, powerful men. Men like me.

I've never seen her pick up a cell phone or talk to a friend. She's a loner in every sense of the word.

I went over the plan again this morning with Dimitri.

Capture the girl.

Marry her.

Take her inheritance.

Get rid of her.

I swallow another sip of coffee and watch Sadie through the sliding glass doors of the library.- Today she's wearing an ankle-length navy skirt that hits the tops of her shoes, and she's wrapped in a bulky gray cardigan the color of dirty dishwater. I imagine stripping the clothes off of her and revealing her creamy, bare, unblemished skin. My dick gets hard when I imagine marking her pretty pale skin. Teeth marks. Rope marks. Reddened skin and puckered flesh, christened with hot wax and my palm. I'll punish her for the sin of hiding a body like hers. She won't be allowed to with me.

She's so little. So virginal. An unsullied canvas.

"Enjoy your last taste of freedom, little girl," I whisper to myself before I finish my coffee. I push myself to my feet and cross the street.

It's time she met her future master.

Chapter Two

Sadie

I breathe in the comforting, familiar scent of well-worn books and newsprint, and sigh. The anxiety I struggle with assaults me and begins its insidious attack whenever I leave the library. When I return, the smells and sights soothe me. My frayed nerves calm.

I knew from a very young age that I would want to work in a library one day. I discovered books as a means of escape when I was six years old, living in the abusive foster home that mars my memory like an ink stain. The family I stayed with could barely afford to clothe their own children, much less me, and I was treated like little more than a servant. One day, when I failed to serve breakfast on time to her screaming baby, Mrs. Enry locked me in the second-floor closet. There I found a stack of books likely forgotten by the previous owners, for I knew Mr. and Mrs. Enry never bothered to read. Some of the words were too big for me, and I still trailed my index finger along the lines like I was reading primers, but eventually I learned to escape into my books.

I'd learned to read in school, but the books we had there were simple and dull, likely chosen for emergent readers and not for someone like me. I picked up a copy of *Little Women*, read it in a day, and never looked back.

My books are my friends. They take me on journeys to places I'll never travel. My friends know what I think, what I feel, what I long for.

I was in eighth grade by the time I discovered romance novels, and by high school, my fantasies took an entirely different direction.

Scottish highlanders. Swashbuckling pirates. Earls and lairds and scoundrels. They sweep me off my feet, and I dream about the type of romance I find in these pages. It's easier knowing these stories don't take place in the modern world. I can fantasize about being dressed in the gowns of the era. Wearing the dainty shoes. Being wooed by a rogue. When we have the library book sales, I sneak in early and buy all the books I can priced at only twenty-five cents. When I'm given a budget to order books for the library, I order all the new books from the catalog. They come in, I enter them into our system, then I'm the first one to check them out. Today, a new shipment's arrived.

I glide a finger along the raised golden edge of the title. I fan the pages and inhale the scent of fresh ink. I sigh in contentment when I think about how good it will be to lose myself in these pages. I'm so lost in thought, I don't notice anyone arrive until his deep, masculine voice arrests me.

"Excuse me?"

I stifle a squeal of surprise at the sound of his voice and look into the most mesmerizing brown eyes I've ever seen. I blink. He's so beautiful, it's intimidating.

Though he wears a jacket, I can tell he's muscled and strong. His hair is roguishly long and so dark brown it's nearly black, a little unruly, and he sports a heavy, dark-brown beard. High cheekbones underscore the depth of his eyes. He's got the blood of kings in his veins, and I half expect him to speak a foreign language.

I blink dumbly for a moment before I find my voice.

"Yes, sir?"

My cheeks heat. It's uncustomary for us to call our patrons *sir* or *ma'am* but there's something about the way he looks at me that makes me instantly respect him. When he smiles, revealing white teeth and full lips, my belly gives a little flip. His brown eyes dance at me.

He speaks in an accent I can't quite detect. Something European? "Can you help me find the biography section? There are several I'm looking for."

His accent gives him an air of power that takes me by surprise. He's a man fit to rule armies. Fight battles. He'd look every bit at home dressed in a soldier's uniform wielding a sword and commanding his men to victory as he does here. Perhaps more so.

"Oh, yes," I tell him. "Of course. Which do you want? Allow me to see what we have."

I ignore the trembling of my hands while I type the names he gives me into our search database. I should be able to handle a man looking at me. I shouldn't let it scatter my nerves and mess with my head.

I really should read fewer romance novels.

When I locate the books, my stomach drops. I forgot our catalog system lists the biographies at the very back. Though few people come here at this time of day, this section of the library is completely isolated. I usually escort our patrons to find the books they're looking for, but I don't want to be alone with him.

"It's in the 900s, and easy to get to," I tell him, feeling the heat of my cheeks travel all the way to my neck. I can't be alone. Not with him. I don't trust myself not to make a fool of myself.

"Ah," he says. "I see. Thank you." But he doesn't go.

I swallow. I really need to control my imagination. My hand travels to my throat and my fingers graze the tender skin.

"Yes, sir." Damn. There's that *sir* again.

He smiles, making my belly warm and my breasts tingle. God, I'm a mess. I inwardly scold myself for being such a fool.

"Your name?" he asks.

"Sadie," I whisper.

"Sadie," he repeats. Oh I like hearing him say my name. "Show me, please?" Though he asks me, it sounds more like a command.

No. He wants me to walk with him. I groan inwardly.

"It's very easy to find," I stammer, which isn't quite true. I'm trying to dismiss him, and I fear I sound rude. The biographies are fairly hidden. I wave my hand in the direction of the of the back of the library. "Just all the way down, take a left at the elevator, then a right at the periodicals. It's the fourth section on the right, behind the local maps."

He raises a brow, and I'm not sure if it's my imagination, but his look grows a bit stern, and when he speaks, there's an edge of austerity that makes my heartbeat race. My cheeks flame.

"Are you too busy to take me there?" His lips thin, and he crosses his arms on his chest, raising a brow questioningly. The simple question feels like a scolding, but any correction I've gotten before never made my pulse race like this.

"Of course not, sir," I rasp in a voice just above a whisper. "I—I'll take you." Do I have a choice?

He graces me with a smile that warms me through. "Very good," he says, his voice lowering just a bit. "You're a very good girl."

I like how that makes me feel, and I smile softly to myself.

I grab a stack of books that need to be put away so I have something to do with my arms, but when I turn to him I promptly lose my grip. The books slip and cascade down around me, onto his feet and mine, scattering along the floor in a helpless mess.

"Oh, I'm sorry," I moan, tears pricking the backs of my eyes. I'm such an idiot. Who cries over such a stupid thing?

I swallow hard and lean down to pick up the books. He kneels and gathers the ones nearest him.

"No need to apologize," he says. "Allow me."

I can't very well sit here and watch him pick the books up on his own.

"I can help you—" I begin, but he gently grasps my wrist, just the press of a thumb and forefinger.

"I said allow me," he says, his voice lowered. My

mouth is stuffed with cotton, my head spinning in a dizzy confusion of excitement and fear.

This man is used to being obeyed.

I want to obey him.

Has he hypnotized me?

Tempering his stern gaze with a half-smile, he gives a curt shake of his head, then reaches for the book in my hand and stacks it with the rest in his left hand.

My mind reels. I've met a man out of one of my books. His commanding stature. Powerful presence. A voice that could melt ice. I'm enamored and terrified all at once.

I watch him in silence, my arms dangling awkwardly as I squat beside him, watching him collect the fallen books. I don't know how to handle being in his presence like this.

After he's stacked the books, he reaches for my hand and lifts me to my feet. Awareness courses through me at the warmth of his hand.

"You were showing me the way," he says quietly, seemingly unaffected by touching me. He points toward the back of the library.

I blink. "Yes," I murmur. Where is the poised, intelligent heroine from my novels? Haven't I read enough that I could assume the grace and dignity they possess? Clearly not.

I walk in silence next to him, and he has to slow

his strides so he doesn't walk too fast for me. My mind whirls. It's just a simple task. I shouldn't feel afraid like this, but the further we get from the entrance to the library, and the more isolated we become, the more nervous I become. The little hairs on the back of my neck rise and my skin prickles with awareness. I'm not sure why. He's done nothing to earn my distrust, and yet my instincts are warring with my need to be near him. Something inside tells me *run*.

On the one hand, I like being near him like this. He's magnificent. Handsome. And I like the attention of this beautiful, dangerous man. On the other, I can't help the instinctive desire to get away from him. My body thrums with need and pleasure while my brain screams at me in warning.

"Are we near?" he asks, taking a step closer to me. I inhale the masculine scent of expensive cologne that takes me by surprise. He's dressed in workman's clothes yet he smells like he stepped off of Wall Street. It's incongruous. Disarming.

"Yes," I whisper. "It's just three or so more rows ahead."

"We're so far away from everyone else," he says, his voice dropping to a husky whisper. He laughs. "They really hide these books."

My pulse quickens, but when I look at him, he's looking away, and not interested in me at all. My imagination is insanity. I quicken my step. He gives me a tight smile.

"Yes, here we are," I stammer. "Biographies." I nearly choke out the words. "Please, take your time."

He smiles and nods his thanks. "I will get what I came for," he says, giving me a curious look, "and then I'll help you put that stack of books away." He places the stack down beside him and nods to the books. "Leave them until I'm finished here."

No. I need to get away from him. I can't handle my loss of control while in his presence.

I go to protest but the look he gives me makes my words freeze on my lips. As if bewitched by his power, I have to obey him. I stare at the books, trying to compose myself, but my gaze wanders. I watch as he peruses the titles and carefully chooses a few.

Stalin.

Lenin.

Robespierre.

"Light bit of bedtime reading," I murmur before I clamp my mouth shut. I didn't mean to say that.

His brows rise heavenward and his lips tip up, but the smile doesn't meet his eyes. He's surprised. Curious.

"Revolutionaries," he murmurs respectfully. "They were the greats."

"Some were terrible, though," I say, curious about who he is and why he admires tyrants.

He looks with interest at the books in his hand. "Some of the most powerful leaders we've ever known have been terrible," he says, before he places the books under his arm and bends to take my stack as well. I don't offer to help this time, though I want to.

"Show me where these go," he instructs. I show him, and he lets me put some away. If he notices the trembling in my hands, he doesn't let on that he does. When we're done, he follows me to the front and checks his books out. I glance at the name on his library card, but it's smudged and illegible.

"Kazimir," he says, when he catches me staring at his card.

I raise curious eyes to his. "Excuse me?"

"My name," he says, those eyes smiling at me. "Pleased to meet you, Sadie. Thank you for your help. Until tomorrow." He reaches for my hand and gives me a brief shake, before he leaves.

I stare at his retreating form and wonder what on Earth just happened.

Maybe I'll be sick tomorrow.

I think of him as I go about my duties. When I begin my latest Highlander romance, I read in rapt attention, as this hero sounds a lot like Kazimir, with his heavy beard and commanding presence. I'm somehow both intrigued and afraid of the tall, stern man who looks like he could've descended from the leaders of old. Sometimes I let my imagination get the better of me, and as I drift off to sleep, I wonder when I'll see him again.

I consider not going into work the next day, but when the sun rises, in the light of day, I realize how foolish that is. I get very few vacation days, and I can't take a day off because of a maybe visit from a patron.

When I open the library the next day, he isn't there. I feel simultaneously let-down and relieved.

He was just a patron, I tell myself. Not unlike the dozens and dozens of people who grace the doors of this place every hour.

Except… he is unlike every one of them. I know there's something different about him. Something dangerous. Powerful. Mesmerizing.

I stock the shelves as I normally do. Check out books and talk with my boss. Answer the phone calls and research the latest bestsellers we need to order for our shelves.

But I make mistakes. I lose my train of thought. I accidentally order ten copies of a book I meant to order once.

I shake my head and get to my feet. It's nearly lunch time, and I need to get some fresh air. When I leave the library, I inhale deeply, needing to cleanse my thoughts. I can't let myself get derailed like this.

I'm not even sure where I'm going, but when I find myself outside the nearest coffee shop, I take a tentative step in. I never come in here. There's free coffee and tea in the break room at the library, so it feels indulgent to purchase a cup for myself now. I really can't even afford to splurge on a four-dollar cup of coffee with the bills I have this month, but when the woman standing behind the counter sees me, she smiles, and I take a step toward her.

"What can I get you?" she asks.

I mumble something off the menu, and don't even realize I'm ordering a specialty drink. It costs more than I'm expecting, so I fumble in my bag for loose change, my hands trembling because I'm embarrassed. I don't belong in a place like this. I try to dress in a way that doesn't attract attention, yet being here in my long skirt and thick sweater sets me apart from the well-dressed business people.

My fingers finally find one last coin that I need, but a deep voice behind me grabs my attention.

"I'll get her coffee."

I know it's him before I turn to look. The moment I hear him, my body reacts. My breathing hitches and my pulse accelerates. My cheeks warm, and there's a strange tingling sensation along the back of my neck.

I turn to face him and smile in a way that I hope appears casual.

"Good morning," I say. "Thank you."

Today he's dressed in the same work clothes he wore the day before. His hair's still damp from a shower, and he runs his fingers quickly through it before he smiles back at me.

"Good morning, Sadie. Enjoy your coffee." He takes the cup of coffee from the girl behind the counter, hands it to me, and to my disappointment, leaves.

I take the coffee and stare off at him.

"He's beautiful, isn't he?" says a voice to my right. I turn startled eyes to see a young woman dressed to perfection in a navy business suit and heels, staring after him.

"Yes," I reply in surprise.

She smiles sadly. "Beautiful and dangerous, like a prowling lion." She looks to me. "You must be a special girl," she says. "He never speaks to anyone. And yet for you, he called you by name and bought you coffee." She sips from the cup in her hand while she scans my worn, drab clothing, my hair twisted into a bun at the nape of my neck, my pale, makeup-free face.

"He's come in here every day for a week," she says. "It's interesting. There isn't a construction job for miles." She takes another sip of coffee then stares off toward the doorway. "I wonder why."

Then her gaze comes back to mine and she sobers.

"Are you related?"

I shake my head dumbly. I know why she asked. Surely a man who looks like a god wouldn't have a romantic interest in a girl like me.

"Well, finish your drink," she says. "It's not every day a man like him buys you a drink." She gives me a wink and leaves.

I take a sip from my cup and look out the door. I wonder if he'll come back. But he doesn't. I decide to head back to the library oddly disappointed, but curious.

Why does he come here? Where did he come from?

On my way back to the library, I enjoy my coffee, but I'm plagued with curiosity. Who is this mysterious stranger?

Chapter Three

Kazimir

My plan was to get her to fall for me. Seduce her, as it were. I can get what I want from her by force, or I can do it with seduction.

I prefer both.

But when Dimitri calls me, he explains the need for me to come home sooner than later. When the *Pakhan* gives an order, we obey. He's our leader. The father of our group. A man who rules with an iron fist but pledges loyalty to the men beneath him. In turn, we swear our allegiance to him.

He rescued me when I was a poor boy on the streets of Moscow. He took me in. Raised me as his own. He taught me the ways of the Bratva.

Over the years, I've risen in stature and power, the

Brigadier. I'm the commander of our small army, the one who assigns jobs, oversees their completion, and pays tribute to our *Pakhan.* I assure Dimitri of our loyalty with fastidious adherence to his expectations. Any man who steps a toe out of line in obedience to Dimitri answers to me.

So when Dimitri tells me to jump, I ask how high.

"*Prikhodite seychas,*" he orders, *come now,* in the familiar harsh yet harmonic language of my homeland. There's no more time to dawdle. He continues, explaining to me that circumstances have changed and he needs me here. I frown but nod, even though he can't see me. This was not how I wanted to orchestrate her abduction. I had a plan, and it was working perfectly, stunned by my attention and eager for more. My plan was to slowly goad her toward the trap I set, but now I'll have to act more aggressively.

I glance at the clock and note that she's off of work in just under half an hour. My plan was to take her to a fancy restaurant. Ply her with wine. Speak to her of the things that are on her mind. Ask questions about herself and feign interest in what interests her.

I don't have time for the slow seduction now. I curse to myself as I think about my options.

She's out of money for the week and will have little to eat until she's paid next Thursday. In her home, she has several packages of noodles, some bread, and peanut butter but nothing more.

Poverty I can work with. Obedience will be harder.

But I know my way with a woman like her, and I always get what I want.

Chapter Four

Sadie

I'm punching the time clock when a shadow darkens the doorway behind me. My heartbeat quickens when I recognize his profile.

"Kazimir," I greet him, startled. "You scared me."

He leans against the doorframe. "I'm sorry," he says with a smile. His voice is soft but deep and husky as it carries across the quiet room. "I didn't mean to frighten you. I wondered if you had dinner plans tonight?"

I nearly drop the books I'm holding. I checked out a couple that I planned on reading tonight.

"Dinner?" I ask stupidly. No one's ever asked me out. Is this a date?

I look down at my clothing, dotted in dust. Today

I spent time dusting the archives, and I must look a sight. "I... do I have time to go home to change?"

"No need," he says with a smile, his piercing eyes giving me a quick look over. "Nothing fancy, really."

Well, then.

"Alright," I say, but the words of the woman in the coffee shop come back to me.

Beautiful and dangerous.

It's an apt description. A prowling lion, predatory and powerful.

Am I making a mistake?

But when he reaches for the books in my hand and takes them into his, then smiles in that way that makes my tummy flip, I silence the doubts in my mind. I won't let my imagination get the better of me. Not this time.

"Where are we going?" I ask, trying to keep calm and not act silly like I did the day before.

"Oh, I have a place in mind."

We leave the library and talk easily to one another. He asks about the books I'm reading, and I tell him about the book of Irish poetry I checked out a few days before. I omit mention of the romance I'm reading. It feels so silly and frivolous around him. He doesn't miss anything, though.

"But that isn't all you're reading," he says, with a look both curious and corrective. "What else is there?"

"Oh," I say, flushing. "There's—well, I read romance."

"Mhm," he says. He leads me into a tavern and the smell of steak and potatoes makes my belly churn with hunger. "Tell me."

"It's silly," I say, shaking my head, but he merely looks at me. Waiting.

And so I do. I go on and on about my books while he orders us drinks and dinner. The wine is pink and sweet, and tastes so good after the long day I've had. Soon, a large platter with a sizzling steak, baked potato, and wilted spinach sits in front of me. I look up at him in surprise. I was so busy talking I didn't notice he ordered for me. He never asked me what I wanted.

My mouth waters.

He waves a fork at my dish. "Eat," he instructs, slicing into his own steak. I'm normally self-conscious but somehow, he puts me at ease.

I eat ravenously as he plies me with wine. He asks me about my family and friends, and I'm getting comfortable with him. I tell him I have no family and no friends to speak of.

"My books are my friends," I tell him, laughing easily when I drink the third glass of wine. Now it doesn't seem so sad and lonely when I'm relaying my life to him. I'm warm and comfortable with a full belly.

He asks about school and college, laughs at all the right places, and goes strangely quiet and brooding when I tell him how I was bullied in school.

"Bullied?" he asks. "Tell me."

And I do. He commands, and I respond. It feels easy. Almost natural. Feeling freer to speak of the past now that I've had my wine, I tell him about foster care and moving schools and about the way some of the kids I went to school with treated me.

"Children can be cruel," he says with a scowl. "I'd like to see any of them treat you that way when you are with me."

I blink, surprised. "I'd like to see that, too," I say with a smile.

But he closes his mouth as if he's said too much. When he tears the roll in his hand in two, crumbs spray onto the plate. He takes a savage bite and chews the bread in silence, swallows it with a large pull from his drink, then waves a hand and gives me a forced smile. His sudden anger surprises me and I almost sober, but not quite.

"Tell me more about you."

He asks about my hobbies and interests. But the whole time we talk, he tells me nothing of himself. We talk about literature and movies, and what sorts of music we listen to. He's an animated conversationalist, and I'm highly entertained with everything he says. I continue to ask him questions about himself to the point where it's borderline rude, but he deflects most of them.

"Where are you from?" I ask him.

"Moscow," he says, slicing into his steak.

"How long have you been here?" I ask, sipping my wine.

"Oh, a while," he says, before he waves the waiter down and asks for the check.

I avert my eyes when he takes the check, and whisper a thank you. This dinner cost more than I can afford, but I don't want to seem silly or foolish, so I keep my thoughts to myself while he pays. I'm sleepy from the wine, and pleasantly full of food.

My head feels a little fuzzy and heavy. I wonder if I've had too much wine. I'm suddenly sleepy. So sleepy. I drop my fork and look up at him.

"I'm very tired," I say to him, disappointed. I like how I feel when I'm with him now. I don't want our night to end. "Will you take me home?"

"Are you alright?" he asks, leaning across the table. I nod, blinking my eyes furiously to keep them open. I'm vaguely aware of him standing, taking out his wallet, and removing a stack of bills. He tosses some on the table and reaches for me.

"Come, now, Sadie," he says in his deep, accented voice. I look at the large hand offered to me, and wonder. What does he see in me? What could possibly interest him in a boring, dowdy, far younger woman like me?

"Thank you," I tell him, my eyes growing so heavy with sleep.

I'm so tired, I slouch against his arm, and he half-drags me out of the restaurant and to his car. The door clicks open and he slides me into the seat. My head falls to the side and my eyes close.

"It's warm in here," I tell him. "Very comfort-able." But I'm asleep before I hear his reply.

When I wake, I blink in surprise. I don't know where I am, and sudden fear hits my chest with a surge of adrenaline.

Am I dreaming? Or am I awake?

What happened?

My head hurts and my eyelids are heavy. It takes an effort to pry them open.

I blink, but it's so dark I see nothing but inky blackness. Panic wells in my chest when I try to move my limbs. I'm bound with something, my wrists and ankles locked tight. I open my mouth to scream but there's a gag in place. I scream and scream against the gag, but all that comes out is a muffled garble.

I close my eyes and will myself to still. I need to

find out where I am and what's going on. Panicking won't help me.

Where am I?

I fell asleep. In Kazimir's car.

He drove me, and I fell asleep.

Did he drug me? He must have, as I almost passed out after the dinner. I want to groan, but I stifle the need. I've been stupid and naïve. So stupid.

A door opens and light floods the room. I blink, momentarily blinded. Harsh voices speak to one another in a foreign language. My breathing stills. I recognize Kazimir's voice but I don't understand what he's saying. I want to scream and cry. It was all pretend. He meant nothing.

A man steps over to me. I blink up at him, and when he meets my eyes, he scowls. He's wearing a knit cap and a black coat, a muffler pulled over his mouth, but all I see are his cruel black eyes.

He spits something out in Russian, and there's a scuffle of footsteps, then Kazimir looms into view. I don't know Russian, but whatever he says to the man has him scurrying away so the two of us are alone. I look at his eyes when he stands over me and quickly look away when they blur with tears.

He betrayed me. But there's no repentance in his gaze. My pulse races when I realize this was what he intended all along. He's scowling and stern when he bends down to pick me up, and his

The Bratva's Baby: A Dark Mafia Romance

accent is thicker than I've ever heard, barely intelligible.

"Do not fight me," he says. "No screaming or flailing. You do exactly what I say."

Even when he was friendly I knew he was a man to be obeyed.

He stands with me in his arms easily and walks toward the exit. Where are we going? My breath goes ragged and my eyes water. I'm helpless and terrified, trying to talk but the gag muffles the sounds I make.

"Silence, Sadie," he growls, walking with large, purposeful strides. But I can't. I can't stop trying to stop him. I shake and twist, trying to get away, begging and pleading against the gag because I don't know where I am or where we're going, but I know if he takes me, there will be no coming back. I can't let him do this.

A man behind him mutters in Russian, and Kazimir swivels to give him a piercing look. He rasps out a few sharp words. The large man challenging him bows his head like a chastened puppy and walks away. Kazimir commands this group of men, and I'm at his mercy.

We're in the dark, cold night, but the moonlight glances off the gleaming silver body of a plane.

No.

Panic explodes in my chest as Kazimir takes us closer.

No.

I've never been on a plane. They terrify me. And I know in my gut that if he takes me on that plane, I'll never escape. Without contact with the familiar, I'll be his prisoner. Maybe I already am. The knowledge makes tears leak from my eyes. I double my efforts, shaking and twisting, trying to scream, but I can't get away.

With a growl, he flips me over his shoulder and his large palm smacks my backside once, twice, three times.

"I said no fighting," he says. "You are mine now, Sadie. You will obey me."

I'm quickly subdued by shock with the rapid spanking he gives me.

Shocked into reluctant submission.

Chapter Five

Kazimir

My timid librarian isn't so subdued anymore when she sees the plane, but her flailing body responds to my correction. My palm tingles from spanking her shapely bottom, and the brief correction ignites in me the desire to punish her more. Harder. Harsher. I inhale the cool air deeply, and control my impulses. There will be time to train her. First, I get her home.

Her little body trembles over my shoulder and I tighten my grip. I will not coddle her, but her submission is for her own good.

When I begin the ascent toward the plane, she flails again.

"Enough," I rasp out. She stills. "You will come with me."

All she can do is moan, her speaking silenced by the gag. My men stand at attention, ready for my command. One eyes her shapely form over my shoulder, but a sharp look makes him tear his eyes away. None of them will touch her. None will even look at her. Sadie belongs to me.

At the top of the flight of stairs leading to the plane, I slide her down so I can cradle her in my arms, the heat of her body pressed up against mine making my stomach tighten. I hold her close, clutching her arms. A warning to obey that feels much too similar to an embrace. When her eyes meet mine, I read more than fear. If I take her gag off, she'll assault me with a litany of profanity from her virgin mouth. I'd have to punish her if she swore at me, and space is limited on a plane like this, so for now she'll remain gagged.

I slide my palm against her scalp and weave my fingers through her hair. Gripping. Warning. I inhale the scent of her fear and sweet feminine innocence. I want to take her mouth with mine until her knees buckle.

At the tight pull, she stills. I glide my second palm to the small of her back. So delicate. So fragile. I want to lick that sacred place and mark her. I swallow hard and issue a ragged command.

"Be a good little girl and no harm will come to you." My accent thickens when I'm aroused. "There will be time to teach you your place, and I can be an exacting master. But for now, obey and you will find our trip easier to endure."

Though she's silenced, her eyes communicate two words very clearly.

Fuck you.

If she stated those words, I'd have to punish her. The gag, for now, is for her own good.

"You want to curse me out," I tell her. "The sooner you learn your place, the better it will be for you."

I turn to face the men outside who wait like soldiers for my command.

"Come," I instruct in English. While they obey, I carry her to the back of the plane, drop her into a seat, and buckle her in. I unfasten her cuffs and give her a look that dares her to defy me. But I don't take my place beside her yet. I need to be sure everything goes according to plan.

Though it's dark out, bright lighting outside the small window illuminates what I need to see. Luggage secure and fastened, neatly packed and tucked under our aircraft. Our pilot sits up front with his co-pilot, silent and ready to obey. We pay him amply for the work he does. He asks no questions.

I have two men traveling home with me under my command: Demyan and Maksym, as twin brothers Filip and Vladak will travel apart from us since they have work to attend to before coming home. Each have various roles of support in our small army of brothers, though Filip and Vladak are the only blood relatives.

Demyan sits to the left of Sadie. With his blond hair and blue eyes, he attracts the ladies easily, but he never settles down. The lives that we live are dangerous, and our lifelong allegiance to the brotherhood of the Bratva means most of us choose not to raise a family. Maksym, Demyan's closest companion, as both of them are the main protection in our brotherhood, is the one exception to the rule. He's broad and heavily bearded with long hair and black eyes that often grow wistful, likely thinking of the woman he's left at home.

All men pay tribute to Dimitri, the father of our group, and all men defer to my authority.

Sadie observes everything, but my instinct says she's only observing every detail she can. At this stage, she's likely plotting her escape. An attempt would be futile, but I still expect her to try.

The five of us men converse in rapid-fire Russian. I watch the frustration in her eyes when she realizes she can't understand a word we say.

Demyan mutters something about Dimitri being pleased we left on time, and says the girl looks compliant enough. With a jeer, he makes a comment about sharing our loot and wares when we return.

Maksym's jaw clenches. He always has a soft spot for any girl under our command or instruction,

The Bratva's Baby: A Dark Mafia Romance

and I give Demyan a look that makes him immediately silence.

"The girl is mine," I tell him in Russian. "You do not look at her. You do not touch her." I give him a piercing look. "Am I clear?"

His face pales when he nods and mutters, "Yes. I'm sorry."

I instruct them all to settle down and stay seated until we're allowed up, allowing the anger that flared through me at his insinuation dissipate. We've covered all manner of business, and soon will undertake the ten-hour trip we have ahead of us. It's evening, and I wish for Sadie to rest as much as she can.

The sole attendant that meets our needs during air travel joints us in the back with a small cart of food and drinks after I escort Sadie to use the restroom. Once she's comfortable, she'll be seated by me. I order a drink for me and one for Sadie, remembering her fondness for wine back in the restaurant. She shakes her head when I offer it to her, and for a brief moment I consider allowing her to decline. But I only have ten hours to teach her. To begin her training. Neglecting to make her obey now would not be in her best interest.

I remove her gag with a quick tug and scowl my disapproval for her defiance. "Abstaining is not an option."

Her face registers surprise with her raised brows and parted lips. "Excuse me?"

37

"You must sleep tonight, so I would like you to do so as easily as possible. The wine will help us avoid harsher sedatives. Drink."

"You drugged me," she accuses.

"I had to."

She huffs out a breath and turns away from me, but I don't let that stop me. I reach for her chin and grasp it between my thumb and finger, forcing her gaze to mine. "You will do as I say, or I will punish you in front of my brothers. Is that what you wish?" I don't moderate my tone. I don't bother to hide the fact that I will punish her. Sooner or later, she will defy me and earn a punishment I'll be forced to administer. If my plan goes as expected, eventually she might like it, but she will learn to obey. She might as well learn now how little choice she has in this.

"Punish me?" she asks, her pink cheeks flushing even pinker than before. "In front of them? What... how"

She's so innocent, it's almost endearing. Almost. The fire in her eyes makes my dick hard even as I yearn to punish her. The sooner I strip her of her defiance, the sooner she submits her will to mine.

"Do you need a demonstration?"

She frowns. "You kidnapped and drugged me, and now I'm supposed to accept a drink from you like you're wining and dining me in a restaurant?"

"Yes," I tell her without apology. "Now choose. Drink or punishment."

I watch as her pouty lips thin. I can almost see her internal battle.

Leaning in, I whisper in her ear, this time only for her to hear. "You have a choice, Sadie. Have a drink, or I take you across my knees and punish you like a child. You'll sit on a sore backside for the rest of our trip, and know my brothers watched your chastisement, and likely it got them hard as fuck." The humiliation will likely be worse for her than the actual physical pain of my punishment. Still, I watch with interest as she grits her teeth and narrows her eyes at me. With a frown, her gaze roams the length of my body then back to my eyes, and I watch with pleasure as a faint blush colors her cheeks and neck.

"You'd spank me?"

"With pleasure."

She has much to learn.

"Fine," she finally hisses out, turning away.

I nod and hand her the drink. It isn't exactly compliance, but it'll do for now. I'm observing her every move. Her body language. She's been eyeing Maksym and Demyan since they got on the plane, and I can feel fear emanating from her like heat from a fire.

"You're afraid," I tell her. "Why?"

Blinking at me, she turns with a look of incredulity. "Excuse me? What part of normal human behavior are you unfamiliar with? You abducted me. You put me on a plane. I have no idea what you plan to do with me. In fact, I'll admit to utter confusion as I'm sure normal abductions don't typically happen the way this one did."

My instinct to teach her manners bolts through me but I temper the need to correct her physically. For now, I'll instruct her.

"What about this has been abnormal?" I ask casually, taking a sip from my drink. I know, of course, but I want to hear her take on this.

"I'm drinking wine," she says. "You've threatened to punish me, but you've otherwise not abused me. And you haven't raped me yet."

My hands clench into fists. Her eyes travel to my white-knuckled attempt at composure. The very idea of rape disgusts me, though there are men in my brigade who have no such disgust.

"You are drinking wine because you need to rest, and if I give you another sedative, you'll be groggier than I wish. When we arrive, we will make an appearance. I prefer for you to be lucid when that happens." I take another sip of my drink and let her think about what I said before I continue. "Though I have no compunction about punishment if you earn it, I will not beat you," I tell her. "In fact, my eventual goal is that you'll crave it.

The pain, at least. Eventually, you will learn to want to please me."

"Never," she hisses. "You're *delusional* and utterly arrogant."

I allow her to have her petty little tantrum. To think she still controls any of this. I dismiss the look of disgust that crosses her features. I have no doubt the very idea repulses her now, though deep down inside a part of her wonders what I have in mind. Morbid curiosity?

"I will not rape you," I repeat with a smile. "But make no mistake. I will fuck you, Sadie, and when I do, you'll like it."

"The idea of being touched by you disgusts me," she says, but her body betrays her. The pink at her cheeks and neck deepens, her pupils dilate. She's an unblemished virgin, ignorant of the pleasure I can command from her body. I'll take my time, though. I'll enjoy her while she's mine, for a little while. Permanent relationships are not for men like me, and anything beyond what I plan to use her for will destroy Dimitri's plan.

I will marry her. Obtain her inheritance. Pay my tribute to Dimitri.

Then I'll be rid of her, as women only complicate our mission.

After a while, the wine makes her eyes grow sleepy, and the hum of the plane and dimmed lights makes her eyelids droop. Her head lolls to the side, but she blinks her eyes rapidly, like a child trying to stay awake past bedtime.

"Rest," I instruct. I snap my fingers to our attendant and obtain a blanket for her. I open it and spread it across our laps, tucking it in beside her. When I touch her, she stiffens, but I ignore that. The sooner she grows comfortable with me, the better.

"Put your head on my shoulder," I order. I wait for her compliance, but she sits stiffened by my side.

"Sadie," I warn. "Do you think I don't mean what I say?" I reach for her leg and give her a warning squeeze.

Her training would be a lot easier if we had more room in the cabin. Taking her across my lap for a spanking would likely subdue her, but it could get a little trickier in here. We normally travel with more luxurious aircraft than this, but we left too quickly to make arrangements and had to settle for something smaller.

"I don't want to *snuggle* with you," she spits out. It's so cute, I can't help but smile, but I quickly sober.

"I'm not asking you to snuggle." What a stupid American word. "When I get you to my bed, there will be plenty of time for that. I asked you to put your head on my shoulder. Now do so. I'm not going to ask a second time."

With an angry little huff, she finally does as she's told and rests her head on my shoulder. Her body's stiff and unyielding. I smile to myself. I'll enjoy watching her reserve slip away as I mold her will to mine and show her the pleasures of submission. Eventually, her breathing calms, and she's almost asleep when we hit a pocket of turbulence. The plane rocks like we're a toy shaken in the hands of a giant. Sadie lets out a little scream and bolts upright, but I only hold onto the armrests and wait for news from the pilot. This might be just a pocket, or we could be hitting a serious patch.

Demyan curses and Maksym looks green around the edges. The plane roils and tumbles. Sadie whimpers beside me. Instinctively, I take the hand closest to me in both of mine.

"Breathe through your nose," I command. "And close your eyes."

Her eyes close and her lips purse. Inhaling, her shoulders rise and fall with the intakes of breath.

"Good," I tell her. "This is just a little turbulence. We'll find out what's going on as soon as the pilot can tell us."

Silently, she nods. The plane settles to a steady hum.

Such a pretty girl. I admire the slope of her nose and curve of her chin, the disheveled hair that looks like she just got out of bed. The image of "just fucked' hair makes me hard. She may look like a nondescript nobody, but to me, I see nothing but her hidden potential. I revel in my plans for her, and when I close my eyes, my mind wanders to images of what I'll do to her.

Lips, teeth, tongue. I'll explore her intimately. Dominate her mind and body. Submit her will to mine.

I wait until she falls asleep before I close my eyes. As I drift off to sleep, the plane vibrates and dips. Sadie sits bolt upright, and even Demyan and Maksym look troubled by the sudden change. I reach for her hand and expect her to pull away, but instead she holds on tighter, her face paling.

"What's happening?" she hisses. "God. You took me from my home and against my will and now you're going to kill us." The staid librarian has a temper.

"Quiet," I order. "Sit and hold my hand and focus on your breathing." I don't have the patience for her anger right now.

"Yes, *sir*," she says in mockery. My hand instinctively tightens on hers. She quiets.

I issue rapid commands in Russian to our attendant, who quickly goes to the front of the plane for details. She returns a moment later and comes straight to me.

"There's nothing we need to fear, sir," she says. "The pilot says we'll settle soon."

"Thank you."

The Bratva's Baby: A Dark Mafia Romance

She leaves. Demyan closes his eyes and Maksym looks out the window.

"Head on my shoulder," I order Sadie.

"Fine," she whispers. "Might as well order me to kiss you or tell you I love you. If ordering people to do things they should do of their own free will gets your rocks off, lucky you."

I dislike her rudeness, and console myself with the knowledge that soon, her temper and sharp tongue will be trained. Soon, we will be home. Still, I won't allow her to run her mouth at me.

"Quiet. You've lost your privilege of speaking. Do so again and I'll gag you."

Though she fumes, she obeys.

I'll give her a better use for that mouth. In time.

Chapter Six

Sadie

With his shoulder as hard as a coffee table, I don't expect to actually relax, but since sleep is the only escape for me, I'm grateful when it finally comes. I'm not sure how long I'm asleep, but when I wake, there's a crick in my neck and the sun is rising out the window. I lift my head and try to stretch. Kazimir's hands are folded on his lap, his eyes closed, but I doubt he's really asleep. Does a man like him, who commands people and steals women just because he wants to, really ever sleep?

The blond man to my left is eyeing me in a way that makes my skin crawl. Kazimir seduced me, tricked me, then took me, and yet this blond guy is creepier. There's something about those eyes that look predatory, and it unnerves me. The other man, the burly, dark-haired one, seems more of a

The Bratva's Baby: A Dark Mafia Romance

gentle giant. There were others where he brought me, but it looks like we're the only ones who came aboard this plane.

How many of them are there? What will they do with me? What purpose do they have for a girl like me?

My mind reels with the need to escape, the need to formulate a plan. I have no friends at home, my only contact my boss. Whatever country we're going to must have an American embassy, or some type of police I could go to.

How will I know who to trust? How will I know who's on their payroll?

The books he checked out of the library were about Russian military leaders, and a name like *Kazimir* definitely fits the bill.

Are we going to Russia?

My stomach drops. Russia is so very, very far away from home. The only image I have in my mind of Russia is what I know from my youth: cold, distant, and communist. Are they still a communist country? I frown, trying to remember. I really should have paid more attention to these things.

Escape will be difficult with these huge, muscular men everywhere I turn. And then there's the matter of how far away from home I am. My heart sinks. For now, my purpose is survival. Though I long to be home, I can't get home if I'm dead.

Will he kill me, though? Does he want to? Why would he? He's told me he doesn't wish to harm or rape me, though he doesn't seem to have any reservations at all about punishing me.

I shiver when I remember his threat. Something tells me punishment is unavoidable at some point. What exactly will that entail?

I was a fool for trusting him. So hungry for human companionship and attention, I ignored every warning sign my intuition sent my way.

I've been a fool. Such a fool.

While I've been musing, the rest of the men have all woken. Kazimir stretches and looks around the plane, noting that his companions and I are awake. He checks something on his watch and signals for the attendant. They speak in Russian, and when she turns away from him, he looks to all of us.

"We land in twenty minutes. Prepare."

The other two put their phones away and sit upright, preparing to land. I sit in silence. For now, it's better that I observe. I'll wait for instructions, and comply. For now. Fighting when I have no means of escape, and when I'm significantly dwarfed by size and strength, makes no logical sense.

"Do you fear landing?" Kazimir asks. It takes a second for me to realize he's speaking to me.

"Me?" I ask.

The Bratva's Baby: A Dark Mafia Romance

He nods.

"I have no idea," I tell him, looking away. "I've never been on a plane before."

I've never traveled much beyond the county where I grew up, my only moves involving which foster home would take me next.

"Never been on a plane?" he asks. "You prefer traveling by other means?"

I blink, surprised. "Well, no. I don't travel at all," I tell him. "I work and live on my own. There's no time or need to travel."

I watch his face register surprise. Why does this shock him so? Why does he care?

"They don't give you paid vacation at your work?"

"Well, of course they do," I tell him. Why does this embarrass me? "I just don't like to use it for travel. Travel is expensive. I can't afford it even if I wanted to go."

I look away shyly. I don't want to talk to him about what I can and cannot afford anymore.

"When we land, you'll feel a dip in your belly as we descend," he tells me. "And a jolt on impact when the wheels hit the ground."

Oh, ew. Jolt? Dip in my belly? Why do people do this for fun?

"Okay."

"Okay?"

"Well, was I supposed to say something else?"

He shrugs and looks away. "I suppose not. I expected a bit more fear is all." This man confuses me.

As he predicted, the plane dips and sways and my belly does a somersault. His companions curse and squirm, but I watch us descend as placidly as I can. Below us, outside my window, the sun rises over the horizon, illuminating rows and rows of dull gray houses. Beyond the houses lies a vast patch of green.

The plane lurches and bounces when we land. I hiss out a breath but grip my armrests when the plane races along the runway at a breakneck speed. I breathe in through my nose, steadying my nerves until we come to a halt.

When we've landed, the men get to their feet. Kazimir says nothing but points his index finger at me, a silent command to stay seated. What was I supposed to do, help him carry the luggage? I shrug and sit, observing every detail I can.

I don't know what to do. What to think. I haven't fully processed where I am or where we're going.

I need to take in every detail I can. I'll never be able to orchestrate an escape if I don't note everything. It isn't until I watch Kazimir's men get our bags from beneath the bottom of the plane that grief strikes me. I have none of my belongings. Though I didn't own much, there were things I'd

The Bratva's Baby: A Dark Mafia Romance

come to love. My journal that I wrote in. My bag of crochet hooks and soft, pretty yarn. The books that were my companions. I have nothing but the clothing on my back. A sad sort of longing makes my belly ache. I look away from them. I can't watch them take their things off any longer. I sit and wait for Kazimir.

Outside the tiny window, a sea of men come swarming to the aircraft. Kazimir shakes hands with one of them, and for a moment, I watch in awe. The man he's shaking hands with is a politician. I can't remember his name or what his rank is, but the men here are high-ranking officials. If I could speak to one of them… if I could just give a clue…

Kazimir comes back to me, bends, and unfastens my belt.

"I can do that myself," I tell him.

He ignores my protests and helps me out of my seat.

"You will meet my friends and companions now," he says. "Behave yourself. Don't do anything stupid, or my threat to punish you will become a reality when we arrive at our home."

Our home.

Is this supposed to look like a domestic arrangement?

"Fine."

His hand tightens on the back of my neck. "Yes, sir," he corrects.

A strange thrill of reluctant curiosity zings through me. I clear my throat. "Yes, sir."

Without responding, he leads me off the plane, and I see the men who are waiting for us to leave. The politician, a tall man with white hair and a gray suit, watches us exit. I need to tell him what happened. I need him to save me. If I go with these men now, I know I'll never escape. America… my home…will be but a distant memory.

"Prime Minister," Kazimir says. "Meet my girl Sadie." I'm curious why he speaks in English. Does he want me to understand this conversation?

I nod to him.

"Welcome to Russia," the man says. "You look tired. Go with Kaz, and he will see to your getting some rest. We will meet again."

I open my mouth to tell him that I'm not here of my own accord. That I was kidnapped. To act on behalf of my safety and contact the American government.

"Thank you," I say. I try to rile up the nerve to defend myself, but the words stick in my throat. Kazimir leads me past the man and toward a waiting car several yards ahead of the aircraft. "Good job," he said. "The others usually try to tell him they were kidnapped and ask him to take them home. As if somehow a politician isn't

The Bratva's Baby: A Dark Mafia Romance

corrupt. Isn't on my payroll. It's a futile attempt, and they always have to bear the consequences of their actions when we return home. You did well."

I blink. "I see."

So this man knows who Kazimir is. And I'm not the first woman Kazimir's abducted.

There really is no one I can trust.

On his instruction, I fold myself into the back-passenger seat of the car that awaits us.

The ride is longer than I expect, and it takes us two more hours before we finally pull into a large estate. Exhaustion suffuses my limbs. Several buildings loom in front of us, frosted with ice, patches of snow along the pathways leading to the main house.

It feels like a dream or a nightmare. It's so surreal. I'm tired and hungry and scared, but trying to be as unobtrusive as possible.

The place he's taken me to is gated all around with thick metal gates, as if this is some sort of sanctuary or fortress with armed guards at every entrance and exit. My stomach falls. This will not be a place that's easy to escape. And what goes on within these walls that they need to be so heavily guarded? My stomach twists with fear. I don't like this. Not at all.

"Who are you?" I ask Kazimir when we get out of the car and he leads me to a side entrance to the house.

53

"My name is Kazimir Romanov," he responds. "I'm brigadier of my brothers, the Bratva. I answer to Dimitri, our leader. He's like a father to me. He's the one we go immediately to now."

"Your father?" I ask him, they share a last name. And what is the Bratva?

"Yes. Of sorts," he says, but he offers no further explanation.

I shiver when we enter the massive house. It's freezing cold, and I'm not dressed for this weather. But soon, Kazimir ushers me into an entryway. People I assume are servants stand at attention, dressed in black uniforms. Their spines are as stiff as swords, their eyes focused beyond us. This is no warm welcome reception. Kazimir issues commands in his native tongue, and people run to retrieve the bags. He takes me by the elbow, a sterner gesture than by the hand, and guides me down a narrow hallway toward a doorway that stands closed.

"You will meet Dimitri first," he says. "You will speak to him with respect and defer to me if you have any questions. He commands the Bratva and is like a father to me." He leans in and brings his mouth to my ear. "You have many questions. Now is not the time to ask them." His voice takes on a stern, corrective tone. "Respect, young lady." I'm tired and cold and this is ridiculous.

"Fine," I say, not sure why he's making such a point to be so demanding about this.

His hand crashes on my thinly-clad backside so swiftly, I'm breathless with shock. "You will refer to me as sir," he says. "You will behave demurely and respectfully in the presence of Dimitri."

My stomach churns with nausea and my backside throbs. What sort of alternate reality is this? Am I some sort of slave? I look discreetly around us, looking for signs of chains or devices he'll use to hold me hostage. That's what I am. Held hostage. A prisoner.

Chills skate down my spine.

"Sadie," he warns.

"Yes, sir," I say, though it feels weird, and I'm a little confused.

We stand outside the office door. The floors are covered in thick carpet, and gilded frames line the wall, pictures of snowy landscapes and beautiful mountains, but an air of coldness pervades our surroundings.

"Pay very close attention to my commands," he says. "Your training has already commenced, and Dimitri will expect that I've already bent your will to mine." A muscle ticks in his jaw. "And I haven't had the time I usually do."

My training? Bending my will?

He says it as if it's so normal. Expected. I'm just some twisted notch on his belt.

"And let me guess," I say, ignoring the warning in

my belly that tells me to curb my temper. "If I disobey you'll *punish* me." I've heard the threat and felt the smack of his palms now that I know what he'll say next. I spit the words out. I'm angry at him for taking me. I'm angry at him for betraying me. I'm angry that the one man who ever showed an interest in me at all only meant to manipulate me. And I'm getting sick of the threats of punishment, like I'm some sort of lapdog who should cower under her master's whim under the threat of a rolled-up newspaper.

I close my mouth, half expecting him to snap at me and hurt me, but his face barely registers any reaction at all. Instead, his jaw clenches and he eyes me for so long, I wonder if he'll speak at all. Finally, he shakes his head.

"It's a shame," he says. "But the situation can't be changed."

"What are you talking about?" I ask in angry confusion.

"You have the makings of such a beautiful submissive." The cold tone of his voice makes me shiver. "But your defiant attitude shows me I don't have the luxury of the training I'd have chosen."

I blink in surprise, dread pooling in my belly when he cuffs my wrists with his fingers and holds me to him. When he nods at a man standing guard by a door, the guard goes ahead of us, returning a moment later to welcome us in. He speaks in Russian, but his bowed head and welcoming gesture are clear enough. I don't know what to expect, or how to prepare. So when the door opens, I scream as Kazimir grabs hold of my hair so roughly I feel the ache flare along my scalp. I try to get away but he's too powerful, too tall, his hand on the back of my head unreachable. Tears blind my vision as I claw helplessly forward. He drags me in front of a large black desk cast in shadow, shoves me to my knees, releases my wrists, then cracks his hand on my backside so hard I fall forward and land on my hands. My heart stammers a crazy beat in my chest. My eyes fill with tears. I'm suddenly the little girl beaten by the ones in power over her again.

"Stay there," he snaps in English. "If you move, you'll feel my belt."

Trembling, I do what he says, the threat of being beaten with his belt too real.

Is he doing this for show? Or is he really so cruel? I'm humiliated, on hands and knees in front of this man who sits at the desk and doesn't even flinch. His face is cast in shadow, but when he turns to face me, I cringe involuntarily. A scar runs down the side of his wrinkled, aged face, one eye staring blankly at me. The one eye that sees looks at me with cold detachment. This must be the man he calls Dimitri. His silver hair is cut short, his formidable jaw clean shaven. Though he's dressed like a businessman, he has the air of an executioner.

"Welcome home, son," he says to Kazimir, in a

thick accent, though his gaze is on mine. "I see you found her."

So this man knew who I was and was party to my abduction. I begin to tremble.

"Yes, sir," Kazimir responds. "As you can see, she's not responded well to my brief training and has much to learn."

"Clearly." The older man chuckles. "This girl," he says, his accent so thick it's barely coherent. "She's not one you will share with your brothers?"

"She is *not.*"

The older man softly chuckles at Kazimir's stern tone.

This is all for my benefit, for the next few minutes they converse in rapid-fire Russian. I can't tell what they're saying at all, of course, but it seems like a casual conversation. Kazimir speaks respectfully to the older man, and after a short discussion, he bends down to me again.

"You need a collar," he says. "I'll have my men make one." He squeezes the back of my neck. "Then I can use a chain when appropriate."

I grit my teeth but don't respond. It seems he's determined to keep me humbled, so I'm not giving him a reason to hurt me again.

I let out a yelp when he grabs the back of my head again, tugging my hair back so painfully my eyes water.

"Stand, woman."

He's pulling me upward. I quake and whimper, trying to alleviate the pressure on my scalp by complying, but it doesn't do much good as he holds me tighter and turns me to face the man he calls Dimitri. He doesn't need to tell me about his past for me to know it's painful and sordid, that he's seen and orchestrated evil. But when he looks at Kazimir, there's pride and warmth in his gaze that quickly vanishes when he looks at me.

"Kazimir is the most exacting master we have," he says with pride. "You would do well to obey him." A brief nod dismisses us before Kazimir drags me out of the room by my hair. I whimper and beg, but my pleas fall on deaf ears.

He takes me to a gleaming glass elevator behind him, barks out commands to a uniformed guard, and the guard nods and presses a button. Tears of humiliation and pain blur my vision. The whole time, I try not to move, frozen in place with the death grip on my hair. I consider turning and kneeing him in the groin, but I have no doubt I'd be swarmed with guards then suitably punished by Kazimir. So I don't fight. If I stand still, it doesn't hurt quite so much. Fighting him now would ache.

The elevator opens, and he drags me in. The doors to the elevator close and he finally releases my hair. I instinctively massage my scalp, trying to ease the sting and burn. I blink back tears, but one escapes and rolls down my cheek. I turn away from him, unable to look at his cruel eyes. I don't want him to know how he affects me. My heart hurts. He betrayed me. For such a brief time, I trusted him. Hoped. And now…

Reaching over to me he sweeps the tear off my cheek with his thumb, and to my surprise, he brings his damp thumb to my mouth.

"Suck it," he orders.

Grimacing, I do, tasting the essence of my own salty tears, strangely unsettled by the command to take his thumb into my mouth. My tongue teases his rough, calloused finger. I watch as his gaze grows molten, an animalistic growl filling the interior of the elevator.

"You will swallow your tears," he rasps, in a low voice affected by our exchange. "Swallow your pride." He leans closer to me, his breath hot on my cheek. "You'll learn to obey until the thought of defiance terrifies you. Until obedience comes as naturally to you as breathing."

I stumble back when the doors slide open, as if he held me by his mere voice and released me when his talking ceased.

I'll never obey the way he wishes.

I can play at many things but true subservience isn't one of them. He can whip me, humiliate me, punish me. He won't take my dignity. The more he hurts me, the harder I'll make my heart toward him. He will only ever get outward compliance from me until I can escape.

The Bratva's Baby: A Dark Mafia Romance

We exit the elevator and enter a long hallway, decorated in opulence. A thick, cream-colored carpet lines the floor, the walls adorned with large, oval-shaped painting. One bare, gleaming cherry wood end table sits by a door. When the elevator shuts behind us, I realize I'm completely free. He isn't holding me. I'm not restrained. I looked about me in confusion until I realize we're isolated on this floor, and a cursory glance at the elevator shows a slim, mirror-like panel I assume is meant for thumbprint identification. Though there's a small, circular window at one end of the hall, I can only see clouds. We ascended four floors.

He doesn't need to restrain me anymore. There's no escape from here.

The door swings open when he swipes his finger on a panel identical to the one by the elevator. Silently, he ushers me into the room first, as if he's a gentleman and not a monster. When we're in, he slams the door with a bang and begins to remove his tie.

"Clothing off," he says. "Fold each item and hand them to me."

I blink at him. I should have expected when we had privacy he'd strip me naked. What else did I expect? He abducted me.

He'll do whatever he wants with me now.

Chapter Seven

Kazimir

I'm weary from travel but invigorated by the job that lays before me. I crave control and power, and look with eager anticipation to Sadie's training. Each woman I train is different. Each has her own fears and wants and needs. Each brings with her a past that affects her responses to my methods. None was mine for the keeping, though.

This one is.

Her training will be different.

It isn't just her training, though, because Sadie herself is different. Her defiance is bred of something other than pride, but I can't quite figure out what it is yet.

I will.

I take a seat in my comfortable chair, the large leather armchair that's the focal point of the living room. Here, in my private penthouse, no one is allowed access but my servants, and only when I grant it to them. Even Dimitri asks for entrance before coming to me, and most of the time we meet in another place. This is my sanctuary, my castle. When I return, the weariness of my work and demands of the day begin to seep away. Returning to Sadie will ease my comfort eventually.

My suite is as private as a high security prison. Sadie, like all the other women I've brought in here before, will explore and try to find a means to escape. She'll find none.

I watch as she begins to undress. Still clad in the abysmal clothing she wore the night before, she looks like she belongs in a convent. I swallow hard, my mouth dry at the prospect of seeing her undress, as if I'm on the verge of opening a precious gift.

"Top first," I rasp out, when her fingers roam her clothes questioningly.

"And naturally, if I don't..." she begins, but as her eyes roam our surroundings, she stops talking. Sadie may be a virgin, but she's a smart girl.

We sit in the entry room, a sprawling living room outfitted in black leather furniture. My armchair. A matching sofa. A black leather ottoman where I keep tools I like to use in this room. On the opposite side of this room is my bedroom, and from where we sit we can see the rings on the bed made for cuffs or a makeshift whipping post, a black leather bench and horse.

She may not know what these things are, but she's smart enough to know they're not designed for hospitality.

When she's stripped, I'll give her the tour.

Scowling at me, she grasps the edge of her top. To my surprise, there's no hesitation. No trembling hands or shaking limbs I expected. With furious yanks and tugs, she tears her clothes off, rending them from her body like a woman in tortured mourning. I freeze, watching her, my body heating with the need to both punish and claim her.

Her training will be the pinnacle of my career. I stand on the precipice of something monumental. Sadie is unique. Women do two things with me: tremble in fear or curry my favor. Sadie does neither.

As she strips, buttons pop, fabric tears, and she pulls her clothes off her body so rapidly and with such anger, she leaves red marks on her neck and her face flushes. Somehow, she's trying to gain control by obeying me in anger.

I fold my hands on my knee and nod.

"Good girl," I say, refusing to give in to her temper. "Now dress again."

The Bratva's Baby: A Dark Mafia Romance

She blinks rapidly, as if trying to process what I've said. "What? In these clothes?"

"Yes."

Our eyes meet in a battle of wills. I'm stronger than she is. More powerful. I have the potential to hurt her with hardly any effort. And yet, her will must be extracted from her. Broken. Molded to mine.

I can train her. I can break her. The one thing I can't do is predict her behavior. It's too erratic, too impetuous. The only way to respond is by meeting her with an unexpected response.

She's a challenge.

I'm so intent on her act of defiance I haven't fully processed how beautiful she is naked before me. As she yanks her clothing back on, I take in every detail. The way her plain cotton panties glide over the curve of her backside. The clasp of her ugly bra encasing her full, exquisite breasts. The rough fabric of her skirt pulled up over her creamy thighs. The hideous top stretched over beautiful, unblemished skin. It's like hiding a masterpiece in a burlap bag. Sinful.

But I'm well acquainted with sin.

And she'll do penance for this.

When she's fully dressed, I give a nod of approval.

"Now finish stripping."

Hands on hips, her eyes flash at me, light pools of anger. "Again?"

I nod slowly, not breaking eye contact. "Again. This time, fold every piece of clothing you remove and hand it to me and if you have another tantrum while you undress, we'll do this all over again."

Though she removes her clothing with tugs and tears as she did before, she's growing fatigued, and her movements are less jerky. The top comes off first. She folds it like a toddler, and hands it to me rumpled. I eye it and silently disapprove. With a huff of anger, she folds it again until it's presentable, then hands it to me. I take it and place it upon my knee, then nod to her skirt. That comes off next, but this time as she shimmies out of it, I watch her breasts bounce and swing, and I swallow hard, my dick tightening in my pants. My mouth waters. I want to devour her.

Folding the skirt neatly, she places it on the top, then removes her underwear, socks and shoes, until a neat little pile lays on my lap. Training doesn't always involve pain and tears.

"Good girl," I approve. I wave a finger in the direction of the corner of the room. "Now go stand in that corner while I get rid of these." I want her well occupied before I give her the tour, and I'll take every opportunity I can to train her.

"The corner?" she repeats. For the first time, the anger dwindles and her eyes widen. I'm surprised by this turn of events. Is she afraid of the corner? What a silly thing to be afraid of.

"Yes," I say, impatience imbuing my tone. "The corner. Are you hesitating, young lady?"

She looks once more to the corner of the room. Her chin trembles, and she looks as if she's about to cry. I don't like that she hasn't obeyed me. Tucking her clothing under my arm, I grasp her elbow, spin her around, and give her a sharp spank.

"Corner," I repeat.

Tears welling in her eyes, she obeys. I'm so confused by her response, I stalk away from her, angry at my lack of understanding and her failure to obey. That instruction should have been the easy one. I eye the fireplace and consider burning her clothes, but cheap, synthetic clothing will melt and smell. It's a shame to merely dispose of them. These terrible things need to be destroyed. I toss her clothes in a garbage bag and leave it by the barrel for the cleaners to fetch.

I expected her to watch me, but when I turn to her, I'm surprised to see she hasn't even moved. Her forehead is flush against the wall, her shoulders slumped and shuddering.

Is she crying?

I thought I'd hardened my heart against tears. They don't garner sympathy. Hell, I like them sometimes. But now... there's something about the way she cries that threatens to break my resolve.

Standing a few feet behind her with my feet planted apart, my arms crossed on my chest, I call her name.

"Sadie, come here."

She jumps at the sound of my deep voice resonating in the quiet room.

When she turns around, her tearstained cheeks pull at me. Wordlessly, I crook a finger at her, and she approaches me. She's so beautiful. So perfect, like a virginal Eve in the Garden of Eden. Not a freckle graces her body, and I reason she hasn't bathed in the sun or played with other children outdoors. Her full breasts swing free, her nipples slightly hardened.

The slope of her hips. Curve of her ass. Full, creamy skin at her thighs. I observe every beautiful detail to distract me from those tear-filled eyes. I could handle her tears of pain, and her tears of anger. But these... these tears are from something that breaks me a little. I mask my concern with my rough tone.

"Why are you crying? I haven't even whipped you. Save your tears for when you earn my lash, woman."

Swiping at her eyes, she looks down and doesn't respond, not even startled by the threat of punishment.

The Bratva's Baby: A Dark Mafia Romance

I fight the urge to draw her to my chest and hold her close. To wipe her tears away and kiss those tear-stained cheeks. To punish those who made her cry. To avenge her.

"I asked you a question," I remind her, chucking a finger under her chin so her eyes meet mine. "And I expect an answer."

"I hate the corner," she says. "And I'm just tired and hungry, and I lost my resolve. You're not exactly the nicest person."

"I'm not." My people speak the truth, so I'm not angered by her honesty. "But that's not why you cry. Why do you hate the corner?"

Even though she looks at me, I watch as her eyes shutter. "I don't know," she lies.

I yank her chin so her gaze swings back to mine. "That isn't the truth."

"I don't know," she repeats, meeting my gaze but closing herself off from me.

"Then behave yourself so I don't send you there," I say sternly, dismissing the small lie I'll revisit until I know the truth. "You need food and rest, and so do I. Come with me."

I'm tired of this. The tour of my place can wait until later.

Taking her hand in mine, I half-drag her to my room. I'm vaguely aware of her eyes widening when she sees the cuffs, chains, and rings on my bed, the comfortable leather furniture and equipment, the wall of tools hanging on hooks. Many have a playground. My playground is in my bedroom.

My servants have prepared my bed as instructed, the sheets turned down and freshly cleaned. I tap a text on my phone to order food brought up, then point to the bed.

"Lie down."

She climbs onto the bed, scowling.

"There's one bed," she says, her anger returning.

"Smart girl," I say, barely stopping an eye roll. If she thinks she gets her own bed, she has a lot to learn.

I strip out of my own clothes, standing just in my boxers, and make a call on my phone before I return to her. The weariness of travel settles in my bones. I never rest during the day but she needs to, and I need to commence her training. I'm curious how it will be with her.

"On your back, Sadie." I watch as her back goes rigid, the wheels in her mind turning before she decides if she'll obey. She isn't comfortable naked in front of me. But when I take a step toward her to correct her, she quickly obeys, flipping onto her back so I can't reach the pretty little backside that needs to feel the sting of my palm.

"Why the hesitation?" I ask her.

"Because I don't trust you," she says truthfully between clamped teeth.

"Ah. I thought perhaps it was because you're uncomfortable being naked."

Her cheeks flush a vibrant shade of heated pink but she doesn't respond. My guess was correct, then. There's that, too.

I prowl closer to her, taking in her the luscious curve of her hips, the swell of her breasts, the peaked nipples. I swallow. Oh, the ways I will bring this girl pleasure and pain.

"Keep your hands by your side," I instruct, my voice ragged with arousal. "Do not move them."

Her hands slowly fall to her sides as she stares up at the ceiling. I watch as her jaw tightens and her lips become so thin they're barely visible. Her spine is ramrod straight.

I kneel on one knee beside her. The large bed is a high-quality affair I had imported. It barely moves when I press my weight into the mattress. "I wonder what's on your mind," I muse, tracing my index finger down one bare shoulder. She shivers. "I wonder what you're thinking. What you fear."

I let the words settle like softly fallen snow. She's so quiet, I'm surprised when she speaks.

"I wonder why you took me," she whispers. "What a plain, boring girl like me could offer a powerful, beautiful man like you." It isn't a compliment. She's truly bewildered.

Weaving my fingers through her hair, I shake my head. "Is that really what you think, Sadie? That you're a plain, boring girl?"

She snorts. "I don't think. I know."

"You're wrong," I tell her, allowing my fingertip to roam over the swell of her breasts. I watch her beautiful pink nipples stiffen as she bites her lip. You're never to say a thing like that again," I whisper. "Not ever again. If you do, I will punish you. Am I clear? Respond correctly."

"Yes, sir." But her response is tight. Angry. "Fine."

I take her nipple between my fingers and pinch it. She howls and writhes. So sensitive to pain. My dick hardens at the thought of what I could do to her. What I *will* do to her.

"Try that again," I order.

"Yes, sir," she screams. "Yes!"

I release her nipple and watch with pleasure as the tight bud reddens and swells. Leaning down, I brace myself with my hands by her side and lap my tongue along the punished flesh. I pull the nipple into my mouth and suck, watching her eyes go wide and her lips part.

"What are you doing?" she says in a hoarse whisper.

I release her breast and lock eyes with her. "Pleasure or pain, Sadie. Both are on the table. The choice will be up to you."

Her beautiful brow furrows and her lips pucker. "You're a monster. Twisted. Sick. Why would I choose pain?"

She has so much to learn.

"Be quiet, now," I order quietly. "I'd like to truly look at you now that you're not dwarfed by that ridiculous clothing."

I ignore her sputter of protest, and begin my careful, meticulous inspection. I run my hands over her shoulders, feeling her strength and soft skin. Her body is tense, like a spring, but I continue. The soft hollow of her neck begs to be touched and kissed. I imagine how beautiful her breasts will look dotted in beaded wax and adorned with raspberry-colored teeth marks. I moan, my hard cock throbbing against her thigh.

So fucking beautiful. So fresh and new and virginal.

I flick a thumb over one nipple and inhale the sweet, heady scent of her reluctant arousal. I release her breasts. Next, I smooth my palms over her thighs, kneading the soft, tender skin. She trembles beneath my touch.

"Are you cold?"

"No."

"Then why do you shiver?"

"You terrify me," she whispers. I like that she gives me the truth.

JANE HENRY

I lift her legs and bend her knees so her thighs part and I get a full view of her pretty pink pussy. I can't help but groan, my mouth watering to devour her.

"I understand terror," I tell her. "But I haven't done much to scare you—yet." She hasn't been whipped. Hasn't seen the inside of a cage. She's never seen me truly angry.

Shaking her head, her eyes meet mine. "You abducted me," she whispers. "That isn't scary?"

I shrug a shoulder.

Leaning down, I lay kisses from her belly to the tops of her thighs, then back again, wafting in the fragrance of her arousal and need. If I touched her right now, she'd be soaking wet for me and she'd hate that she was.

For a few moments, as I continue my exploration of her beautiful body, she doesn't say anything. I move down the length of her leg, cradling first one then the other in my hand.

"Beautiful," I murmur.

"What is your job here?" she asks.

"I'm the enforcer," I tell her. "*Avtoritet.*"

"What does that mean?" she whispers.

"I believe the best word in English is authority."

She swallows. "Not a surprise. And what exactly is your job description?"

"I basically run our organization," I say. I can't help it. I lean down and lap my tongue along the inside of her thigh and groan. She's damp with arousal even here.

Her breathing is ragged and hitched. "You… run it," she chokes out. "Do you lead people?"

"Of course. I often assign jobs."

"And if they don't do them, you punish them," she says with more than a little disdain. "Do you beat them?"

"Yes."

"Torture them?"

"Yes."

She pauses, then, "Kill them?"

"When necessary."

A bell rings, indicating our food has arrived and interrupting her interrogation. I don't bother instructing her to stay, as I know she has nowhere to go, and I'm curious if she'll try to run. It's better if she attempts this now, while I can respond with my full attention. I lock my bedroom door behind me with a casual swipe of my hand along the panel. It's better for her if she stays confined for now. Every entrance and exit to this suite is securely fastened, my bedroom no exception.

Lydia, the youngest and quietest member of the staff, stands on the other side of the door when I look through the peephole. "Leave it there," I order, then watch as she quickly obeys before I get our food. When I come back in my bedroom, Sadie is gone. I stifle a chuckle. So predictable.

"You have until the count of ten," I say nonchalantly. "If I have to come fetch you, you'll sleep behind bars tonight."

I place the tray on the table and begin counting out loud. "One. Two. Three…"

On seven, she slides open the closet door and walks timidly in the room, wearing one of my robes.

"Take it off," I order, buttering a roll. "And come sit down."

"People don't eat food naked," she protests.

I look up from my plate. "You do."

Frowning, she obeys, then pulls out a chair, but a *tsk* of disapproval freezes her in place.

I beckon to her. With a curious glance, she slowly walks my way, and when she reaches me, I slide her onto my lap.

"Kazimir," she fusses, squirming, but a sharp spank to her thigh settles her.

"I'll feed you."

"Little lapdog," she mutters. "You brought me all the way from America so you could have a little lapdog. How quaint."

It's time she learned to curb her mouth.

Chapter Eight

Sadie

I don't really know what's gotten into me. I'm so out of my element, scared and angry, it's like the only control I have here is my ability to speak. He's drawn me out into the open so there's nowhere to hide. At home, I've always blended into the background. Avoided eye contact. Assuming the role of the timid recluse made it so much easier to avoid people. Relationships. And the inevitable pain those relationships bring.

And now he's yanked me out of my comfortable hiding.

I knew it was inevitable he'd punish me eventually. He's given me a few swats here and there, and threatened punishment. So when he pushes away from the table, his corded muscles around me flexing and bunching, and he turns me over his knee with effortless ease, I close my eyes in anticipation of what I know will come.

My cheeks heat when he turns me over his lap. Before his palm connects with my ass, I'm clenching and cringing in anticipation. Still, it hurts worse than I expect, his palm slapping my naked skin so hard it echoes in the quiet room. I hold my breath and brace for the second sharp spank. My eyes are closed, my only means of escape from the humiliating punishment. He gives me a series of rapid spanks before he speaks, and when he does, his tone isn't angry but disapproving, like a stern father.

"You'll speak respectfully to me from now on, or you will not speak at all," he says simply, underscoring his words with sharp smacks of his palm. "You're a little girl under my control who will learn her place."

I don't fight him. There's a lump in my throat, and my body feels strangely heated and energized. I don't know how to respond, so I don't respond at all. Apparently, he thinks I'm sufficiently chastened, for he rights me with a fluid grace that surprises me. I blink, sitting upright on his lap, and he turns me to face him. His eyes are cloudy and severe, probing me.

"If you speak out of turn again, I'll gag you. Do you understand me?"

The Bratva's Baby: A Dark Mafia Romance

"Yes, sir," I say through clenched teeth. The audacity of this man infuriates me.

He stares at me a moment before he shakes his head.

"Do you have any idea what I could do to you?" he asks, his accent thick with emotion.

"No," I tell him honestly. He's a veritable stranger to me. I know almost nothing about him.

"I could hurt you," he says, but he isn't angry. His tone almost registers surprise. "Whip you. Put you in a cage and make you eat from a bowl."

I wrinkle my nose at him. "Does that appeal to you?"

Taking my face in one of his large, rough hands, he grips me so tightly it hurts. "Your submission appeals to me," he growls. "Your obedience. And I'll do whatever it takes to get that from you."

I meet his gaze squarely and give him the bald truth. Stripped and punished, I have no pride left. I have nothing to lose with stark honesty.

"I've seen cruelty in my life. I was raised on a constant diet of humiliation. If you think a spanking and the threat of more punishment will bring me to my knees in blind submission to you, you abducted the wrong damn girl."

I've been beaten and starved, shoved in a closet and tormented. I hate thinking about my past. I hate remembering the pain and humiliation I've felt. But I learned how to withstand humiliation and never relinquish my dignity. He won't get it from me this way.

"A spanking and a threat?" he asks quietly. Too quietly.

I shiver in fear when I feel something beneath my backside harden. Oh, God. I've given him an erection. I squirm in uncomfortable fear. This... *this* will be my undoing.

Leaning in from behind, his mouth brushes my ear. "Have you ever had your defiant mouth gagged with a cock?" he asks. My belly twists uncomfortably, and I try involuntarily to pull away from him but he's too close, too strong. "Have you ever been spread on a bed and brought to the edge of climax so long and so intensely the very breath you released caused you pain and torment?" I close my eyes to shove the image away, but he continues his relentless torment. "Have you ever been forced to orgasm again and again not for pleasure, but punishment? No? Learn to obey me, and you may never experience the variety of punishments I have at my disposal." Brushing my hair off my neck almost tenderly, he kisses the skin there. "This was no accident, *krasotka,*" he says. "I didn't abduct *the wrong girl.*"

What does *krasotka* mean?

A ringing sound outside his room makes his body go rigid, and though I don't understand the words he utters, I can easily tell they're some form of

The Bratva's Baby: A Dark Mafia Romance

curse words. He shoves me to off his lap and I topple onto my feet.

"Eat," he orders. "That is an order. I will check when I return. And put this on." Opening a wardrobe on one side of his bed, he removes a silky bathrobe.

He yells to the door in Russian, while pulling on his pants, then he gives me a warning glare before he leaves the room to answer the door. I slide on the robe, eager to cover my nudity, when I hear the door open. He's left his bedroom door ajar.

From where I sit, I can see two men bring in a third between them, the third man's face bloodied and bruised. One eye's swollen shut, the other black and blue. His nose is clearly broken, his clothing tattered. Kazimir curses when the men throw the other at his feet, but my vision is obscured by the doorway so I can't see the faces of the two men who brought this one in. They both bow their heads in respect.

One of the men standing speaks in harsh tones to Kazimir, the other interrupts him, and Kazimir silences them with one sharp word and a swipe of his hand. They all fall silent, while Kazimir kneels on one knee in front of the man they've dragged in. He grabs the man by the chin and asks a question in that low, dangerous voice I've already learned to fear. I'm held in horrid fascination as the scene plays out.

The man begins to sob and beg. I can't understand

81

a word he says, but his pleas are pathetic. Kazimir's dispassionate look seems to make the man even more desperate. He begs and sobs, before Kazimir rears back and slaps him across the face. I wince at the crack of flesh hitting flesh, then he does it again and again until blood spurts from the man's nose. I cover my mouth with my hands when Kazimir lifts the man and knees him in the belly, before he throws him halfway across the room so effortlessly the man could be a small animal. With a casual flick of his wrist, he issues an order then makes the man howl and try to claw his way to freedom, but the other two grab him and drag him out of the room.

Kazimir watches, his eyes furious slits, when I realize he's dismissed them and coming into me. I've eaten nothing. My stomach is tied in knots, but I don't want to find out what happens if I disobey him. I grab a hunk of bread from the table and shove a large bite in my mouth. My mouth is too dry. I feel like I'm chewing on cotton balls. I chew and chew but when I finally swallow, my belly churns with nausea and I'm afraid I'm going to vomit. I never could stomach violence.

The doorway darkens with his form. I grab a glass of water and wash down the bread, then quickly eat a few bites of some type of soup. I taste nothing, and my stomach still threatens to empty.

Walking past me, he goes to the bathroom. I hear the faucet being turned on, then he's muttering to himself as steam billows up around him and he scrubs at his hands. From where I sit, I can see the dark shadows of tattoos all over his body, though I can't see details. They scare me, but it can't be denied that some are works of art. A skull graces the bulging muscle of one large bicep, a rose with something stuck in it is along another arm, a spider crawls along his back, and other intricately woven lines join them all together. These tattoos mean something. I make it my mission to find out what.

I've always been afraid of men with tattoos, like they were somehow dangerous and had to be avoided. Now, looking at Kazimir, I can see my fears aren't unfounded.

When he returns to the room he's scowling at me. I've slopped soup on the tray and sprayed bread crumbs all over the place in my attempt to eat hastily.

"Why was the man crying?" I ask. "What did you order?"

Without blinking, Kazimir replies. "His execution."

A cold shiver of dread skates down my back. "Why?" I whisper. "What did he do?"

"He betrayed me," Kazimir says. "That's all I will tell you."

"You don't perform executions yourself?" I ask.

"Eat!" he snaps at me. I jump, nearly knocking over the water.

"I did," I say in a small, offended voice. "I'm not very hungry. You don't have to yell."

With a scowl, he looks at my tray and grumbles to himself. "That will do," he says, which I suppose is his pathetic attempt at an apology. "Now get in bed and rest until I call you to me."

Before I can respond, he leaves the room, shutting and locking the door behind him. Fruitlessly, I turn the knob and try to open the door, but it's impossible. I hate that I've been locked in here like this. The room is huge, but everywhere I turn there's another reminder of him. His smell hangs about the place like an omen, dark and dangerous and to my utter disgust, erotic.

I'm alone, though. Blissfully alone. Solace is where I find my peace, the only place I'm comfortable, and this time it seems almost like a tease. I'm by myself, I have no privacy. And I don't realize until he's gone how badly I wished for this. How badly I wanted to be by myself for a little while. I haven't been able to even think through what's happened to me.

I assume if he's left me in here, there aren't many things I can get into that will aid me in my plan of escape. A cursory glance around the place tells me I'm not wrong.

There is no window in the bathroom. The bedroom's ceilings are so high, I can't even reach them. There is nowhere to climb to. No means of escape. The windows are large and airy, but too high to reach, and likely monitored or secured in some way. And even if I got to them, we're too far up for me to escape.

Next, I walk to the door I assume is a closet but find it locked. There are two dressers and a bedside table, but when I open them and inspect the contents, all I find are women's clothes. I shiver involuntarily. Who lived here before me?

The room is sparsely furnished. There is no television or a tablet, no cell phone or computer. Not even so much as a book. It's like a prison, really. I try the door one last time, and give a little scream when it opens, only to find Kazimir standing on the other side, scowling at me.

"I told you to rest," he says, his lip curling in a sneer. "I knew you'd want to snoop. They all do. But you'll do what I tell you." He takes me by the arm, spins me around, and gives my ass a sharp crack. "Now go."

He might not break me with a spanking, but I have no interest in getting another one, so I do what he says and climb into bed, feeling a bit like a chastened child. Kazimir points a finger in my direction.

"Do not get out of bed again without my permission."

Then he's gone and the door clicks shut again.

I roll my eyes. I'm fuming but exhausted, so I mutter to myself and think about crazy means of escape while I lay there in bed. I don't know how to get away from him, and even if I did, I don't know how I would contact anyone who could help. He has connections everywhere. I know *no one*.

My eyes grow heavy with sleep, and I finally doze off. When I wake, the room is slightly darkened, and the door is open. Kazimir stands in front of me dressed in a suit. I sit up and shiver, pulling the blanket up around me. I didn't even hear him getting dressed.

"Time to get up," he says. "You'll find your evening gown hanging in the bathroom for you to wear. Shortly, I'll have an attendant come and get you dressed. This evening, you will dine with me and Dimitri."

"Like some sort of date," I mutter, but a warning look from him makes me freeze. I won't get myself punished again. Not now, anyway.

"You belong to me, Sadie," he states. "Therefore, when I eat with Dimitri, you will join me." He's adjusting a tie around his neck as he speaks. "This is part of your training."

Frowning, I get out of bed, strangely sleepy and disoriented. My stomach churns with hunger. My mouth is dry and I long for something to quench my thirst.

When I'm three steps away from the bathroom, he calls my name.

"Sadie, *stop.*"

I freeze mid-step.

"Come back here."

I turn to face him and give him a curious look. Crooking a finger at me, he points at the floor in front of him. With a sigh, I obey and walk until I'm standing in front of him.

"Good girl," he says. "You respond to your training better than I expected. Now go lie on the bed on your back and spread your legs."

I blink. "What? You just told me to get dressed."

"Do it."

My cheeks flame. What does this mean? When he uncrosses his arms and takes a step toward me, I quickly scurry to the bed and do what he says. My legs shake, my pulse races. I didn't expect this, and remember his admonition about his particular methods of punishment with vivid clarity.

I can hear the sound of a drawer beside me opening, but I can't see what he's doing. I shiver in anticipation, my whole body trembling.

"You are a smart girl," he murmurs, running a hand appreciatively along my side. He stands above me. I close my eyes, needing to shut this out. It's shameful to lie before him naked and vulnerable, and I can't get away.

"Open your eyes, Sadie," he orders. Reluctantly, I obey, my gaze finding his. He stands between my legs, his hands on my knees. Gently, he guides my legs further apart and to my surprise, kneels. His mouth, his eyes, the intimacy of his tongue and gaze so close to the most private parts of my body terrify me.

"Kazimir," I whisper, begging. "Please, no."

"No?" he asks. "You don't even know what I'm going to do."

That's what scares me the most. I don't respond, though I beg him silently.

Shaking his head from side to side, he smoothes his hands up my naked inner thighs. "*Krasotka,*" he says. "Your very tone of voice and straight spine speak defiance. It imbues your thoughts and words. And I've already explained to you," he pauses, bending down and nipping the sensitive skin of my inner thighs. "I will train you to obey me."

He drags his tongue along my thigh upward. My body clenches in fear and anticipation.

"No," I whisper, but when I try to close my knees, he pinches my bottom so hard I scream in pain.

"Yes," he breathes, the heat from his mouth tickling my sensitive skin. "If you close your legs again, I'll whip you before we leave for dinner." His gaze boring into mine, I know he means what he says. Hell, he's eager. Without another word, he continues his exploration of my inner thighs with his tongue and lips and teeth, nipping, grazing, licking, suckling. I've never touched myself, but as

The Bratva's Baby: A Dark Mafia Romance

he continues, the need to relieve the pressure between my thighs builds to almost painful.

"Mmm," he whispers. "My little *kisa's* pussy weeps for me. Let's see what those pretty lips hide." I cringe. It sounds so vulgar, but I can't focus on this as he sweeps his hand upward and parts me. Holding tightly to my thighs, so tightly I can't close them, he flicks his tongue between my folds. I want to die of embarrassment, as if he's stripped me naked in front of an audience. It's so intimate, so personal, I can't handle the intensity of this.

"Please, Kazimir," I whisper. "Sir," I plead, giving him what I hope he wants. "Nooooo."

Ignoring my pleas, he licks and suckles. My hips writhe, my back arches. He's mastering my body without my consent. "Nooo," I beg, but my pleas fall on deaf ears. Blood pumps through my veins and my pussy tightens, contracts, throbs, until finally he stops. Though I begged for him to stop, my body hangs on the precipice of something blissful, and to my horror, the sudden cessation of pleasure makes me long for more.

Standing, he wipes a hand across his mouth and groans. "Anything else I taste tonight will pale in comparison, *krasotka.*" Bending down to the bed, he lifts something he retrieved from the drawer. It gleams in the overhead light. Some sort of metal?

"On your knees," he orders, encouraging me with a slap to my thigh.

"What are you doing?" I ask him. "What is that?"

89

A scowl and shake of his head is my only warning as he reaches for the clasp of his belt and unfastens it. With a rapid tug, he yanks the belt from the loops, doubles it in his hand, and before I can process what he's doing, he lifts my legs straight up in the air. The leather lash falls on my naked backside once, twice, three times.

"On. your. knees," he thunders.

I scramble to my knees to obey and escape the flare of pain. I fall to the bed and cringe, as my backside is now on full display. But he doesn't punish me further with his belt. I hear him slide it through the loops of his pants and fasten it. He wants me to know he can. "If you think I'll hesitate to strap you with my belt in front of any of my brothers or Dimitri, you are mistaken," he warns, fisting my hair. I scream when he yanks it. "In fact, the very idea makes my cock throb."

"Chest down." He presses his palm on the small of my back. I fall to the bed and lie prostrate. I can't defy him, can't question him any further. Maybe I was wrong when I told him he wouldn't break me with punishment. He's done nothing but punish me, and here I am, putty in his hands. The knowledge both terrifies and saddens me and I don't try to stop the wail he tears from me. I've overcome so much in my life that I can barely protest when he forces himself on me, forces me to obey him. The sadness comes from the loss of hope. I hoped he would be the one who wouldn't do this to me. I hoped he would be the one to treat me with dignity. And I was wrong. So wrong.

"When you sit at the table with me and Dimitri, you will be reminded of your submission to me," he says. I freeze when something cold pushes at my asshole. Oh, God. This isn't right. He shouldn't be doing this. Without warning, he plunges his thumb past the muscle, fingers gripping the fullness of my ass. Pushing, pulling, stretching me, I arch my back and scream, but he continues his onslaught. Something cold and liquidy glides along my ass, then the cold metal pushes inward. I scream out loud, but when he speaks, his voice is surprisingly gentle.

"Relax, *krasotka*," he says. "You must relax. Close your eyes and breathe in through your nose." With no other choice, I do what he says. He's stroking my lower back, easing me into this while he glides the metal into my ass. I whimper and cringe at the very thought, but when his fingers come between my legs and he begins stroking my swollen folds, I am overcome with a fullness. I can't breathe at first until he reminds me.

"Inhale."

I take in a ragged breath as he strokes me.

"Exhale."

I let the breath out.

"Good girl," he approves, leaning down and whispering in my ear. "While you sit in that dining room dressed like a queen, you will feel the reminder of my control. I will feed your mouth while I master every part of you. Your pussy will throb for me. Your ass will clench in fear and need. Your mouth will water. And tonight, if you behave yourself, I'll grant you a reward."

And then his touch is gone and he's at the door. I freeze, not knowing what to expect.

"Nikita. Come in."

Chapter Nine

Kazimir

This is almost my favorite part of training. Everything is new to her—my mouth on her pussy, the gleaming, beautiful plug between her full cheeks, the stripes of my belt on her naked skin. My cock strains against my zipper. There's just enough fight in Sadie. She's perfect. Blind submission would leave me wanting, and too much fight makes my job that much harder. Sadie's curiosity and stubborn refusal are the ideal pitch.

I watch as Sadie's eyes fly open at the sound of Nikita entering the room. Nikita doesn't even blink at the sight of Sadie's submissive posture. Bowing her head, she greets me.

"Sir. What is it you wish from me tonight?"

Nikita has worked for the Bratva for four years.

JANE HENRY

Dimitri rescued her from dire poverty where she lived in a little shack, fed her, clothed her, employed her. We quickly came to see she was a woman to be trusted. She is our most faithful staff member, and the one I bring in first when I have a new woman to train. Her quiet nature and easy way of speech make the girls relax a little, but her loyalty to me means I can trust her not to betray me.

A petite woman with short, black hair, almond-shaped eyes, and a pert little nose, she takes in every detail with shrewd precision.

"Sadie will join me and Dimitri for dinner in an hour," I tell her. "She is unaccustomed to any type of pampering, so it will be your job to introduce her. She may not appear before Dimitri until she's been sufficiently prepared. Her gown hangs in the bathroom." Nikita nods. I take a step toward Nikita, getting her attention. "The appeal of this woman is her innocence. Her wholesome appearance. Enhance that," I instruct. "None of the exotic appeal of our native women. Do you understand me?" Russian women take pride in their appearance and slim figures, many choosing vibrant make-up and revealing clothing. I want Sadie's beauty underscored, not hidden.

"Is she allowed to leave the bed, sir?" Nikita asks, her eyes twinkling at me. She knows it's impossible to dress Sadie when she's still lying on the bed.

I merely growl at Nikita and narrow my eyes at her. "Do not overstep, woman," I warn.

The Bratva's Baby: A Dark Mafia Romance

She bows her head in apology. "No, sir. I'm sorry, sir." Turning to the bed, she calls to Sadie. "Come with me, please."

Sadie hangs her head miserably and drags her feet, wincing when she walks. I don't care about her embarrassment. Perhaps it will ease my training. She doesn't make eye contact with me at all, which is just as well. She should be humiliated and chastened right now, after the brief spanking and plug. If she behaves, she'll learn I'm not always a cruel master.

I sit at the table in my room while the women do their work, checking my emails and messages on my phone. The door to the bathroom stays open on my instruction, but their voices are muted. At first, Sadie doesn't speak to Nikita, but as they continue with their primping and preening, she begins to talk. I don't pay attention to their words until I hear Sadie ask in a hushed tone. "What is *kisa*?"

"Kitten," Nikita says.

"Oh." I smile to myself.

"And *krastoka*?"

I look casually to where Nikita stands behind Sadie, brushing her hair. "It means beautiful," she says. "If he says that to you, he's calling you beautiful woman."

Sadie doesn't respond, but I can see the faintest flush of her pink cheeks. I'd forgotten she wouldn't know what I said, the words coming unbidden.

But she is so beautiful. Untarnished by the touches of other men, unencumbered with pride and vanity.

I focus on a message from Maksym and give him a detailed reply when I hear Nikita clearing her throat. I look up and blink in surprise. Sadie stands before me, biting her lip, her eyes cast down as if she can't bear to look at me.

A sequined black evening gown hugs her curves, dipping low in the front to reveal cleavage. Sleeveless, her bare arms slope gracefully downward. I want to kiss my way from the top of one arm to the tips of her fingers. Her soft brown hair is arranged on top of her head in loops and swirls, elegant but simple. Natural hues enhance her cheeks and lips, her eyes emboldened with black and browns. I knew she was a diamond in the rough, but this... she's mesmerizing. Gorgeous.

I beckon wordlessly, swallowing hard as she makes her way to me gingerly, the plug still keeping her quietly submissive. Nikita beams. She knows she's done her job well.

When Sadie stands between my legs, I take her hands. "You look stunning, *krastoka*," I say, watching a pink flush bloom on her cheeks now that she knows what I mean. "I hope you choose obedience at dinner, for it will be my pleasure to reward you this evening."

"It would be a smart choice," Nikita chirps up from the corner.

I scowl at her. The woman oversteps. "You are dismissed, Nikita."

Giggling to herself, Nikita gathers up her things and leaves. I stand and arrange Sadie's hand on my arm.

"Walk with me, Sadie. Remember your place." I pat her backside firmly. She winces and cringes. She won't forget.

I lead her out of our room and to the exit, giving her instructions along the way. "You are not to speak until spoken to. If Dimitri asks you a question, you respond promptly and reverently. You do not speak out of turn or disobey me in any way. And you eat from my hand."

It isn't until I give her the last instruction she balks. "What?" she asks.

"Did I stutter?" My patience grows thin.

"I just… how am I to eat?" she asks.

"From my hand," I tell her, pushing a button on the elevator and watching the doors slide shut. "When I feed you." Eventually she'll be allowed to feed herself, but for now, one of her methods of obedience is to learn to accept food from my hand. Controlling her primal needs will help me train her to my satisfaction.

I was a poor boy on the streets when Dimitri

found me. Skin and bones. My mother worked herself to death to meet our needs, doing menial tasks that barely kept our bellies fed. My father was a weak man who left the two of us to poverty. I stole for food and begged for a doctor's help when my mother became ill. He refused.

The doctor who refused to care for my mother was the first man I killed when I had the power to do so. My useless father was the second.

Dimitri took me to his home. Raised me as his own. Fed me. Clothed me. Trained me to be the man I am today. A starving man learns to respect the hand that feeds him, the one who cares for his most primal needs. So when I begin training a woman, my plan is intentional. I strip her of the most basic necessities. Food, clothing, shelter. Though her needs are contrived by me, the cumulative effects of my training will not be in vain.

The utmost floor of the large mansion we occupy belongs to me, the entire apartment private and secluded. Dimitri's office, and the other rooms are where business is conducted—interrogations, meetings, and the like—lie in other parts of the sprawling building. Dimitri lives off-site in a small, humble home he occupies with his wife of thirty-five years. Yana is like a mother to me, but I haven't seen her in some time. Dimitri prefers to keep his family life and business separate.

Sadie notes everything as we descend to the dining hall. In the past, when I've been in the position of training a woman held captive, it took days to get

The Bratva's Baby: A Dark Mafia Romance

them to where Sadie already is. Like silly little mice caught by a cat, they try to flee when their tails are already pinned beneath my paw. They can't get away. None ever have. But they always try.

Not Sadie, though. I can tell by the way she takes everything in she misses nothing. This girl isn't impetuous and foolish. Not like the others. She knows if she runs from me, I'll catch her. She knows if by chance she got away from me, I have so many men surrounding this estate she wouldn't get far. And she knows an act of defiance would earn her punishment.

So I don't have to watch her the way I've watched the others. My observance of her involves more intricate methods. The way she shifts—uncomfortable with the metal between her ass cheeks, or the clothing she wears. The way she darts looks at me as if she doesn't want me to see. The way she nervously fidgets and crosses her arms over her chest. Cold, or uncomfortable with the exposure?

This is no simplistic task, though. Training her will have to be a complicated, well-orchestrated project. We will marry, and after we've settled legal details, I'll pay the tribute I owe Dimitri.

"How many floors?" she asks.

"The only one you need to concern yourself with is my floor," I tell her. "You will not leave unless escorted by me."

Pursing her lips, she doesn't reply.

The doors to the elevator slide open, bringing us to the large entry hall. Huge, crystal chandeliers hang from the ceilings so high above our heads they're like stars in a night sky. Attendants stand waiting by the exit to the elevator, uniformed servants and armed guards. Sadie trembles when I take her hand and place it on my arm. When she steps foot off the elevator, she wobbles.

"Do you not know how to walk in heels?" I ask her. Of course she doesn't. Why didn't I think of that?

"Kazimir, you saw the way I dressed. Do you think I've ever dressed like this before?"

I groan. She's such a klutz in the heels, I'm growing impatient. I'm half-tempted to carry her, but when I catch sight of a nearby servant, I get another idea.

Snapping my fingers at a young woman standing to my left, I point to the floor in front of me. She rushes forward. "Yes, sir?"

"What size shoe do you wear?" I ask her in Russian.

"Thirty-five, sir." Equivalent to an American size five, it's too small.

I shake my head and point my finger back to the line of her peers, then beckon a second woman to me. "Shoe size?"

"Thirty-seven, sir."

I nod. "That will do. Trade shoes with my woman." In English, I order Sadie. "Take off your shoes."

I wait for the two of them to obey me. Sadie looks at me in consternation, but the woman who works for me hastily bends and removes her shoes, handing them to Sadie.

"Did you just tell her to take her shoes off?" she asks me incredulously.

"No," I reply, "I told both of you to. Do it or I will."

Her pretty lips cast down in a scowl, but she obeys, stepping out of the heels and pushing them to the side, before she slides into the flats the woman hands her. I hand her heels to the servant.

"Bring these to Nikita, and tell Nikita to order you new shoes. You have the night off."

I dismiss her when she nods, then take Sadie by the arm. Leaning in to whisper in her ear, I hold her arm firmly in my grasp. "You never question me. But if you do so in front of Dimitri or my brothers, I promise you, you will never do so again." My dinner this evening will be of secondary importance. Her training will be the first. I give her a firm smack on the ass, feeling the satisfying metal beneath the thin fabric on my palm. I enjoy watching her cringe and clench her teeth. Her defiance simmers under the surface like molten lava, boiling and bubbling.

"Yes, sir," she says, but her teeth are gritted. She's giving me the mere show of obedience. I decide to take another tactic.

With a flourish, I spin her out and pull her to my chest, placing my hand on the back of her neck. The wide-eyed look she gives me makes my cock lengthen. Without her heels, she's a full head shorter than I am, so diminutive I could overpower her with one arm. My hand at her neck, I feel her rapid pulse against her soft, silky skin. I pull her so tightly against me, my hard cock presses into her.

Parted lips. Rounded eyes. Quickened pulse. Labored breathing.

I squeeze the back of her neck while I whisper in her ear. "If you behave at dinner, I'll reward you tonight with pleasure. I'll work my way up and down your body. Mark every inch of you with my mouth. Touch and lap your sweet pussy until you climax so hard you'll forget your name." I squeeze tighter, making her wince, then release her and whisper again. "And if you disobey, you'll get my lash before I cage you."

I let the words sink in. She closes her eyes, her small fingers holding onto my arms.

"Do you understand, Sadie?"

Her desperate nod tells me she understands quite well. She licks her lips and nods again.

"You'll get one warning, woman. If I squeeze your

knee, you've had your warning. A second squeeze, you'll face punishment."

She says my name as if begging for mercy. "Kazimir."

I kiss her forehead, a reminder of what's in store for her if she behaves. "Yes."

"I—don't know what you expect me to do," she says. "I'm in a foreign land and no one speaks my language. I'm in clothes I've never seen, much less worn. And even if I want to obey you," she cringes when she says this, as if the idea of obeying is physically painful, "I'm not sure what you expect."

"It's simple," I tell her. "You do exactly what I tell you." Her spine straightens, her lips thin. But she doesn't reply.

We walk into the room with her on my arm, her eyes so wide she looks as if I'm leading her to execution or hell. For her, maybe I am.

Dimitri stands when we enter. The table is laid with bread and butter, and glasses of wine and water. The food we eat is prepared in our massive kitchens, everything made from scratch with quality ingredients. Her stomach growls with hunger, and a small part of me yearns to feed her.

"We eat breakfast in my suite," I tell her. "Eight o'clock promptly. Our midday meal is the largest of the day, which you'll often have with me at one o'clock. We eat dinner at what you Americans call eight in the evening. Sometimes we will eat alone. Sometimes, we will join Dimitri. If I am away on business, you'll eat alone."

A short nod tells me she heard me, but she does not reply.

We reach Dimitri, who stands watching us in the quiet benevolence of a father, save for the way a muscle twitches in his jaw.

"Kazimir," he says, taking my hand. He shakes so firmly, when I was a young man it made me wince. Now, I meet his firm grip with one of my own.

"Dimitri."

"I see you've had Nikita attend to your woman?"

I'm not even sure he remembers her name, and for some reason that grates on me. Typically, I wouldn't care. But Sadie is different.

"Yes," I say. "Sadie has met Nikita."

When he reaches for her she involuntarily takes a step back. This will not do. Placing my hand on her lower back, I move her toward him. "Greet Dimitri properly, Sadie."

But when he leans in to kiss her cheek, something in me revolts and I hate the idea of him touching her. I brace for it, putting up a wall between my feelings and the respectful actions to the man who calls me son, but my hands involuntarily clench by my side. I pull her back to me quickly, and don't meet his eyes.

"Sit," I growl at her, pulling out a chair so quickly it scrapes along the floor like skates on ice. With the grace befitting a queen, she folds herself into the chair, wincing only slightly when her backside meets the wood.

I take my place beside her.

"You are hungry, my son," Dimitri says in broken English, his eyes glinting in the candlelight.

"We both are," I say in Russian. I don't like her here with him. I've seen what he's capable of, and if he treats her the way I've seen him treat our other captives… I pull the basket of bread to me, take out a piece, and butter it.

"Have you ever had rye bread?" I ask Sadie.

She shakes her head and reaches for a slice, but a firm shake of my head warns her. I watch as her hands slide into her lap and her jaw tightens.

"We take pride in our staff's bread," I tell her. "They bake it in small batches and knead it by hand. The locals order it from our kitchen for banquets for our leaders. It is renowned here."

I'm not sure why I'm telling her this. Dimitri's lips twitch, but he sits in silence while he eats a buttered slice of bread and follows it with a sip of wine.

Tearing off a corner of the bread, I hold it in front of her. She swallows, but her mouth remains closed.

"Open," I instruct. Though she obeys, her eyes slice to mine, suddenly defiant. I slip the bread between her lips. To my surprise, she closes her mouth before I've removed my hand, her teeth just grazing the tips of my fingers.

With a scowl, I reach my other hand to her knee and squeeze. Inhaling, she straightens.

Warning number one.

Dimitri speaks to me of the business he's conducted this week. We have associates laundering money in various countries in Asia, a large shipment of illicit jewels coming from overseas, and two political officials he's had to pay off this week. Many are already on our payroll, so it's a matter of pulling our resources together. We speak of these matters as if we're discussing the stock exchange or investments. And in many ways, we are.

Sadie's eyes focus on the basket of bread. She sits quietly, not speaking. Not moving. Her eyes don't even roam when the door to the kitchen opens and three uniformed servants come in with large silver platters.

Dimitri continues our discussion while they unveil oval-shaped dishes laden with *zakuski*. We take our food seriously in our country, and Dimitri likes his appetizers. Sadie eyes the pickled cucumbers and beets, salad of diced onion and cabbage, and stuffed eggs, with a curious eye. My stomach rumbles with hunger. It's been some time since

I've eaten at our table, and I've missed my favorite dishes.

I place several items on a plate in front of her but shake my head to remind her not to touch them, then fill my own dish. As Dimitri brings me up to date, I take a small bit of salad on my fork and hold it in front of her mouth. She eats it politely, chewing and swallowing, then following it with a sip of water, while Dimitri watches our interaction.

"Have you had enough?" I ask. She nods, so I eat my own food.

"Does your girl have a tongue?" Dimitri asks in English for her benefit, his humorous tone laced with disapproval. "Or must she always sit so mute?"

Beside me, Sadie's fingers clench into fists.

"She can speak when allowed to," I respond in English. "Do you have anything to say, Sadie?"

"I'm not sure what to say," she replies. "So perhaps it's best I stay mute."

Dimitri's eyes darken. "The chatter of women amuses me," Dimitri says. "Do speak, Sadie."

"No, thank you, sir."

"Sadie," I warn.

"What is it you wish to hear?" she asks Dimitri through gritted teeth.

"Tell me of your family," Dimitri says, giving me a curious look.

"I know nothing of my family," Sadie says in a little voice. Her eyes travel over his head when she speaks, as if she's giving a recitation. "I was raised in foster homes by people I don't care about. I prefer to be alone."

"I see. No siblings?" he asks. He already knows all of this but wants to hear it in her own voice. I want to tuck her into my chest and carry her away, not just to my room but far, far away from him.

She shakes her head. I watch her closely. I'm a man of my word and she's out of warnings.

Dimitri's eyes meet mine. "How fortunate."

I finish my bread and swallow before I reply. "Very."

"Are you shy?" he asks her, ripping his bread with savage tears of his hand.

Inhaling, she takes a breath as if to calm herself before she replies to him, her voice soft. "Yes. I don't like people. They've never been nice to me, so I prefer not to socialize."

He smiles. "Are you a virgin, then?" He draws out the question as if he mocks her. My temper flares. If he were any other man, I'd level him. Make him bleed. How dare he ask this of her? I have to remind myself who he is and curb my temper with a steady intake of breath.

But Sadie doesn't balk. "Of course."

He leans across the table and eyes her thoughtfully. If he asks her anything else, I'm liable to hurt him. Before he speaks again, and before I say something I might regret later, the dining room door opens. The waitstaff bears several platters laden with fish, potatoes, and wilted greens.

I'm grateful for the interruption. I want to gather her up in my arms and shield her from him, and it angers me that she softens me. Full grown men cower in my presence, but here... here I am, wanting to protect her. I want to see her smile.

I take double the portion onto my plate, and hand her empty plate to the staff. She watches me warily as I take small bites and feed her bites of food. I'm enthralled by her full lips closing over the fork, the way her tongue darts out and captures every last drop of food. The way she chews and swallows with grace, her little voice when she thanks me for the food.

"Good girl," I croon, and for one brief moment it's just the two of us until Dimitri speaks up. I'm so mesmerized by Sadie, I almost forgot he was here.

This will be the last meal we take in the dining room for a good, long, while. She'll sit on my lap in my room and eat from my hand, unencumbered with clothing and social expectations. Away from the eyes of everyone but me.

Dimitri goes on and on about a meeting he had

JANE HENRY

with the Prime Minister, his wife's birthday wishes to travel to Paris, and a new investment he's made. I listen, but I'm preoccupied by the soft breaths she takes. The feel of her leg beneath my hand. The soft, warm skin beneath my palm beckons to be kissed and bitten and licked. I squeeze her leg on impulse, so taken by her beauty. Soon, I'll have her alone in my room.

I decline dessert for both of us. I don't want her sleepy after this, and I'm ready to leave. When I rise and take Sadie by the elbow, her face looks troubled. Cloudy. She chews her lower lip and fidgets. I dismiss it, because we've had a long day and both of us are tired. When we get to the elevator, her eyes are cast down and her lower lip sticks out in a pout.

"Why so forlorn?" I ask her. "You behaved well at dinner. I'm not sure why you look like someone just ran over your cat."

When she looks up at me, her gaze is confused. "Did I?"

"Did you what?"

"Behave myself at dinner."

"Of course," I say, confused. "I told you I'd warn you if you didn't."

"You squeezed my leg twice," she says quietly, casting her eyes own. "You told me the second would mean punishment. I've been wondering

110

The Bratva's Baby: A Dark Mafia Romance

what it would be like sleeping behind bars and feeling your...your lash, as you call it."

I blink and think for a moment as the elevator sweeps upward. Christ. I did squeeze her leg a second time, but it wasn't a warning.

I shouldn't have done that.

I shake my head. "That wasn't a signal of punishment," I tell her. "It was an appreciative squeeze."

She sputters and blinks. "*What?*"

I take a step toward her and slide my hand through her soft, fragrant hair tucked up on her head, then pull her close to me. "I didn't mean to frighten you."

Not this time.

She closes her eyes, her tone a breathy whisper. "I wasn't frightened." But she's lying. And though a part of me stiffens at the lie—she'll learn to speak nothing but the truth to me—her reaction tells me that she wants to submit. She dislikes the idea of punishment.

I'll use this to my advantage.

Chapter Ten

Sadie

After dinner with Dimitri—the man my captor obviously reveres and respects, though one look at the man tells me he's capable of wicked, terrible cruelty—I'm sickened. The food was richer than what I normally eat, and though Kazimir fed me a moderate portion, my stomach churns. Maybe it's not the food but something else.

My nerves are frayed, my mind as confused and twisted as tangled rope. In such a short space of time, I went from dread of the punishment he would mete out to relief that I wasn't in trouble. But as I think about the very fact that this man can, and likely will, punish me, my hands clench into fists so tight my knuckles whiten.

And yet... and yet a twisted, deviant part of me wants to know what that looks like. What he'll do.

His utter control makes my pulse race with more than repulsion.

I'm afraid, but it's the type of fear one feels at a horror movie. It's unnerving, yet... something more.

A normal person would by plotting to find a way to escape. I've been kidnapped and held against my will in an unknown place. The men who orchestrated this should be arrested. But where would I escape to? Who could I trust?

I've always been a logical person. Even when I was a child, I was unnaturally practical. It annoyed my teachers and peers, but I didn't know how to shut off the part of my brain that chose logic over emotion. So instead of trying, I chose to be alone.

And until Kazimir, that worked perfectly fine for me.

I think what I hate most about what he's done to me is that he's robbed me of the solace I crave. My privacy.

The elevator cruises to a stop on his floor, and my belly swoops right along with the elevator. I stare unabashedly at Kazimir.

He runs a hand through his short, dark hair, so that it's a little untidy. A neatly-trimmed beard makes him look formidable, but it's his eyes— danger and power lurk in his gaze. He looks away from me, but I'm not sure why.

Taking my hand in his, engulfed by his large,

JANE HENRY

rough palm, he pulls me off the elevator and into the hall that brings us to his suite.

"You lied to me, Sadie," he growls.

I blink as I skip to keep up with him. With a sweep and flourish, he opens the door and half-shoves me in.

Why is he so angry? He told me I behaved myself, and promised to reward me.

"What did I lie about?" I ask in earnest curiosity when he slams the door behind him. There's nowhere to run. Nowhere to hide. I'm alone with this large, powerful, angry man, who's accusing me of lying and promised to punish me.

"You said you weren't frightened," he says, prowling closer to me so that I take a step backward.

"I… well…" I stammer, but I don't step back again. I decide to stand my ground. He's so close to me, the tips of his shoes hit mine. Was I lying? "I didn't mean to—to lie," I try to explain. "I suppose the truth is, it isn't just fear I feel. It certainly wasn't the predominant emotion."

It might be my imagination, but his eyes look like they're twinkling a bit. Is he amused?

Wordlessly, he cups my jaw and holds my gaze steady with his. "Not the predominant emotion," he repeats, his accent so heavy I can hardly understand him. "You speak like a walking dictionary."

He's criticizing my word choice? Really?

"Well. So?" I ask.

"So?" he repeats.

"Am I supposed to repent for my vocabulary?" I ask. Now I'm getting angry. What a silly thing to criticize. "I'm an educated woman who's read far more words than she's ever spoken. And you never mentioned my word choice in your instructions."

He shakes his head, his warm, calloused palm under my chin making it difficult to speak.

Leaning in closer, his breath caresses my cheek. "Then tell me, *krastoka,*" he says. "If fear isn't your *predominant emotion,* what is?"

I think for a moment. I have no reason to give him anything but the bald truth, but when I realize what the truth is, I feel a little bashful.

"Curiosity." I decide to tell him. Maybe a part of me wants him to shed light on this. "This is all... so wrong. Yet... surreal. It surprised me I felt let down when I thought you were signaling you'd punish me. And though I feared being put behind bars, I wondered what it would be like being degraded like that."

"Degraded?" he asks curiously.

"Yes," I continue. "Humiliated."

I watch his eyes narrow. "I know what the word means."

I say nothing in response, but swallow my emotion, waiting for him to make his next move like we're playing a game of life-or-death chess and he's about to say, "check mate."

"What else," he growls.

"What else?" I whisper. The timbre of his voice reverberates through me, making my palms grow sweaty and my pulse race with expectation. The masculine, spicy scent of his cologne. His warm, rough hand against my skin, holding me hostage with his eyes that promise punishment, pain, and pleasure. I don't get a chance to respond before his mouth hovers over mine. A flash of panic warns me he's about to kiss me, and that it's wrong, I'm not his lover. I'm a woman he's stolen, a woman he's going to hurt, and kissing is for the people who do things right. But I can't stop him any more than I can stop my heart from beating. I can't help leaning into him.

I need to know what those lips taste like.

I inhale in anticipation the second before his lips hit mine.

I never knew why people close their eyes when they kiss. But when he kisses me, I know. I'm so overcome with feelings, so wrapped up in this moment, I need to shut out everything else around us. When our lips meet, my body jolts and hums with pleasure. I need more. Deeper. Longer. My hands reach for his neck, scrambling for purchase as he pulls me toward him, his warm, strong hands on the small of my back. I moan. I'm drowning but it's a thrilling struggle, the beat of my heart and rapid pulse in my veins making me feel more alive than ever.

Too soon, he pulls away. He blinks. It's the only time I've seen his eyes register shock. He's as surprised as I am. He mutters a guttural curse in his native language. I have no idea what he says, but I know by his tone it can be nothing but cussing.

"And now, *krastoka*," he whispers. "What is your *predominant emotion?*"

I shake my head, unable to put into words what's happening right now. I'm spiraling out of control, afraid of being attracted to a man I should hate. How could I? I feel as if anything less than hatred and revenge betrays every woman who's ever walked this Earth, and yet—

My mind stutters to a halt when he yanks up the fabric of my dress, bunching it carelessly between his rough fingers, I freeze when his palm glides down my lower back and over my backside, coming to rest where he's put that god-awful metal. I close my eyes, my cheeks heating, when he traces a finger between my cheeks.

"Kazimir," I beg, knowing before I utter a thing that my pleas will fall on deaf ears. He has to stop. This is too much.

"Hush," he commands, caressing the outer edge of the plug. It makes me feel so full I might split apart, and so utterly under his control, it's as if he holds the switch to my will in his hand. I'm a marionette, and he holds the strings. Orchestrating my every move. My every thought. "You want to know what it's like," he says, a statement without question. "I'll show you what it's like."

Panic sweeps through me. "No," I tell him, shaking my head. I lost myself there for a moment, but now the thought of meeting "his lash" as he calls it, or the bars of a cage, make real panic surface. He only looks at me with a wolfish grin and shakes his head.

"Silly girl. As if you have a choice."

He's sliding out of his suit jacket, his eyes fixed on me. Silky fabric on the edge of a chair. Sleeves rolled up to the elbow, revealing strong, powerful forearms. Hands that dwarf mine, reaching for the clasp of his belt. I pedal backward. If he takes his belt off…

"On the bed," he commands, tugging his belt through the loops of his pants and folding it over. He points to the bed with the folded leather. "Now."

Somehow, I obey. Is "his lash" his belt? It hurts so much.

"Remove all your clothing, and hand it to me," he instructs. Standing to the side of the bed with his arms crossed on his chest, he points. "When you're stripped, I want your hands on the bedpost."

The Bratva's Baby: A Dark Mafia Romance

When I'm naked, will he whip me? I freeze. I can't move. I'm terrified of what he'll do to me. How stupid I've been.

"Kazimir," I say, shaking my head. My gown hangs down around me and I'm on my hands and knees on the huge bed. "No, I can't. Please don't—"

His belt swishes through the air so quickly I don't have time to react. A line of fire lights up my backside and I scream out loud.

"Now."

I reach for the hem of my dress quickly, my hands shaking. I don't want him to hurt me, and he's so close, holding his weapon in hand, he very well may. I tear at the clothing, every twist and turn making the metal in my ass feel deeper. I'm full. So full.

The dress comes off easier than I expected. I fold it hastily, hand it to him, then remove my silky undergarments. He says nothing, just takes the clothes silently. When I'm naked, he points his belt to the bedpost, and I can tell from the way his jaw clenches, this is my only reminder.

I freeze, waiting for the belt to strike again, and jump when I feel him beside me. He takes his belt and loops it around the post, fastening my wrists. I blink in surprise, watching as he expertly weaves the leather in an intricate knot, my hands secure but comfortable. I'm kneeling, my hands restrained, my ass still burning from the lick of his belt. He no longer holds the belt, though, as he's restrained me with it instead of striking me again.

What will he do next?

"Bow your head, Sadie. You won't be able to unfasten your wrists. When I start, there will be no way to stop me. So the sooner you decide to surrender, the longer you'll enjoy yourself."

When he starts? What was this, then?

I nod. A firm pinch to my naked bottom makes me amend my response. "Yes, sir," I manage to croak out. He pats my ass almost affectionately.

I have read the wrong romance books. The wrong damn ones. I've been spending all my time in regencies and contemporary comedy, when I should have been reading the ones with the hand-cuffs on them.

Are those even the right ones? I always had a vague idea that the play in those books was consensual.

This is nothing of the sort.

Kazimir stalks past me and heads to the large closet to the right of the bed. I try to turn my head to look, but can't turn enough to see. Instead, I wait. I let myself feel the cold leather on my wrists, inhaling the fragrant, rich scent. I let my eyes fall closed so I can focus better on what else I feel. I'm warm, despite having no clothes on. He must keep the temperature regulated.

And deep inside I know I'm one defiant step away from incurring his anger, and something tells me I don't want to anger him.

But there's more to it. Between my legs, pressure builds, hot and insistent. Instinctively, my body knows this is something more than what I've experienced before. That he could teach me oh so many things—pleasure. Pain. I've read about sex so many times, I've almost convinced myself I know what it feels like. But I don't. Hell, I don't have the first clue. I've never… climaxed before.

I can hear him walking around the bed, as he takes in every detail of the scene in front of him. I'm glad he's made me bow my head. I have to close my eyes. Knowing I'm helpless to him and utterly naked makes me quake with nerves. It isn't fair. I do my best to hide from people, and he's taken that from me.

I lose track of time as he circles me. With my eyes closed, I try to take in every detail I can. A drawer opens and closes. A clink of metal. Steps retreating, a door opening. Steps returning back to me, along with his heat.

"Focus." The sound of his voice so close to me makes me jump, and my eyes fly open. He holds something gleaming in his hand that looks almost like a spur.

"What is that?" I ask, trying to pull away, but the restraints hold fast. He shakes his head and places

JANE HENRY

it on the bed behind me so I can't see it. I notice a black length of silky fabric in his hand.

"No more speaking," he orders sternly, as he loops the fabric around my mouth and ties it behind my head. "I don't want to be distracted by the sound of your voice." I close my eyes and taste the fabric with my tongue. It's soft but tight, so it pulls back the corners of my mouth. I suck in air around it, but find it easier to breathe in through my nose. I take in one deep breath, then let it out again. A second. A third. But I can't relax. I'm too tightly wound.

I was scared when he took me, but now... my whole body quakes, tremors rippling through me as if I'm naked in the cold, but I'm comfortably warm.

I hear the rustle of fabric. Craning my neck to look, I watch Kazimir slowly removing his shirt, his stern gaze fixed on me like he's a professor and I'm the naughty student he's about to punish. Jaw tight. Lips thinned. Eyes crackling with heat.

Why is he angry? Why does he look at me like I'll pay for the sins committed against him?

He starts speaking to me, but it's in Russian and I don't understand a word. When he shrugs out of his shirt, he stands before me in just a t-shirt. The stark white contrasts against his swarthy skin, covered in a map of tattoos before he tears his t-shirt off. The skull stares at me with foreboding, another one a head with an open-mouthed scream. They run together so they're barely distinguishable, the black rose the only reminder of his humanity.

Taking the white shirt in his hands, he folds it neatly in a little square, smoothing out the edges while his eyes are on mine.

Daring. Warning.

My belly dips and my pulse races. He hasn't touched me, but he holds me in his power—the fabric in my mouth, his belt holding me in place, the throbbing line of fire where he spanked me, the degrading metal between my ass cheeks. My whole body is under his control, though he stands a few feet apart.

Reaching down to place his shirt on the bedside table, I watch the large muscles in his neck and back bunch together. When he stands straight again, I'm struck with how magnificent his body is. So strong. So powerful. He towers over me vibrating with energy. I take it all in—broad shoulders, bulging biceps, sculpted abs with a dark line of hair that dips low, tucked into his pants. My gaze travels downward when I notice his erection. I turn away, suddenly shy.

Again, he speaks in Russian, like he's saying an incantation, reminding me that I'm a stranger in a foreign land, and even speaking English to me is only a kindness he grants when he wishes. He controls every bit of this, including my comprehension. I have no choice but to bow my head and wait.

When he picks up something off the bed, my body tenses. Waiting. Fearing. The prick of metal on my shoulder makes me yelp, but the sound is muted against the silk in my mouth. He wraps one large hand around my mid-section, holding me in place, while he traces the prickly metal along my shoulder. Goosebumps rise on my skin and I shiver, line after line of bristles trace along my back. He sweeps the hair off my neck and traces the metal on the tender skin. It's such a surprisingly erotic move, my back arches and I throw my head back. I freeze when his lips meet the primed, prickly skin, and he sucks my flesh into his mouth. The hand on my abdomen skirts up, and one rough knuckle brushes the underside of my breasts. I whimper.

Then he's back to the prickly metal, zigzagging it along my back to the very top of my bottom, back and forth, my flesh crawling at the feel of it. My breasts swell, and suddenly I need him to touch me. There's pressure between my legs that's almost painful, and even though I've never had sex, never even brought myself to climax, I instinctively know I need him to. I can't fully breathe until he does.

Ragged breaths and trembling limbs. Arousal. Fear. All swirls together in an incomprehensible cocktail he stirs in me. After he's thoroughly primed my skin, the pressure builds, the metal spokes digging deeper into my skin. On and on, the slightly painful prickles scour my body until I imagine angry pink railroad tracks dotting my skin.

And then he stops. I tense. Waiting. I have no idea what he'll do next.

"Sadie."

I snap my head up and open my eyes. He kneels on the bed beside me, but he doesn't touch me.

I can't speak, so I lift questioning eyes to his. My eyes catch the glimmer of metal in the light. The wheel that looks like a spur sits beside him.

"Remember to breathe," he warns.

Rearing his arm back, he brings something swishing through the air. I don't see what he's holding, but the fire he lights on my ass makes me scream against the gag. But he only strikes once. Leaning close to me, I'm overcome with his masculine, powerful scent when his hand anchors on my waist as he did before.

"You wanted to know what it was like," he whispers against the shell of my ear. His warm breath tickles, and a shiver runs through me. "Taste my lash." An invitation.

I brace, knowing he's going to strike me again before he does. He stands behind me, one hand braced on my lower back, before I hear the whistle of leather through the air and feel a line of pain on my backside. It stings, it burns, but before I

125

JANE HENRY

recover, another flare of pain follows. With slow, steady blows, he whips me. I've never experienced this before, but I know intuitively that he's holding back, and that he could strike much harder than he is. The large hand on my back trembles slightly, as if he needs to hold onto me to temper the blows, and the spanking continues.

Red hot pain crisscrosses my ass. I wince when the leather strikes metal, the fullness in me flaring. Instinctively I try to turn away but a harsh word I don't know makes me pull back to the position he put me in, the next strike of his strap the hardest he's given me yet.

"Do not twist," he raps out. Three rapid, vicious swipes of the lash correct my behavior, reminding me to keep my position. I tug on the restraints at my wrists, but the belt holds fast.

I cry, but the gag mutes my cries. My cheeks are wet. I blink, surprised, when I realize I'm crying. He doesn't stop, but the tempo of his punishment changes.

The hand that braced him slides down my abdomen. My hips rise automatically, silently pleading for him to touch me where I need him to. His strong fingers glide through my folds.

"You like this," he whispers in my ear, stroking faster. My hips buck. I push against his fingers, needing him not to stop. I shake my head. Denying. I can't like this. Why would I like something like this?

126

My response is met with another lash from his strap, my muted scream crying out in pain.

"Do not lie to me." He ceases stroking, and rests his hand on my inner thigh, so close to where I need him, the top of his hand creates torturous pressure. "Do not *ever* lie to me, woman. What I give you now is a taste. Mercy. If you lie to me, Sadie," his mouth is at me ear. "I will not show mercy."

His hand crashes onto my naked skin on the underside of my heated bottom. I wince and cry.

"You like this," he repeats, not asking, as his touch comes back between my legs. The feel of his fingers makes me moan. I slump against the restraints, spreading my legs wider. Silently begging him to touch me.

"Mmm," he groans. "There is my answer." He expertly strokes me with his fingers. "Such a very good girl. I promised you pleasure tonight if you behaved, but your pleasure will be on my terms. Do you understand me?"

I nod, my eyes closing as I succumb to the delicious friction he builds between my thighs. Stroking, stroking, my need builds more intensely with every second that passes.

"No climaxing without my permission, Sadie," he orders, never stopping the endless pleasure he brings. "If you feel you are close, you are to ask permission."

I feel him unfasten the gag. It falls, my mouth free. I open and close it and lick my lips.

"Do you understand?"

"No, sir," I tell him honestly. I'm not defying him. I really don't understand. I hang my head, ashamed.

He freezes. "Excuse me?"

"I—I don't know how to tell if I'm close, sir." When he doesn't respond, I go on. "You told me I should never lie to you. So I'm telling you the truth. I've never—cl—climaxed before," I stammer. I'm shivering, and suddenly cold. "So how would I know I'm getting close?"

"Never climaxed before," he repeats.

I shake my head. "No, sir."

He swears. Then he's silent for a moment before he speaks again. "You mean to tell me you've never even brought yourself pleasure?"

My cheeks flush. I'm mortified. I can't look at him. "No, sir," I whisper.

The heel of his palm rests between my thighs, and I throb against him. I want him to stroke me again. I *need* him to stroke me again. "You mean to tell me," he repeats, his voice getting deeper, gravelly. "You've never experienced any sexual pleasure?"

How else am I supposed to explain this to him?

"No, sir."

"I knew she was perfect," he murmurs to himself, then he's muttering in Russian again. His hands are gone. If this is how he'll punish me—bringing me to the edge of pleasure and leaving me there? —I might have to obey him after all. I fear being brought to the cusp and left far worse than I fear his lash, even now that I've felt it.

My wrists swing free when he unfastens the restraints on my wrists. He's hovering over me, his muscled torso at my back, as he catches my arms and rubs the wrists with his thumbs. I cringe in mortification when he brings his hand to my ass, easing the metal out. It's such an invasion of my body I cringe. The fullness is gone, but my feminine parts, swollen and primed, pulse with need.

He knows exactly what he's doing.

To my surprise, he gathers me in his arms and turns me, so that he cradles me against his chest. "Never experienced sexual pleasure," he says, shaking his head. "Then your first taste of pleasure will not come from my mouth. I'll worship that sweet pussy in time," he promises. "But not tonight."

I don't know what to think or do, as he carries me past the little table and chairs, to the overstuffed chair that sits in the corner of the room. I fold myself into his warmth because I'm cold now. I don't need his comfort, I tell myself. I just need his warmth.

JANE HENRY

Though I'm stark naked, he's fully clothed from the waist down, so when he sits in the chair and slides me onto his lap, my bare ass brushes against his pants, underscoring the dichotomy of power here. I want to hide from him but I'm laid bare.

"Lay your head back," he orders.

Reluctantly, I obey, the back of my head nestling in the hollow of his neck. When he opens his legs, he places me between them.

"Part your knees."

Still shivering, I obey.

Chapter Eleven

Kazimir

I keep it warm in my bedroom, since she will rarely be allowed to dress, and yet she shivers. I hold her to my chest. So soft. So sweet. So innocent and unblemished.

So perfect.

I will own everything that belongs to Sadie. Her pleasure will be no exception. Every spasm of pleasure I wring from her body will be mine and mine alone.

My dick lengthens under her punished ass when I hold her to my chest, cradled in my lap.

I introduced her tonight, a whisper and a promise of things to come. My Wartenberg wheel coaxed sensation to the surface. The small plug she wore reminded her to obey. The brief spanking reminding her what happens if she doesn't obey. I'll reward her with the climax she's earned, a fitting ending to our session to show her she's mine. To train her will.

I never dreamed I'd grant her first climax to her. Knowing her virginal body belongs to just me, I couldn't bring myself to do what I planned to do —lay her out and eat her sweet pussy until she writhed in pleasure. It's too intense for a first time. Instead, she'll need the support of me behind her when she chases her pleasure.

On my command, her legs have fallen open, though she trembles at the knees. So pretty. So soft. I glide my knuckles along the tender skin between her thighs and inhale the heady scent of her arousal.

She denied liking this, but it's no matter. She will learn to speak truth to me, but first she must accept the truth. They always deny my dominance brings them pleasure, even the most wanton of them. Sadie is the most innocent, so it only stands to reason that she denies it. Likely, the thought of being aroused by my sadistic manipulation of her body appalls her.

Up and down her creamy thighs I trace my way, putting enough pressure so I don't tickle her, but just enough that she'll long for more. I hold her against my chest with my left arm, my right hand teasing her. Her back arches when my hand comes close to her sweet pussy. She whimpers when I skirt it away.

"You are beautiful," I croon in her ear. "Your eagerness pleases me."

She's adapted quicker than any other woman I've taken before, but I suspect it's partially due to the fact that she's smarter than the rest. A clever one, she's likely already accepted the futility of an attempt to escape, instead observing as she plans her move.

I'm under no delusion that her acquiescence comes from real obedience. No. Sadie's tenacious. It will take time. Time and skill to break her. Mold her. Make her mine.

"Please, Kazimir," she whispers, tilting her head to the side, against my chest, her cheek resting against the coarse hair. "Sir, I know you can soothe this ache between my legs."

So innocent, her pleas sway me. With my left hand, I lightly touch the underside of her breast before I cup the full breast in my hand, first one, then the other, my thumb flicking over the furled nipples. A tremor runs through her. I continue the gentle caress, then bring my hand between her legs.

"Close your eyes," I whisper in her ear. She obeys. While fondling her nipples, I slowly give her what she wants, gliding my fingers through her wet folds. I curse when I feel her arousal, my mouth watering to taste her. With deft strokes, I work her closer to orgasm, patiently letting her build. If she's telling me the truth, and my instinct says she is, she doesn't know what waits for her on the other side of this pleasure. The unknown might frighten her, which is why I'm holding her close like this. A climax apart from me might be overwhelming, and I don't want to overwhelm her yet.

Soon.

Her breathing hitches, her body tensing against mine. I work her faster, circling her clit and stroking her breasts, lightly pinching her nipples before I plunge two fingers in her slick core. Her breaths become ragged, her nipples hard as rocks, and I know she's on the very brink of coming when her back arches into me.

"This," I whisper in her ear. "This is the verge of orgasm. Your body dangles at the very edge of bliss. Your breathing changes. Your heartbeat races. The pressure and longing will build. This. This is when you ask my permission. The first few times I'll allow you to learn your body's cues. But once you know them, if you come without asking, you'll earn punishment. Do you understand me?"

"Yes," she chokes out, hips bucking. She writhes, her head whipping from side to side when I feel her climax rip through her and her low-pitched moan fills the room. I ease her through her orgasm, gentling the strokes of my fingers when she passes her peak. She falls against me. Gasping.

The Bratva's Baby: A Dark Mafia Romance

Panting. Her body heated and no longer trembling from cold. Her head lolls to the side, her eyes closed. She's exhausted.

I hold her to my chest.

"How did you like your first orgasm, *krasotka?*" I ask.

"It was… more than I'd hoped," she whispers. My chest swells with pride at her words. I drop a kiss to one bare shoulder.

"Good," I tell her. "Obey me, and you will learn to crave pleasure."

"Mmm," she says, her eyes closed. "I get it. Disobey, it will be the opposite." I growl. It's no joking matter. She'll see, though.

I rise with her against my chest and carry her to the bed. My cock presses up against her hot ass, but I won't take pleasure from her tonight. I'll rub one off in the shower to ease my aching balls. I long to claim her, but I can be a patient man when I want to be. After years of exacting revenge and biding my time, I've learned patience.

"I don't trust you," she says, when I lay her down on the bed. Her eyes are closed, a faint pink flush coloring her beautiful cheeks. It would be a travesty to dress her now, when she still wears the marks of my session, lines across her back and shoulders and crisscrossed pink on her full backside. The marks will fade quickly, and in the morn-

135

ing, no residual reminders of our session will remain. I pull the sheet up over her body, covering her, then pull up the thick duvet cover and place that over her as well.

"Of course you don't trust me," I tell her. "I do not demand your trust. I demand your compliance."

She doesn't respond, but tucks her hands under the pillow and sighs.

"I'm tired," she says on a yawn.

"Get some rest," I tell her. This night could have ended so differently. Every one of them defies me at this point and earns the night behind bars by my feet. Sadie hasn't yet. I wonder if she will. But as I stare at the gleaming metal, sitting in the corner of the room in shadow, a part of me dislikes the idea of putting her there. I want her full ass pressed up against my cock as I sleep. Her breasts within reach should I decide to touch them. Her mouth ready to service me when I demand it.

I sit by the bed and thread my fingers through her hair. It would be an almost gentle gesture, if I wasn't touching her to remind her that I'm here. That even though she has the freedom to move around the room without restraints or shackles, she still remains confined with me. So when she falls asleep by my side, she knows who she belongs to and that freedom no longer exists for her.

I rise and retrieve the wipes Nikita keeps in the

bathroom, then come back and sit on the edge of the bed. Cradling Sadie's face in my hands, I wipe away the remains of her makeup until she lies with her eyes closed, her simple beauty making my heart swell.

I watch her soft brown hair ease through my fingers and fall. Over and over, a mesmerizing repetition, combing through her fragrant, silky hair, until her breathing slows. I stand, and stretch, my cock painfully hard. Lifting my belt in my hands, I double it and lightly smack the belt against my hand. When I fantasize about hurting Sadie, this is what I conjure up, my belt in my hand, doubled over and ready to punish her.

I lay the leather on a chair, where I coil it like a length of rope, before I unfasten my pants. I push them down my hips, step out, and fist my thick cock while I look at the sleeping form of the girl in my bed. I want to jerk myself off until I mark her with my come. I throw my head back at the image of her breasts dripping as she kneels in front of me. I stop just before I come and turn away.

In the shower, I ease my misery, imagining her presenting herself on the bed for me, striped with my leather, her body welted and marked by me. When I finally come, I roar out my release, bracing myself on the wall. I jerk myself off until there's nothing left. I slump against the wall, panting. Christ, how I want to bury my cock balls-deep in that virgin pussy of hers.

I lather up and quickly finish the shower. I towel

off, slide into a pair of boxers, and lie down next to her.

Soon, we will marry. She has no choice in this. The marriage is one of convenience, and by the time we say our vows, I'll have her trained well enough that she shouldn't cause a problem. I will take my place as her legal husband. Reap her inheritance. Pay my tribute to Dimitri.

And what happens when I pay my tribute?

Typically, the women we use for our own gain disappear, never to be seen nor heard from again.

And as I drift off to sleep, I know this time will be different, just like I've known Sadie was different. This time, everything changes.

Tomorrow will be her real test. Tomorrow, she meets the rest of my brothers.

She tosses and turns all night, murmuring to herself until the sun finally rises. I rub the sleep from my eyes, exhausted.

"For the love of God," I growl. "Will you rest and get some sleep?"

"I tried," she says petulantly, her back to me.

Irritated, I give her a sharp crack to the ass. "You didn't try hard enough."

The Bratva's Baby: A Dark Mafia Romance

"Ow," she says, rubbing her ass. "What was that for?"

"Because I wanted to." I don't like her tone of voice and today's an important day.

"Well, good," she mutters. "It seems foolish to spank someone for not sleeping."

My dick is hard waking up to her beside me. I lean closer to her. "I'll spank you for any reason I want."

She doesn't respond. I reach out to her ass and give it a good squeeze, so I can tell if she still feels the residual effects of our session last night. The hiss of breath she releases confirms to me that yes, she definitely does. Good. Sometimes a reminder to obey is most effective.

"You didn't tie me up," she says, in a curious tone. "If I wanted to, I could have just walked about the whole apartment if I wanted?"

"Yes," I tell her.

"And what would happen if I tried to leave?"

"Do you want to find out?" She's like a child pushing boundaries. She can push all she wants. I'm prepared to handle her when she does. Hell, I'm eager.

She silences.

"Don't be silly, woman. I won't restrain you unless necessary since there's nowhere for you to go. No way to escape. But make no mistake. You belong to me."

Still, she doesn't respond.

"Are you hungry?" I ask, taking another tactic.

"Very," she admits.

I get out of bed and make a call on my phone, ordering breakfast to be sent up.

"Take your shower," I tell her, jerking my finger toward the bathroom. "There are towels and all the toiletries you'll need. If you need anything else, tell me."

Nodding, she gets out of bed and goes to the drawers that hold all her clothes, looking around the room. "This is weird," she says.

"What is?"

"You have clothes for me and toiletries to keep me comfortable. And yet, I'm your captive?"

I remove my own clothes from the drawers and lay them on the dresser. "Yes."

Turning wide brown eyes to me, she cocks her head to the side. "Why?"

"Why what?"

Her brows knit together. "Why me?"

I shrug, not meeting her eyes. I won't tell her the real reason, but it won't hurt to give her a partial truth. "Because I was mesmerized by you. And I have my reasons."

Frowning, she continues asking probing questions. "Why didn't you just… woo me?"

"Woo you?" I furrow my brows, not understanding. "What does this mean?"

"Pursue me," she says. Her cheeks flush a deeper shade of pink. "It's an old-fashioned term, I suppose." Those silly historical romance novels she reads.

"Charm me," she stammers on. "Heck, date me." Now she's adorably beet red. It bemuses me what things make her blush and what doesn't. She tries to cover it up by turning to the dresser and removing the clothes I put there for her. "You didn't have to steal me and keep me prisoner. I maybe would've responded well to a little… oh, forget it."

"Look at me." I will not have her hiding her shame. It all belongs to me. Every last bit of it. When she doesn't turn around right away, I cross the room to her and tangle her hair in my fist, spinning her around. I'm impatient for her immediate obedience. I thirst for it.

"I said *look at me*," I repeat.

Her wide brown eyes flash angrily at me.

"This afternoon, you'll meet my brothers," I tell her. "They will push you. Test your boundaries.

JANE HENRY

And I'll expect you to behave. Why do you hide now?"

I watch as tears well in her eyes. "That hurts," she whispers, her fingers delicately touching my wrist.

"I know," I respond, not caring.

"It's embarrassing to think of," she says, closing her eyes so she doesn't have to look into mine, but a sharp tug makes her eyes spring open again.

"What are you talking about?"

"A man like *you*," she says through watery eyes, "pursuing a woman like me. I don't want to talk about this anymore. I shouldn't have asked you." I probe her gaze with mine, searching, but I don't know what I'm searching for. Clarity? Something inside her that will explain why the monster inside me rages, tempting me to do more than pull her hair?

There was no time to court her. No time to win her favor. But the truth is, I wouldn't put myself in the position of growing attached to a woman I was going to destroy.

Finally, I release her and continue getting ready. Ignoring what plagues me.

"It shouldn't be embarrassing," I tell her, my temper stoked. She thinks so little of herself that she can't imagine a man like me wanting her? It's bullshit. But when she sees my temper flare, her own eyes heat.

The Bratva's Baby: A Dark Mafia Romance

"I'm as boring as they come," she seethes.

"So?" I step into my pants.

"I dress like a nun," she spits out. Her temper's rising, making my own blood simmer. How quickly she got over the little hair pull. The knowledge both impresses me and makes me want to stripe her ass again.

"Your point?" I ask, piercing her with a stern gaze that makes her back down a little. She looks away.

"You're strong and powerful and rich," she says to the wall. "The women in this country cultivate beauty."

"Yes," I agree, fastening my pants. I reach for the belt coiled on the chair beside me and begin threading it through the loops on my pants. I watch her eye the belt and swallow hard. She twists a strand of hair in her fingers.

"It doesn't make sense," she snaps.

"It doesn't need to." I don't owe her an explanation. I keep my hand on my belt to make a point. She won't get the truth out of me. Not now. Not ever. And if I'm honest, there's more than money in this bargain.

I need to ask her a question.

"Last night was your first orgasm, Sadie," I say, my eyes focused on her eyes that go from narrow to wide. When she captures her lips between her teeth, my cock aches to remind her what that felt like. "Have you ever been touched by a man?"

She shakes her head.

"Is that the truth?" My tone sharpens.

"Yes."

"Good," I mutter to myself, and ignore the question in her eyes. "Have you been kissed before?"

The pretty pink flush I've already grown accustomed to heats her cheeks. "No."

My chest tightens with pride. I captured the victory flag and stumbled upon a treasure. I own all her firsts. Her first kiss. Her first orgasm.

I'll take her virginity and own that, too.

Her money is only an excuse. I'm greedy for more than what money can buy, and I'm on the cusp of a fucking goldmine.

"Go get ready," I instruct her, dismissing her. Sadie is too perceptive for her own good, and I don't need her to read any weakness. "You'll find everything you need in there. When you're finished, we'll eat breakfast."

I watch her stalk to the bathroom, stomping her way to the door before she slams it shut behind her. On the other side of the door, she fumbles with the knob, no doubt trying to lock it. Silly girl. As if I'd allow such a thing. There are no locks in here. None for her to access, anyway.

The Bratva's Baby: A Dark Mafia Romance

Shaking my head, I follow. This woman will end up over my knee before the day is through.

I walk to the bathroom and open the door, but she pushes it from the other side.

"Hey!" she shouts. "There's a door here for a reason."

"And that reason is to give *me* privacy," I say through gritted teeth. "Open."

She's not foolish enough to outright defy me, so the door falls open and she stands on the other side, her arms crossed over her bare breasts. "Well, that's a double standard," she says.

"Of course," I agree. "Our entire relationship is a double standard. Your point?"

She throws up her hands. "Fine, then. Watch me shower." When she spins to turn to the shower, I reach for her hand and tug her over to me. I sit on the edge of the toilet seat and stand her between my legs. I capture her jaw with my hand and secure her gaze with mine.

"Do you wish to wear a plug between your cheeks when you meet my brothers?" I ask.

I watch the delicate skin of her neck as she swallows. "No, sir."

"Do I need to spank you again?"

Both curiosity and fear light her eyes at that. My cock stirs. "No, sir."

145

I reach my hand to her breast and grab her nipple, making her cry out in pain. She tries to push me away but I hold fast. "Then that's the last time you speak back to me, Sadie." I twist, her nipple heating between my fingers.

"Yes, sir," she cries out. When I let go of her nipple, I send her to the shower with a sharp crack to her ass. A red handprint blooms against her pale skin. I watch as she looks around the bathroom, gathers up a towel and washcloth, and gingerly places them on the small table beside the shower. This is a large bathroom, with a whirlpool tub and full shower all in white marble and gold, a vanity and matching table housing the toiletries she'll need.

"After you've showered, I'll call Nikita up to come help you dress and prepare for the day," I tell her, as billows of steam rise in the shower. I can see she opens her mouth to say something, but doesn't reply, Good. Perhaps she actually listened to my warning this time.

I watch her wash between her legs, and imagine what it would be like to be the one touching her there. My cock tightens in my pants. Steam rises, and my clothes are getting damp, but I don't care. I can't tear myself away from her as she lathers her entire body.

"Is this razor in here mine?" she asks, picking up the pink handled razor I chose.

"Mine aren't usually pink." I shake my head and I

swear I almost hear her giggle. I don't know if I've ever heard her laugh before. The sound intrigues me.

"Let's go," I tell her. "It's time you got ready."

I hear a noise outside the door indicating our breakfast has arrived. I tear myself away, wishing instead I could strip off my clothes and join her.

Hell. Maybe I will. But when I glance at the clock I realize I don't have the time I thought I did.

"Let's go," I yell into the shower, after I've arranged our food.

When she emerges from the bathroom, she pulls a chair out, but I shake my head at her.

"Have you already forgotten how this goes?"

Apparently, she has. She nods her head and walks to me, still wrapped in her towel. I stand her in front of me and with a flick of my wrist, divest her of the towel cloaked around her body. "Wrap it around your hair," I instruct. "I don't want to get my clothes wet. Then sit on my knee."

When she's done what I instructed, she sits on my knee and places her hands in her lap.

I take a bite of egg on a fork and bring it to her mouth, but she wrinkles up her nose. "No, thank you."

"I thought you ate eggs every day, " I say.

"I don't eat them fried," she says, a little furrow of

consternation knitting her brows. "And how do you know?"

I don't answer her question. I hired an investigator to tell me everything about her so I'd be prepared. "How do you eat your eggs?"

"Scrambled," she says. "Or like in an omelet."

"Well, we can have that another day," I say, pushing the eggs away and bringing the porridge over. She takes small bites of the creamy concoction. She eats in silence until I break it.

"When I was a child, I'd never have denied food like this," I tell her, correcting her.

"I wouldn't have either," she responds. "But I'm no longer a child."

"You would eat them if I forced you," I say.

"Yes," she says. "I would. But I also might vomit them back up and then we'd have a mess to clean up, wouldn't we?" Even naked on my lap and eating from my hand, she's feistier than most women I've had in this position.

But have I really ever had a woman in *this* position? I've had women I've taken and trained, but none that affected me the way she does.

There's nothing but honestly in her eyes.

"The porridge is good," she says. "Thank you."

I nod, and feed her another bite. When she swal-

The Bratva's Baby: A Dark Mafia Romance

lows, she turns slightly to me so she can look in my eyes. "Did you grow up poor?" she asks.

Nodding, I offer her another spoonful, and while she swallows it down, I continue. "My parents were destitute. My mother worked to pay for our needs, and my father did nothing to stop it. I could have died from hunger and nearly did a few times."

"You said Dimitri took you in," I say to him. "What does that mean? Did he adopt you?"

"Not legally," I tell her. "But yes. He took me into his home and raised me as his own. He taught me his values, fed me, clothed me, saw to my education."

"And when was that?" she asks.

"Twenty-four years ago," I tell her.

"You were how old?"

"Nine years old."

Frowning, she takes another nibble from the spoon I offer. "Do you have any family, then?"

"None left, but the ones I've chosen."

"Have you ever done anything but work for Dimitri?"

"I've done many things," I say to her, tired of this line of conversation. "But that's enough for now." The sound of ringing tells me Nikita has arrived,

149

so I slide Sadie off my lap and instruct her to finish breakfast while I open the door. When we come in the room, Sadie's draped a blanket around her naked body, and her bowl of porridge is empty.

"That was good," she says.

"I'm glad. Go with Nikita and get ready. You have thirty minutes."

Rising, she takes the blanket with her. This time, I allow it. Eventually... soon... it will be clothes that make her uncomfortable.

I look at the time. Soon, I take her to my brothers.

Chapter Twelve

Sadie

I hardly pay attention to what Nikita is doing to me, my mind is so focused on what Kazimir's just told me. He held back truth when I asked him why he chose a boring girl like me to take. I want to know what his endgame is. Every case of abduction I've heard of featured a man who wanted a very specific thing: usually sex, money, or revenge.

Sex makes no sense to me. I'm hardly a beauty, and a man like him could have any woman he wanted. Money obviously makes no sense, as I'm poorer than a church mouse. Revenge also doesn't add up. I have no ties to anyone of importance.

And yet he has his reasons. The truth lurks behind those angry eyes of his.

I let Nikita dress and primp me, even though it

makes me a little uncomfortable. The clothes I wear make me look prettier than I am. Other women would probably like being all dolled up, with expert application of makeup enhancing the fullness of my lips and brightness of my eyes, but I'm massively uncomfortable. I feel like some sort of human doll he's playing dress-up with. And what do people do with dolls? Use them. Break them. Discard them.

There is no good that will come of this.

The porridge I ate churns in my stomach like a rock tumbler when I think of meeting the men he calls brothers. He has no family left "but the ones he's chosen," so I surmise the men I'm about to meet are the men he's chosen as family. Nikita hands me a glass of water and several little pills. "Take these," she instructs. "They were ordered by Mr. Romanov."

"What are they?" I frown.

She shrugs and doesn't meet my eyes. "Some vitamins or something," she says.

A sharp knock sounds on the door.

"Take them," she insists. "If you don't, I'll tell him."

I frown at her and stare at the vitamins. Is that all they are? But when he knocks on the door again, I toss them in my mouth. She's right. They just taste like vitamins, and I feel fine. I hate that I have to

The Bratva's Baby: A Dark Mafia Romance

second guess literally everything that happens to me.

"Let's go. You're taking too long." It's odd that he knocks. I know the door isn't locked. Maybe he prefers to give me the illusion of privacy, or he doesn't like to interrupt Nikita. Or maybe he just likes to see me when I'm done.

Nikita rolls her eyes in the mirror and whispers, "He's always impatient. We're almost done."

She doesn't seem afraid. Why not?

I stare at the reflection, hardly recognizing the pretty woman that looks back at me. Her hair gleams in waves around her face, unblemished with a faint touch of pink at the cheeks, plump, pinked lips, bright eyes with perfect brows and full, dark lashes. I didn't even know I could look like this.

Small silver hoops hang from my ears, but I wear no other jewelry. The thin, V-neck sweater she's chosen for me is sapphire blue, hugging my curves and dipping so low in the front, I can see the swell of my breasts. I'm wearing a simple pair of black slacks with the sweater, but they're expensive, high quality material that clings to me. Kazimir must have told her no heels, for today, she hands me a pair of black flats to slide on. I look... beautiful. And it's so foreign to me, I pull my eyes away.

When she opens the door to the bathroom, I walk into the room with my head bowed down. Dressed in fine clothes like this makes me so uncomfort-

153

able, I'd almost prefer being naked. And maybe that's exactly what he wants.

Kazimir takes me by the elbow so firmly it hurts a little, and barks out something in Russian to Nikita. Without a word, she nods to him, gathers up her things, and walks out the door. Before we leave, his phone dings. When he reads the message, he grunts, mutters to himself, and shoves the phone back in his pocket.

"It seems Dimitri is delayed," he says through gritted teeth. "I'll have to attend to something before you join us."

I finally yank my elbow away from him and stand with my hands on my hips. "Why are you so angry?" I ask.

"Sadie," he warns, reaching for me.

I step out of his reach. "You wanted me to dress up, and I did. I've done everything you said, and yet you act as if you're half a minute away from a tantrum."

We stand at the threshold, when he spins me around to him and removes something from his pocket. At first, I think it's a collar for a dog, a thick leather band with a sturdy metal ring. But I realize it's for me. A chill, like liquid fear, trickles down my spine.

"I don't want them to lay eyes on you," he grits out while he snaps the collar open. "Tilt your head back and bare your neck for me."

I look at the collar in his hands and purse my lips before I obey. There's no point in resisting him, though. With a resigned sigh, I tip my head back and let him slide it on me.

"I am not angry with you, *krastoka,*" he whispers in my ear. "I'm angry they will see you." I gasp as his teeth clench on my earlobe. He suckles the punished flesh before he continues his confession. "They'll breathe the same air you breathe." With a hand around my mid-section, he yanks me to him so that I'm flush against his chest. "If they lay a finger on you, I'll have to break them. And that complicates things for me."

"Then leave me in the room," I gasp, my breath constricted in my chest by his intensity. "I like being alone. Love it, even."

"I'm expected to show you off," he says. I shiver when his calloused fingers graze my neck, his thumb throbbing against my pulse. "Therefore, you will wear my collar. When we are seated, you will sit by my feet and a chain will dangle between my fist and your neck. A reminder to them and to you that I own you."

He wears worn jeans and a faded t-shirt stretched tight over massive biceps. When he flexes his fingers on my neck, I watch his muscles contract beneath the fabric, his jaw firm. He's no longer the business man of the night before, but a fighter, his tattoos snaking along his neck menacing, and I know when I look at him he forged his way to the top with his fists. Bloodshed. Death. Ruthlessness.

JANE HENRY

A low throb of arousal makes my cheeks flush. I shouldn't be attracted to him. I feel shallow and stupid for letting him affect me.

"That's savage," I whisper. "Degrading."

"*Krastoka,*" he responds, almost apologetically. "That's only the beginning."

To my surprise, his forehead touches mine, as if he's gaining strength from my very presence, which makes no sense to me. But before he speaks again, he leans down and brushes his lips over mine.

"I want to kiss you, Sadie," his voice, molten lava, simmers with potency. "I want to hold you against me, and plunder your mouth. Own your lips. Taste you. Kiss you so long and so fiercely you forget who you are." When he brushes a knuckle under my top, he holds his hand against my belly, the top of his finger grazing my breasts. "You taste like honey and sunshine." My gaze focuses on his full lips, less than in inch from me. I know he could do wanton, wonderful things with that mouth of us. "But we have no time. I'm to meet with Dimitri and the others before I come to you. But I have plans to occupy you in the meantime."

When he steps back I stumble a little. His eyes look no less angry than they did before, slits that promise punishment and pain to anyone who dares get in his way. More out of curiosity than compliance, I take his hand and go with him. What other choice do I have?

We go to the elevator and ride down in silence, while he holds me so tightly against him, my breath is constricted in my chest. With his collar around my neck and a promise of a chain, I wonder what his plans for me involve? Will he chain me somewhere to wait for him until he's ready for me? Does he have some type of dungeon ready for me? It wouldn't surprise me at all. I've seen the bars of his cage and know he's a ruthless man.

Clenching my jaw, I vow that I won't let him break me. If he needs to parade me around and degrade me, I can't stop him. But he won't get my will. No one has ever broken me, not ever. And he won't be the man that does.

The elevator glides to a stop, and a bell rings at our floor. I try to remember the number he hit to see Dimitri, but I can't. All I know is the bottom button on the panel of buttons lights up with the doors swing open. The ground floor. My pulse races and my hands grow clammy. What does he have for me here?

But when the doors swing open, he takes me by the hand and leads me off with the glimmer of a smile.

"You've been a good girl this morning, so I've decided to grant you this. You may occupy yourself here while I meet with the others. It likely comes as no surprise that you won't be able to leave." We stand in a hallway outside double doors with frosted glass, so I can't see what's behind them. When he kneels, I watch what he does. He slides a metal cuff around my ankle and pushes a button, like I'm a prisoner. And hell, I am.

"You are not to leave this room," he says, standing as he pushes something on his wrist. "If you do, I'll get an immediate alert. Understood?"

"Yes," I tell him, as a sense of foreboding builds. What is he doing? Where is he taking me? Why has he put a tracking device on me?

"Good," he says, turning to the doors, still furious but now a little eager. He takes the handles in both of his hands, twists, and swings the door open.

I gasp, my hand involuntarily covering my mouth.

"Kazimir," I murmur. "Oh, it's beautiful."

He's brought me to a library. Dark-paneled shelves line every wall, books stacked higher than I stand. There are small ladders attached to gliders on each wall. Large, black leather couches with plump silver throw pillows sit in the middle of the room, and vibrant Oriental rugs dot the floors. There are two massive fireplaces, several coffee tables, and in one corner of the room, what looks like a fancy coffee machine, mugs, and a silver tray.

"This estate was previously owned by Dimitri's great-grandfather. He purchased this from his family three decades ago. His great-grandmother was English, and she loved books. Though the majority of the books are in Russian, there are a

The Bratva's Baby: A Dark Mafia Romance

fair number in English on one wall." He shrugs, looking strangely bashful. "They likely haven't been touched in years, but you are welcome to take a look around."

"Thank you," I tell him, but I don't meet his eyes. I don't want him to know I'm as enamored by this magnificent room as I am. I already regret showing the initial eagerness. I'm surprised he's brought me here, though a part of me knows he does nothing accidentally. He wishes to train me. The leather at my neck is a stark reminder of his ultimate goal. And if he knows I'm a book lover, he's going to manipulate me in whatever way he can.

"Remember what I said," he warns, when he looks at his phone and glares at the time. His accent thickens and the anger he wears like a badge returns. "I'll know if you do anything you shouldn't."

Without another word, he leaves. I watch in silence as the doors to the elevator swing shut and the numbers indicate he's going up, before I turn and look again at the library. It's absolutely beautiful.

I walk around in a sort of trance, gingerly tracing my fingertips along the spines of the books. The majority are in Russian, the curly lettering on the spines entire worlds that are foreign to me. I'm a world apart from where I've lived, but here, in the presence of so many books, the scent of leather and paper imbuing my senses, I'm home.

What will he demand of me so that I can return? Will I ever? Though there were many things about my home I didn't love, memories in America I'd love to leave behind me, the knowledge he's taken away the ability fills me with a sense of longing I can't deny.

I'm curious about the English books he says are here, so I walk around the room until I find titles written in English. I pull six into my hands and fold myself into one of the leather couches. Time fades as I read and for just a little while, I'm not a captive in a foreign land. My eyes grow heavy, but I fight sleep. I want to be alert in here. I tuck my leg under me, when I feel the pinch of metal.

How could I forget he put a cuff on me? A tracking device? The very idea burns. I plunk my leg on my lap and tug on the metal. Of course, it doesn't budge at all. I might as well be a kitten trying to move a boulder with its little paws. But the longer I try, the angrier I get, and as I tear at the metal at my ankle, I think about what he's done to me.

Have I lost my mind? Just because the man looks nice, and occasionally isn't a monster, doesn't mean he isn't capable of doing very real, horrid things. Have I been mad? As I claw at the metal on my leg, my nails scrape along skin. It feels good, a sort of release bursting in my chest, all warm and tingly. I like the vivid pain that brings me back to reality, like a cold blast of air waking me from a terrible dream, and the trickling warmth that floods me when the pain lessens.

Kazimir abducted me. He brought me out of my home, here, apart from everything familiar to me. I want to smack myself. Here I am, squealing over books, like he's done me some type of kindness, when he's done nothing of the sort. Just because he's made me feel things no one has ever before made me feel... just because he's attractive, and in some weird way, he makes me feel attractive as well... just because he hasn't done the cruel things he's fully capable of doing, doesn't mean the man is anything but a monster.

I claw at the metal until my skin bleeds. Blood smears on my nails like cherry juice, staining the white skin. I blink and shudder, then look down, surprised, at where I clawed at the metal on my ankle. Angry red marks burn my abused flesh, little droplets of blood oozing from where I clawed my own skin. My stomach rolls with nausea. What have I done?

The books clatter to the floor when I get to my feet. This place is a mansion. Surely there must be a place where I can go to wash this off my hands? I tremble, walking around the small enclosure, looking for a door to a bathroom. The need to clean the blood off my hands builds, as my leg throbs from the self-inflicted tears and scrapes.

I circle the library four times before I realize I'm not really focusing at all, and I need to if I'm going to find the bathroom. I stand in the library, and really look around me. I feel like someone's watching me. Without thinking, I flick my middle finger at the walls. I've never flipped someone off in my life, and it feels strangely freeing, even as my heart pounds.

"Screw off," I whisper under my breath, though I might as well be telling a bully on a TV show to leave me alone. He doesn't hear me, and even if he did, my pathetic request would fall on deaf ears. God, I'm so stupid.

I shake my head at myself, when my eyes fall on a mahogany doorway across from me. Where does it lead? I open it, hoping to find the bathroom, but I'm surprised to find myself in a closet of sorts. I step inside, smirking to myself when I think it's pretty unlikely there are any damn monitoring devices are in the closet.

This is a strange closet, with none of the typical storage items one might find in a place like this, and it's huge, like a walk-in closet. There are shelves upon shelves, arranged meticulously in what looks like little storage boxes. I squint at them, trying to see what they're all about. I pull one down, feeling a bit guilty when I open the lid and my blood-stained fingers stain the lid. I wipe my fingers on my pants, hoping to at least hide some of the blood.

I'm snooping, and I know Kazimir would not approve. However, Kazimir is not here, and maybe a part of me likes doing what I know he

The Bratva's Baby: A Dark Mafia Romance

won't approve of in a strange, childish *he's not the boss of me* sort of way.

Inside this box is a bunch of things I don't recognize at first. Pictures. Documents. A birth certificate. School pictures. More recently, a picture of him with Dimitri. Dimitri has his arm around him like Kazimir is his son. Why are these things tucked away in a closet? Does Kazimir know they're here?

I place the box back on the shelf and walk deeper in the closet. There are several shoe boxes just like this. I peak in each, and find each belongs to a different person. I recognize two from our plane trip here. Is this a sort of memory room, filled with the men Dimitri has recruited to his little posse? What exactly do these men do? He's mentioned The Bratva. What does that even mean? I'm a well-read girl, but now I'm regretting not having read anything that would help me understand even a little bit more about Kazimir.

And why do I even care about him? The only thing I need to know is he abducted me and he's my captor. My goal is to find someone who can help me prosecute him for what he's done, and live the rest of my life in peace, without fearing repercussion.

But is that even possible?

I go to the furthest end of the closet, feeling like Lucy in back of the wardrobe about to enter Narnia. All I need to do is reach my fingers to the

163

very edge, and the solid back of the wall will melt into snow-laden branches in a forest. My entire time here feels surreal, and the mystery imbued in the feel of this closet only enhances that.

When I reach the wall, my fingers collide with solid wood, and I feel almost let down. I slump against the wall, my forehead flat against the cool wood. When I inhale, my shoulders rise and fall. I'm imprisoned. Though I walk freely, there's nowhere for me to go. And while I'm slumped against the wall, a sudden realization hits me with the power of a sledgehammer.

In taking me from my home and robbing me of all that's familiar to me, he's taken away my ability to hide. I have no escape. No retreat. He's forced me into the open, into the blinding light. I'm caught halfway between feeling like I'm trapped in a prison and half like I'm on display in a Colosseum. Entertainment for the masses to watch me slaughtered.

A muffled sound of a door opening and closing makes me freeze in place. Footsteps enter the room, but they're not Kazimir. They're too light, not heavy like his.

I listen and try peer through the small crack in the door where it stands ajar. I see a shadow pass the door, but I can't see a face yet. There are muffled sounds of things being lifted up and moved, all accompanied by the patter of feet. It's someone small and lithe. Why do I hide? I could just go out there and see who it is. But something tells me I shouldn't have entered the closet to begin with, and my snooping would not go over well.

The elevator dings, and the movement of the person in the room freezes. My heart longs to hear Kazimir. Though he may punish me for a what I did, he's the only one I trust.

I freeze. *Trust?* How much have I been influenced by him?

It isn't Kazimir's voice I hear the next minute, but Dimitri. Cold fear races through my veins. I shouldn't be in this room. What will he do if he finds me in here? Suddenly the threat of Kazimir's spanking seems fairly benign compared to what Dimitri might do.

I back further into the closet so my back is flush against the wall. Voices approach. They're getting closer. Between the stifling heat in this closet and my panic, I can hardly breathe. I hold onto my breath, standing as still as I can. I can't understand a word Dimitri says to the woman, but his tone is anything but pleased. He barks out a series of commands, and I freeze when I hear her shriek. Through the small sliver at the door, I can see him grab her by the upper arm and wave his hand angrily at the closet. He barks out a few commands in Russian, then practically throws her against the door and shoves his body up against hers. I hear the crack of her skull on the wall and cringe.

Panic sweeps through me when she cries out in

JANE HENRY

pain. My hands shake. Is he going to hurt her? Rape her? What can I do to stop him? He'll kill me.

I watch in horror as he clamps a hand between her legs and growls in her ear. She whimpers but doesn't move, pinned against the wall by his frame. My own hand freezes on the door knob. What will happen to *her* if I interfere? I screw up my face and swallow a cry. I'm torn between right and wrong and the consequences of what happens if I get involved.

I open my eyes and glare at the monster Kazimir thinks of as a father. What would Dimitri's wife think if she saw his hand between this woman's legs? Or is she as cold and vicious as he is? Is he going to hurt her? A second later, he lets her go, but rears his hand back and strikes the woman across the face. He gestures angrily at the closet door and thunders at her. She cries freely now, begging and pleading, and though she speaks a foreign language, her pleas break my heart.

Dimitri turns on his heel and storms away, when he freezes mid-stride. Kneeling, he touches something on the edge of the carpet with the tip of his finger.

Oh, God. My blood freezes in my veins. Did I leave any hints that I'm here? What will he do if he sees me? Not only should I not be in here, I just witnessed him abusing a member of his staff.

The Bratva's Baby: A Dark Mafia Romance

Does it matter? Could anyone really prosecute him anyway?

I hold my breath as he scowls at what he sees. I can't see what he does next, since the small crack in the door is so slim. He barks out an order to the woman, and the next second, my heart sinks. She's on her way to the closet. With a firm slam, she shuts the door. I'm plunged into darkness when I hear an audible *click*.

I'm trapped.

Chapter Thirteen

Kazimir

The meeting drones on and on. Dimitri goes over so many orders of business, I see Maksym yawn, and Filip's eyes wander and begin to droop. I kick him swiftly under the table, and watch as his brown eyes flare with annoyance at me. I give a sharp shake of my head. If Dimitri caught him dozing, Filip would regret it.

"Pay attention," I admonish sternly, when Dimitri pauses for a minute to return a phone call.

Filip looks like he wants to tell me to fuck off, but he knows what happens if he does. Instead, he slouches in his seat angrily but turns his gaze to Dimitri. Good. Like anyone under my authority, I don't care if they like me. I care if they obey. If it were Demyan, I'd cuff him for his arrogance, but Filip is rarely ornery and never challenges my

The Bratva's Baby: A Dark Mafia Romance

authority. It's out of character for him, so I let it go with a warning look.

"Go," Dimitri finally says, after giving out final orders. "Return here in an hour." He looks to Maksym. "Report your findings."

The men stand to leave, but Dimitri's sharp voice arrests me when I rise.

"Kazimir, stay here, please."

I turn to face him, but he waits until everyone else has gone before he addresses me. I wait, impatient to get back to Sadie. When the door shuts behind Filip, Dimitri turns to me.

"When I took my last call, when I excused myself for a few minutes, I went to the library."

Though I've done nothing wrong, or even anything that might arouse suspicion, my pulse races. Why? Do I dislike the idea of him near Sadie so much?

"Oh?" I feign ignorance.

"Oh," he says, his gaze smoldering. "I saw something interesting in there," he murmurs softly. "The floor, to be precise." The floor? He didn't see *her*? Liquid fire courses through my veins. Has someone touched her?

His gaze narrows. I tap my foot impatiently. Waiting. I need to know what he saw and he needs to leave before I can act.

"Yes?" I ask.

169

JANE HENRY

"Fresh blood," he says contemplatively, stroking his chin, as a well of fear rises between my ribs. Fresh blood? In the library?

I try to keep my reaction calm. Why would there be blood?

"Yes," he says, folding fingers pressed to his lips.

"Did you investigate?" I ask, hardly able to keep from grabbing him and shaking him. I hold his gaze with my own.

Until I brought Sadie here, I revered Dimitri. Hell, I might even say loved him, as a son loves his father. But now… now, I feel my body tense with taut nerves. I've seen how he treats women, and I've justified his actions. I blink, as if waking from a dream. Who is this man? If he touches Sadie…

"Mmm," he says thoughtfully, pulling at his chin. "I made the servant who was in there do so but she reported back nothing."

I'm not breaking any rules by having Sadie with me. It's not even a risk. Then why does my temperature rise like this? I hate the idea of him stumbling upon her unawares.

"I see. Well, allow me to investigate."

He waves a hand, dismissing me. "Just beware," he says, standing. "It could be nothing. A servant cut a hand on a piece of glass while cleaning or something. But tell me if you see anything out of place."

I leave, barely tempering my need to run to her.

The Bratva's Baby: A Dark Mafia Romance

To hide her away where no one, especially him, will ever find her.

Why is there blood?

And why do I care?

I wait for the elevator, tapping my foot rapidly. I need it to move quicker. I should have taken the stairs, but didn't want to arouse suspicion when I ran. I watch the lights illuminate on the indicator panel. Finally, I can't wait anymore. With quick, deliberate steps, as if I'm angry and not alarmed, I go to the stairwell and open the door, step through the door, and when the door clicks shut, I race downstairs, jumping to each landing and practically falling in my haste.

I burst through the door and into the library so quickly, I'd startle anyone who was in there.

But no one's here. None of my brothers. No servant.

No Sadie.

"Sadie?" I bellow. "Where are you?" No response.

I know she's in here. Where else would she go?

"Sadie?" I repeat. Still, nothing.

"So help me," I seethe, my temper rising at the thought of her injured, or worse. "If you're in here and don't answer, when I get my hands on you, you won't sit for a week. Do you understand me?'

JANE HENRY

Still, no response.

I was foolish to leave her alone. The people who frequent this home are not trustworthy. I should have kept her locked and caged in my room where no one could get to her. No one except me.

"Sadie?" I ask, prowling around the perimeter of the room. "Where are you?"

While I walk, I hear a knock and a muffled voice calling. I freeze, trying to decipher where it's coming from. Is it her? My pulse quickens as I look around the room. The furniture is vacant, but on a couch lies a stock of books in English. Books she likely put there. Dimitri either didn't see them or lied about it.

"Sadie?" I call out. Louder this time. When I hear another muffled cry, I can tell it's coming from behind a closet door. I step to the door and try the handle, but it's locked.

"Sadie?" I knock on the wood. "Are you in there?"

This time, the responding muffled cries make my heart pound. She's behind this door.

"Why the hell are you behind this door? Are you alright?" My voice is thick with emotion, my accent barely intelligible English. I try the knob again, but it's no use. It's locked fast. I curse and kick the door.

"Who locked this?" I shout but her response isn't clear enough.

172

"Stand back from the door," I order, hoping my words to her are clearer than hers to me. "Now!" I take a few steps back, turn my shoulder to the door, run and ram my shoulder, hard, against it. It doesn't budge. Cursing, I step back again, rear back, and let loose a powerful kick to the center. To my relief, the wood splinters and the door topples to the side. Another swift kick brings it down completely.

I step through, intent on finding her and dragging her ass out of here, when I see her huddled form in the corner, sitting on the floor. Her knees are tucked up against her chest, her wide eyes fixed on me.

"What the hell are you doing in here?" I thunder. I take her by the arm and haul her to her feet, ready to beat her ass for hiding in here. "I told you to stay in the library."

I'm so relieved at finding her unharmed, I crush her to my chest so fiercely, I can hear her struggling to breathe.

"There's like no oxygen in here," she gasps. "I almost passed out." She takes deep breaths, filling her lungs with the clean air that rushes in from the open door. "And he's a monster," she gasps, pushing away from me. "That Dimitri is a monster."

"Hush," I hiss. I can't have him hearing her speak like this.

The door lies in ruins on the floor as I take her

arm and drag her out of the closet. I need to inspect her to make sure she's okay, before I spank her little ass for making me worried. I sit on one of the overstuffed armchairs in front of a coffee table, and haul her onto my knee, then take my phone out of my pocket. I call Vladik, Filip's twin brother. They function as the security for our small team. He answers on the second ring.

I tell him briefly where I am and what I need. As long as Dimitri doesn't come down here before our meeting, Vladik's men will have the closet door repaired before Dimitri sets foot back in here.

"Give me twenty minutes," I tell him in Russian. "I have some business to attend to here, first." I glance at the time on my phone. I'm meeting back with Dimitri in forty minutes, and I don't want to arouse suspicion by being late.

I swing her around on my lap so that she straddles me, one leg on either side. Though her eyes flash in anger, there's something else in those depths that tugs at my heart strings. She looks furious but afraid.

I grab her chin firmly between my fingers and hold her gaze to mine. "You tell me why you disobeyed me," I growl. She deserves punishment for making me fear for her safety.

"I didn't," she insists. "You told me not to leave the library. I didn't leave the library. How was I supposed to know I would get locked in there?"

The Bratva's Baby: A Dark Mafia Romance

I growl, a warning to her, but she doesn't heed the warning.

"And I meant what I said. He's a monster!"

"Sadie," I warn.

"He is! If you'd seen how he treated that woman who came in here—"

"What woman?"

"She was cleaning in here. He got mad that the closet door was open, I think. I don't speak Russian, but he gestured to the door and hit her face." She cringes. "God, he's terrible."

"He's no worse than I am," I say with pursed lips. "I don't want to hear another criticism against him."

Though her lips pinch together, her nostrils flare. She takes in a deep breath before she says through gritted teeth, "You've never struck me across the face, and even though you can be mean, I don't see you ever doing that."

I blink, thinking about what she says. No, I've never slapped her face, but she has no clue what I'm really capable of. I'm no better than Dimitri. If she thinks I am, she's mistaken.

"Not yet, I haven't," I say, though I would never strike her pretty face. Even though I won't admit it to her, I'm not the type of man that would. I'd rather take my belt to her ass or punish her with my cock in her tight asshole. My eyes fall to her

175

fingers stained in blood, and I remember what Dimitri says he saw.

"Sadie," I ask, probing. I no longer fear the sight of blood, but it always stirs something in me. Something savage and violent. I grip her wrist so tight she winces when I ask, "What happened to your fingers?"

Her lips clamp shut and she turns away from me. I give her a little shake.

"Answer me," I demand. But she won't.

Now that I see she's unharmed, I'll have to extract the answers from her. I get answers from men with other methods. With women, I have my preferences.

With grim determination, I flip her over my lap and lift one knee so her ass is perched high in the air.

"Answer me," I tell her, my palm resting on the swell of her beautiful ass.

She lies still before she shakes her head from side to side. I set my jaw, lift my hand, and crash it down on her ass. But her eyes are closed and she isn't saying anything.

"I need to know," I warn her with another hard smack. "Tell me!" I give her four rapid swats, but she refuses to say a thing. I can make this a lot harder for her, though.

Restraining her against my lap, I lay my elbow

The Bratva's Baby: A Dark Mafia Romance

across her lower back to keep her in place while I drag her clothes down and bare her. Though she tries to writhe against me, she's no match for my strength.

"I can do this all day," I tell her, my palm stinging with every smack on her naked skin. Her ass is hot to the touch and flaming red. "You fucking *tell* me." I punctuate my words with hard smacks that imprint on her perfect skin in angry red, but she staunchly refuses to submit.

I can't keep from growling at her resistance. I could spank her all day, but I have other ways to break her iron-like will. With a firm push, I part her thighs.

"Kazimir!" she pleads, panic in her tone now. "Don't!"

"Tell me," I order, my fingers poised at her entrance.

But she clamps her mouth shut.

I glide three fingers through her folds, pumping firmly. "Now," I order, but all she does is moan.

With one hand pushed on her lower back, I finger her pussy with hard strokes of my fingers. Her arousal coats my hand, making my cock stir under her belly. "Do you want my cock there?" I bend my head and growl in her ear. "Do you?"

She shakes her head and begs. "Stop," she whispers. "Please. Fine! I'll tell you. Just stop touching me there. You're violating me!"

177

I roll my eyes.

"We're not on one of your politically correct college campuses," I say with derision and a rueful smile. "What you call violation I call foreplay. Are you going to tell me?"

She pauses too long, so I slam my hand against her ass again.

"I hate that cuff on my leg!" she says. I blink in a second of confusion.

What?

Then realization dawns on me. I lift the cuff of her pants and reveal her torn, angry skin, where she clawed at the tracking device I snapped on her. A new wave of anger rises in my chest. I let the fabric fall, pin her down on my knee, determined to give her a sound spanking she won't soon forget. She hollers and twists, but I hold fast, one leg draped over both of hers.

"Don't you *ever* harm yourself like that again," I lecture, delivering smack after smack. "You belong to *me* and you do not harm what belongs to me. *Ever.*" I spank her until she slumps across my lap and she's crying softly, but don't release her until she gives me what I want.

"Do you understand me?" I ask, my hand poised to strike again.

"Yes," she wails, sniffling.

Frowning, I pull her clothes back on her and turn

her upright on my knee. I expect she wants to march away from me and nurse her wounds apart from me, but I won't let her. To my surprise, though, she doesn't push away, but burrows herself on my chest. She sniffles a bit, but isn't crying outright.

"I know you don't like that tracking device," I tell her. "But what you don't know is that it's for your own good."

I didn't know when I was sent to get her how this girl would affect me. How strong my need to protect her would be. How I'd need to make her mine. Dimitri is so determined to garner her money, if I let her go now, he'd send someone else after her. The very idea of any other man touching her… hurting her… my fingers curl into a fist before I realize it.

"I'm not usually like this," she whispers.

"I know," I say with a rueful smile. "Sit quietly while I make a call."

I pull up Doctor Rothsky on my phone, and dial. I give him instructions in Russian. I want him to dress her wound, but he'll meet me here. I glance at the time on my phone. I have twenty minutes before we need to return to Dimitri.

When I take her hand in mine and examine her fingers, I see they're not injured, just stained with the blood from tearing at her own skin. She must have caused some real damage to actually bleed on the floor. I push her off my lap so she's sitting

JANE HENRY

beside me, and take her leg onto my lap. I ignore when she tries to swat my hand away. I pin her hand to her leg and lift the fabric. Gingerly, I run my finger along the tears on her skin.

"Do you typically self-inflict pain?" I ask her quietly.

When I get no response from her, I bring my eyes to hers. "Do you?"

When she looks away, I have my answer. I blink in surprise. I never expected Sadie would be the type to hurt herself. She's so reserved and self-contained. But sometimes, the quietest ones are those that are wounded. Though Sadie hides it well, deep down inside she's hiding something from me. Maybe even from herself.

"I know what that's like," I say, looking away from her. I do. There are times I punch a punching bag with bare hands until my knuckles bleed just to feel something. And when I have a woman under my control… tied up, in pain, or on the brink of orgasm and begging for release… the power feeds a hunger inside me nothing else satiates.

"I don't want to talk about this," she says, turning away from me with her pretty little chin jutting out. I don't regret for a minute spanking her ass. I do, however, regret leaving her here alone. It won't happen again.

I glance at the clock, frowning. We don't have a lot of time for this. I need the doctor to show promptly and handle her injuries before I snap my

180

leash on her neck and have her sit with me and my brothers.

My phone buzzes. I glance at the screen. The doctor's arrived and needs me to let him in.

"Sit," I bark out, pointing to the couch. Though she pouts, and she's frowning, I know she's not up for trying anything risky. The good spanking I gave her will subdue her for at least a little while.

I walk past the damn closet and open the door to let him in. He's a tall, young man with wire-rimmed glasses, a clean-shaven face, and eyes that meet me squarely. He knows who we are and what we're capable of, but he's paid well to keep his own counsel. His mother hails from Poland and his father from Russia, so he's Russian born and bred.

"Mister Kasamov," he greets. "Why the library?"

I step to the side to let him enter. "This is Sadie. She injured her leg and I'd like you to treat it."

"Kazimir!" Sadie sounds shocked. "You called a *doctor* for a little scratch?"

I scowl at her and take several deep breaths before I reply. "Yes. I want to be sure it isn't more than a few scratches. This is an old place, and untreated wounds could prove dangerous."

Though Sadie huffs out a breath, there's something in her eyes that's a bit bemused. I tell the doctor what I need him to do in Russian. He nods, kneels down in front of her, and examines her injuries.

"Fairly superficial," he tells me in Russian. "Some antibiotic ointment and bandages will help. She must not do that again."

"Oh, she won't," I tell him, watching him with my arms crossed on my chest.

The doctor carefully tends her wounds, and she allows him to stoically. She doesn't speak or say a thing, just watches quietly.

When he's dressing the wound, he leaves me with several clean bandages and instructs me to clean them again before bed. Sadie hangs her head, no doubt embarrassed by what she did when she lost self-control.

I thank the doctor and look at the time. "We need to go," I tell her, but before she does, the doctor holds up a hand and turns to her.

"Do you have any further injuries that need to be treated?" he asks.

With an adorable pout that's far too cute for her own good, she says with a pout, "None that he'll allow you to treat, I'm sure."

The doctor raises a curious brow to me, his lips twitching.

"That's all for today, thank you," I tell him. I take her hand in mine, and with a tug, pull her to my chest. "And that's quite right. If you're referring to the punishment you've earned, the only way you'll get any relief from that is with your obedience."

I watch the warring in her eyes, how badly she wants to tell me to fuck off. And though her eyes remain hard, her tone is soft when she whispers, "Yes, sir."

With a frown, I lead her to the elevator while I dismiss the doctor. I have to take her with me now. How I wish I could lock her up and throw away the key.

Chapter Fourteen

Sadie

This man is an enigma to me. Heck, *I'm* an enigma to me. I shouldn't find it sweet that he had my wounds doctored. I mean, he literally abducted me, then lit up my ass when I wouldn't cooperate with his demands. How can I let the fact he had my wounds treated affect me in the slightest? I shouldn't. And yet… I've never had anyone show the slightest concern for me.

When the doors to the elevator shut, I blurt out what's on my mind.

"It was unnecessary to get a doctor. I'm experienced in nursing my own wounds, you know."

The people who raised me thought traditional medicine a privilege, and they never took me, no matter how sick I was. I was expected to take care

The Bratva's Baby: A Dark Mafia Romance

of myself when sick, and to stay away from them. The idea that he had an actual doctor treat my scrapes is utterly preposterous.

And weirdly compelling.

"I know you'd think that," he says. "But I'd do it again."

"I can take care of myself," I insist.

"Not here you won't," he responds, in a tone that brooks no argument.

I turn away from him, not out of anger, but because something moves me and my eyes are watering. I hate that they are. I'm weirdly emotional about this, and it's embarrassing to me. It's more than that, though.

Every time he touches me with tenderness, he reaches a part of my soul I've never allowed anyone to see, much less touch. Every time he cares for me, it quiets a restless part of me that's been anxious for as long as I remember.

But he is not a good man. He has done, and continues to do, wicked, violent things. My ass still stings from the spanking he gave me, my body still throbbing from his manipulative fingers exploring my most private parts. I've read so many romance books… so many.

The good guys don't act the way Kazimir does.

He's the villain.

How can I be falling for a villain?

185

I shouldn't feel what I do for him, and yet emotion trumps logic when it comes to him.

"He's a monster," I tell myself. *"Don't be fooled by the slightest show of kindness."*

But I'm hungry... so starving for a taste of humanity, for someone to care for me, that the slightest taste evokes a stronger, more powerful hunger that dominates my logical brain. That stokes the romantic in me who wants to be held by him once more. To taste his lips on mine again. I'm as powerless to stop my yearning for affection as I am from stopping *him*. That is... not at all.

When he pushes a button on the elevator, it begins to swoop upward. While we're riding, he reaches into his pocket and removes the thin, supple chain that he showed me earlier.

I shiver, my belly clenching when he reaches for me with a scowl so dark his brows knit together and his eyes look nearly black.

"While we are up here, you'll sit by my side," he growls, his accent so thick I can hardly understand what he says. Reaching for my neck, he tips a finger under my chin so that I look upward. I swallow when my neck feels cool air. Such a vulnerable position, baring the neck, as if waiting for the executioner's axe. The vampire's bite. The intimate kiss of a lover. And now, for me... a collar and chain.

There's a tug and pull when he clicks the chain in place, the weighted heaviness a physical reminder of his expectation of my obedience. I thought I would hate it. I *should* hate it. But we're about to enter a room full of strangers. Even though he's my captor... and I shouldn't trust him... being tied to him like this brings me a strange sense of comfort.

I hate that it does.

The elevator cruises to a stop. As the doors glide open, he murmurs, "You look beautiful with my collar around your neck. Remember your place." My chest warms with the praise. I mentally berate myself, but no matter how hard I try, I can't hate him. I hate myself, though, for allowing the utter weakness of character.

We're at the same floor he took me before to eat with Dimitri, only this time he doesn't lead me to the dining room but takes a right instead, leading me down a hallway. In front of us stands a massive doorway that gleams in the light of the overhead lights, tinted glass and dark-paneled wood. On the other side of the door comes a series of deep, masculine voices speaking in Russian. I hear Dimitri's, but the others are foreign. I shiver and step closer to Kazimir. In my former life, men intimidated me. I feared them, even those who were kind and gentle. And now he's parading me in front of a room full of powerful, ruthless men. It's like dragging someone who fears spiders in front of an aquarium of tarantulas.

"Kazimir," I say, my voice choked and desperate.

My hands shake so badly I flatten them against my stomach to still the trembling. "I can't do this."

I close my eyes, as if shutting out the doorway to my fears will somehow make it go away.

"You can," he says calmly. "You must."

I shake my head, my eyes still closed. I don't pull away or try to run, as I know that would be useless, but I don't take another step forward. I jerk closer to him when he pulls the chain at my neck. My eyes fly open just before I crash into the black t-shirt at his chest. His arms encircle me and he holds me close to him, as his mouth comes to my ear.

"There are no men in that room besides me," he whispers, his warm breath making the skin on the back of my neck rise. The masculine scent, like sandalwood and pipe smoke, envelopes me, when his hand glides up the small of my back, pulling me flush against him. "There is no one whose voice you obey, eyes you hold, body you touch. Your only focus is on me, *krasotka.*"

I nod into his chest, still angry at myself for letting him comfort me, but the reality is... he does. He doesn't have to tell me that if another man looks at or touches me, he will hurt them. And despite the fact that he's a monster... capable of cruelty... in this circumstance, he's my protector.

"Okay," I say with a nod.

I jump when his chuckle startles me. I forgot that

The Bratva's Baby: A Dark Mafia Romance

this large, brooding man was capable of something as human as laughter.

"What?" I whisper.

An upward tug of the chain brings my gaze to his, shining dark eyes that twinkle like gleaming obsidian.

He whispers something in Russian, and this time I want to know what he says.

"What does that mean?" I whisper back.

"I don't remember the exact translation," he says, but I think he's lying before he silences our conversation with a kiss that reignites every electric wire in my body. I come up on my toes when his mouth meets mine, branding me with a kiss that's anything but tender. When he pulls away, a heated whisper in my ear so fierce it's nearly a roar makes me freeze. "Behave yourself."

Taking my hand in his, the chain to my collar tucked between our palms, he turns the handle on the door and pushes it inward. I follow his lead when he steps in the room, my eyes cast to the floor. He told me he's the only man in this room, so I see no point in looking around me. That's my plan, anyway, and at first, it's easy to do as silence descends on the room when we enter. My cheeks flame with heat, but Kazimir walks in proudly and greets them all in rapid Russian.

I follow him as he leads me to a small loveseat

sitting across from another, but when he sits he points to the floor.

"By my feet, Sadie," he orders, his voice sterner than it was out in the hall. When he tugs the chain with a gesture to the floor, I feel my cheeks heat. It's humiliating being treated like this in front of others, like I'm a dog to lie at its masters feet. I fold myself onto the floor, tuck my legs under me and sit quietly. I wish I spoke Russian. I want to know what the voices above my head are saying.

Eventually, curiosity gets the best of me and I discreetly lift my eyes to see who's here. Across from the sofa where Kazimir sits is Dimitri, dressed in a black suit with his hands folded to one knee. When I raise my face, his eyes come to mine. I want to look away, but I won't let him intimidate me. He gives me a predatory smile, turning to Kazimir. He says something approvingly in Russian that makes Kazimir's grip on the chain tighten.

I look to Kazimir, but he won't meet my gaze. He's focused on Dimitri, and when a man next to him speaks, I look to see who it is. There are two other men here, both I recognize from the plane, the blond-haired, blue-eyed man who gives me an appreciative look and the darker one whose eyes are fierce but kinder. I tremble when the blond man's eyes rake down my chest to the full cleavage on display. The brown-haired man doesn't meet my eyes or even look my way, and for some reason it feels like an act of kindness.

Dimitri says something I don't understand, but he says Kazimir's name. Kazimir resounds, then Dimitri says something that makes Kazimir's entire body go rigid. I watch his knuckles turn white. He gives Dimitri a one-word answer, but the other men don't seem to like it.

I jump when their voices rise in volume. The blond man says something that makes Kazimir angry, because he raises his hand and cuts him off with a harsh string of sentences. The blond man sits back in his chair and crosses his arms, brooding. The man next to him says something in a quieter voice, but the blond man interrupts him. Dimitri interjects something, and the other two begin to argue. Kazimir orders a sharp command, and both of them stop speaking.

He's clearly the one in charge here. Though he defers to Dimitri, Kazimir is the one calling the shots. I move subconsciously closer to him. When I do, he gives the chain a little tug and rests his hand on my shoulder. Leaning forward, he speaks with vehemence to Dimitri. I hate that I don't have a clue what he's saying, but I am fairly well versed at reading body language.

Dimitri has just told Kazimir something he didn't want to hear. The other men objected, and Kazimir stopped them. Now Kazimir and Dimitri are making a decision.

At least, that's what I've surmised.

I keep my eyes downward, but when I hear

JANE HENRY

Dimitri say my name, I look quickly at him and shift on the floor. Dimitri's eyes are on Kazimir, but when I look up, he looks down at me and strokes his chin. My skin tingles when he lets his lewd gaze travel down the length of my body, but when he comes to my feet, he freezes. I glance to where he's looking. The hem of my pants has risen with me sitting on the floor, and the bandages are clearly visible.

"Sadie," Dimitri says. Kazimir stiffens. "What happened to your ankle?"

Oh, God. I don't want him to know.

"I cut myself," I say in a barely-audible voice.

Kazimir intercepts in Russian. Dimitri gives me a long look, but his eyes look colder than before. He gives Kazimir a nod, but I know he hasn't missed anything. My stomach feels uneasy. I want to be alone again. Heck, I'd settle for being alone with Kazimir.

I stand when Kazimir does, keeping my eyes cast down. It seems their meeting is over. When he walks to the elevator, he goes so quickly I can hardly keep up with him. I skip to match his stride. The other men sit behind us, no one following. Silent.

He slams the button on the elevator as if to punish it, and curses when the doors don't open right away. Dimitri calls out to him, and Kazimir responds curtly. The doors to the elevator swing open, and Kazimir practically shoves me in.

The Bratva's Baby: A Dark Mafia Romance

When the doors shut, I look to him.

"What happened in there?" I ask. "I didn't understand a word."

"You don't need to," he says, before he clenches his jaw and looks away.

I don't like being dismissed like this. I might be chained and still bearing the pain from punishment, but I want to know.

"Tell me," I ask. "Please."

"There are some things that don't concern you," he says. We stop at his floor. The doors swing open. I yelp when he tugs the chain at my neck and practically yanks me out of the elevator.

"Kazimir—"

"Sir!" he thunders. "You will call me *sir.*"

Tears prick my eyes. Was it just my imagination thinking there was tenderness in this man? A desperate longing that painted my perception?

"Sir," I throw back at him, the hurt in my chest flinging the word at him like an arrow. "It seems you were talking about something that *did* involve me."

With a pull, he spins me out in front of him, the chain yanking against the tender flesh. I cry out when I lose my balance and topple over, but he braces me against his knee and slams his palm against my backside.

"Quiet," he orders. I stand by his side, subdued and a little afraid, as he opens the door and leads me in.

"Remove your clothing," he says, slamming the door so hard behind him, the glass chandelier and mirror on the wall shake audibly. When he lets the chain go, the weight of it tugs on my neck. "All of it," he growls, standing in front of me with his arms crossed on his chest.

"You're doing it again," I seethe. "Furious at me for doing literally nothing."

I expect his anger. A hand at my neck, another slap to my backside. Instead, he silently watches me tug viciously at my clothing. I shove the pants off and kick them to the side, then tug at my panties and rip them off. I pull my top off and whip off the bra, throwing them all in a pile, until I stand in front of him, furious and naked.

"Is this what you want?" I ask him. "*Sir?*"

His Adam's apple bobs when he swallows. "Yes," he says, in a calmer voice than before. Reaching for the chain, he gives it a little tug and leads me to the bedroom. There are silver trays waiting on the table, the smell of something savory and rich filling my senses. My stomach churns with hunger. I didn't realize how hungry I was, but it's been hours since I've eaten.

I know what he'll do next before he does it. Sitting at the table, he draws me, naked, onto his lap, lifts the silver lids, and feeds me in silence. I'm so eager for food and so tired of his mood swings, I take the food from his fingers gratefully. There's buttered bread with thick slices of deli meat, a pretty beet salad garnished with chopped, hard-boiled egg, wedges of cheese, and a plateful of what looks like dumplings. I never eat such a variety of food, and my appetite is quickly sated.

"That's enough, thank you," I say to him politely. When I've finished eating, he tucks me against his left arm and feeds himself with his right. Though he sits upright and eats politely with utensils, I get the decided feeling he's like an animal eating its prey with bared teeth and vicious bites. Food is a mere means to an end for him, and it seems he's lost all the joy in it.

With my tummy full, tucked into his side where I'm warm, safely pulled away from the uncomfortable stares of the men downstairs, I feel emboldened.

"Do you dislike eating, sir?"

He pauses with a large crust of bread raised to his mouth. "No," he says. "Why would you think that?"

"You eat as if it's nothing but a utilitarian effort," I remark. "I'm just curious why."

Nodding, he takes a big bite of bread, chews, and swallows before he replies. "I've got much on my mind, Sadie," he says, "which is preoccupying me. I dislike that you feel my anger when it isn't you I'm angry with."

Something inside me warms, like the tiniest fission of a flame in darkness.

"Oh?" I ask quietly.

"For the past decade, I've been trained to hone my temper," he says. "To channel my anger to do my job. I was trained to do so, and in many ways, it's served me well. Misplaced compassion never sways me from doing my job. I don't waver in the face of danger. There is almost nothing that I fear."

Almost nothing… I long to know what it is he fears, but I know he won't tell me. Not now.

"The women under me before learned to fear me. The men who work for me do as well, and my enemies do. The only one who doesn't is Dimitri, but even he has times when he's close to fear." He takes another bite of bread and chases it with a long pull from a glass of water before he continues. "And I like that. When people fear me, it empowers me." Lifting a fork in his hand, he spears a large bite of salad and places it in his mouth, chewing thoughtfully. "But I don't like that my temper flares around you."

I frown, trying to understand what he's saying. Why doesn't he like that he gets angry around me?

"You don't fear me the way the others do. I suspect I know why, and the reason unsettles me."

"Oh? Care to fill me in?" I ask.

His chuckle makes me jump in surprise, and he

repeats what he did outside the door before we met everyone. "And now I remember what I said earlier means," he says, shaking his head.

"Yes?" I ask. "Do tell."

His eyes twinkle. "It means *cute*," he says. "The little temper from you, the outrage, it's like a little child having a tantrum." Lifting a napkin in his hand, he dabs at something on my lip. "Sometimes, that temper will earn you a good spanking. At other times, it will earn you a sound fucking. And sometimes, you just make me smile."

"Let's keep it at the smile stage, please," I mutter.

He only shakes his head, his eyes sobering. "You are the one that controls what you earn, *krastoka*." With a gentle shove, he pushes me off his lap and stretches. "And now that our appetites are satisfied, I'd like to enjoy my spoils. It's time for my dessert."

I've begun to know what the fire in his eyes means. My nerves are alight with excitement as he prowls toward me and I step backward toward the bed.

"On your back on the bed," he commands. "Keep your hands above your head, and do exactly what I say."

I don't have much of a choice, though my thoughts are confused and jumbled. His kindness toys with me, and when he divulges what's on his mind, I feel as if he's doing something he's never done with anyone else. Or maybe it's the romantic in me that wishes for it to be so. That somehow, I'm special to him.

I feel a tug on my neck when he lifts the chain and secures it to a hook on the headboard. Next, my wrists are suspended and secured so that they're stretched far and immobile. Though it's warm in here, I shiver, now that my body is stretched out and naked before him. What will he do? I suspect I know exactly what appetite he wants to fill. He hasn't had sex with me, though, and he won't rape me. What will he do?

"You are beautiful, Sadie," Kazimir says, circling the bed and taking in every detail of my naked boy. "So beautiful, like a goddess sent to me from above."

"I think there was some alcohol mixed into your drink," I tell him, but his only response is a twitch of his lips.

"I want to taste you."

My knees tremble, knowing now what he has planned for me. He takes his place at the foot of the bed and gently pries my knees apart. "Let them fall open," he says. "Close your eyes. Pay attention to your body, especially how you feel before you climax. Do you understand me?"

"Yes, sir," I say. And I try to do what he says, but the tension in my body makes me clamp my legs together.

He gives me a hard pinch. I squeal and drop my

The Bratva's Baby: A Dark Mafia Romance

thighs apart, just before he lowers his head between my legs. My cheeks flame with embarrassment, my pulse quickening. He's so close to my private parts that I tremble in anticipation. Before, he told me pleasure like this was too intense, so I fear this. My body remembers his mouth, his touch, and the bliss he brought me, even as my backside aches from the spanking he gave me, my neck sore from the heaviness of the chain and collar.

Whiskery kisses flutter along the sensitive skin between my thighs. I whimper when I feel my body rising to meet his. My breasts swell and tingle, and the throb of need between my legs intensifies. I shiver when his warm, wet tongue trails up and down my inner thighs, and he nips his way with little grazes of his teeth. Large, rough hands part my knees further so I feel the pull along my muscles.

"I'm going to eat out this pretty pussy," he says. "Again and again and again. I want the taste of you on my lips tonight and the memory of the pleasure I brought you burned into your memory. Until you are so intimately acquainted with climax, you know when to beg for permission. Until the very thought of displeasing me and being denied the pleasure I can grant you makes you tremble." He continues speaking but it's in Russian, so I have no idea what he says. And now, I don't care, I'm so intent on having him relieve the pressure between my legs.

199

Placing a warm, tender kiss between my legs, I throb with need before he glides his tongue through my folds. I keen with the intensity of his mouth, already so close to the bliss I chase. Over and over he laps and suckles my clit, taking his time with the tip of his tongue at my entrance, teasing and probing, before he swipes pleasure through me once more. I buck beneath him, so tense on the cusp of pleasure. This. This is what it feels like before I explode.

Heat flares between my legs as he eases me to orgasm with gentle yet firm strokes of his tongue. I climax so hard I close my eyes, light flashing behind my eyelids. I can't breathe or speak, bliss consuming my entire being, and just as I reach the pinnacle of this orgasm, a second, more powerful one builds on the first. I fall to the bed a split second before I'm rising again, spasming against his mouth.

"Good girl," he whispers, his heated breath tickling my sensitive parts. Finally, I collapse on the bed, but my eyes fly open with the zip and whir of his zipper. I watch with sex-sated eyes as he fists his cock in his hand. It surprises me that my body feels empty, as if I need him to fill me. With his gaze fixed on me, he tugs his cock, harder and faster, until he throws back his head with a roar, his seed spilling on my naked belly and breasts.

Panting, he leans down and brushes his lips to my ear. "You're mine," he says. "I will wipe you clean but you'll know your skin bears my mark. No

The Bratva's Baby: A Dark Mafia Romance

matter what happens tonight, you will know this, Sadie."

He's gone. I shiver at the loss. I want him here. I want him in me. I want his heat and his presence.

I hate that I do.

Chapter Fifteen

Kazimir

I clean her off with a washcloth and give her a moment to recover, but only a moment. I own her orgasms, and today, I'm greedy.

What she doesn't know is that tonight, Dimitri's filling the great hall with guests from all over the country. He's planned this for months. Fucking *months*. Politicians and military leaders, the richest men in our country, law enforcement, and every member of our group will be here to witness her take her vows, and she's not ready.

Hell, I'm not ready.

So before that happens, I'll bring her every pleasure I can to train her heart toward mine. It's a plan of desperation and hope. Sadie has an unbreakable will, an indomitable spirit that can't

The Bratva's Baby: A Dark Mafia Romance

be crushed. With a mind filled with romance, she's learned to expect that marriage is born of love, and any fool can see we don't love each other. How could we? We don't even know each other.

But love is a foolish notion for the weakest minds. Any true leader knows that empires aren't built on love, but power. And often, destruction.

I set out to break her, but in so doing have realized she has so much more to offer me than blind obedience.

We have so much before us. So very much before us.

I clean her with a thick, ivory washcloth, and dry her skin, but give her hardly any time to recover before I lie beside her on the bed and ease her again to orgasm by fingering her. She doesn't resist this time but rolls into me, and climaxes quickly and hard. After she's come down from her third orgasm, I reach for the bedside table and remove a little dildo I purchased for her training, and a small set of clamps.

"Kazimir," she whispers, her voice slurred and eyes half-lidded. "Have you drugged me?"

"On pleasure, *krasotka,*" I tell her. What she doesn't know is that I'm begging forgiveness for the crimes I've yet to commit.

I watch her eyes widen when I take the rubber-tipped clamps in hand.

"What are those?" she asks, tipping her head to

203

the side. "What are you doing?"

"Hush, Sadie."

I fasten the first clamp to one nipple. Her back arches and she cries out, but her wrists are fastened and she can't stop me. I fasten the second one, and give the chain between them a gentle tug.

"Oh," she moans. "Ow!" But her protests fade to moans when I slide the dildo in place. I work her closer and closer to orgasm, and just when she's on the cusp, I unfasten the clamps. Blood rushes to the abused flesh as she screams with pleasure, and I suckle her nipples one at a time between my lips and let her explode into pleasure.

"Oh God," she pants, her head falling to the side. "I'm exhausted."

"Yes," I say. "You'll get some rest now, but only for a short while." Covering her with a throw blanket, I make some calls and give her a short rest. I watch as she drifts to sleep, then a quarter of an hour later, wake her with my mouth between her thighs.

Her eyes fly open and she yanks at the cuffs around her wrists, but it's useless. She can't get away. I suckle her sweet, wet clit and lap her tender folds until she groans and writhes with her fifth release. Fingering her channel while she comes, I imagine the tight walls of her pussy milking my cock. Soon.

We go on like this for hours, until my own body is

fatigued from having brought her to climax again and again. I'll buy her a Sybian, soon, and sate her in other ways, but for now, I want to claim her orgasms with my tongue, my fingers, anything that will bring her flesh in contact with mine.

"I... didn't know..." she gasps. "The human body could be wrung with that much pleasure." Her eyes are closed but a small smile plays at her lips.

"The human body is capable of enduring a lot more than one might think," I tell her. I let the words hang in the air between us, but she doesn't respond. She's too tired. A little sleep will likely prepare her for the evening ahead, and having been brought to the brink of pleasure so many times will likely help her keep her place tonight.

Maybe. She might need to be forced. She might even try to run. My stomach clenches at the thought of the punishment that awaits her if she runs. I hate the idea of forcing her to do what lies ahead of us.

I storm out of the bedroom and into the living room. I glance at her from the corner of my eye and realize she doesn't even know I've left the room, she's that drunk on pleasure and bliss. Good.

I sit on the black leather chair that faces the large picture window and stare. The sun has begun to set, fingers of orange and gold tinged with red on the horizon. In front of me lies the city, tall buildings and houses crammed so closely together, from here it looks as if there's less than a finger's distance between them.

I came to the city a young man, wild with notions of revenge and power, but I was impulsive and reckless. Dimitri was the one who honed my skills, taught me to master my strength. He taught me everything he knew. Dimitri's wife never had children, and Dimitri mourned the loss of a dream of having a child. He shared this with me after I'd become like a son to him. I was the son he never had.

And tonight, I honor my allegiance to him.

I stalk to the kitchen and pour myself a shot of ice-cold vodka. I throw it back and let the burn travel from my throat to my stomach, burning its way like a line of red-hot fire. I inhale and pull my shoulders back before I take another shot.

I drink only the finest, purest drinks, and rarely. I despise the idea of needing alcohol for bravery. Bravery comes from within, not from a bottle. Fools think anything but internal conviction and strength is what gives a man courage. I drink instead to dull the ever-present ache in my chest. Memories of my past I stoke to keep me sharp and alert when opportunity arises.

I walk back to the window with a third shot and sip this one slowly. Thinking. Contemplating.

I'm angry that we're taking the next step before she's ready. But if I'm honest… when will she be? She likely has misguided notions about old-fashioned concepts like marriage. Sadie probably thinks marriage is a union between two people who love each other. I scoff to myself and shake my head. So naïve. Only fools believe a commitment of fidelity and honor is bound by love.

My fingers clench around the small shot glass in my hand at the thought of what I must do tonight. A few weeks ago, I wouldn't have thought twice about what needed to happen. Why do I hesitate tonight? What is it about the girl that makes me question what I've already decided I needed to do?

I think about my family, to remind myself why I'm here and what I need to do next. I remember being a young boy, rail-thin and dressed in rags, in Dimitri's sprawling kitchen. His wife fed me thick, crusty rye bread and bowls of soup until I couldn't hold another bite. I slept in a small room above their kitchen, and reveled in the small luxuries of family life until the day he decided I needed to learn more.

The first time I realized he was part of an illegal crime ring, I was supposed to be asleep in the loft when one of his associates dragged a man into Dimitri's kitchen in the middle of the night. He was bruised and bloodied and he begged for mercy. I knelt in my loft, peeking down to the kitchen below. Dimitri's wife Yana came into the kitchen dressed in a fluffy white robe. I held my breath, waiting for her to scream in terror or run from the room. Instead, she put on the kettle to boil and made herself a cup of tea.

"Not in my kitchen," she said to the men, carrying her tea cup out of the room. "Be sure Kazimir is asleep, and wait until I've gone back upstairs before you do what you need to. And for the love of God, Dimitri, be sure to clean up any blood."

The bloodied man screamed and writhed in the hands of the men who held him, but no one paid any attention to him.

But Dimitri did not wait to see if I was asleep before he "did what he had to." I watched in horror, the breath frozen in my lungs, when he bared the man's throat. He ordered the floor be covered in plastic, and the man closed his eyes, openly weeping and begging forgiveness from a nameless god.

I watched every second of it. Dimitri's cold, calculating determination as he told the man he earned his death with his betrayal before he pulled plastic gloves on his hands and drew his knife. The glimmer of metal in the kitchen light as he drew the sharp blade across the man's throat. The spurts of blood so dark it was nearly black. The way the man's body writhed and contorted in the dance of death. The sound of his dead body hitting the floor, smeared in blood. Dimitri's sharp orders to the men to clean up the kitchen. Then his proclamation he made that I was sure I was meant to hear.

"A real man doesn't waver in the face of what needs to be done," he said softly. "There are many acts of war. Many battles that take place off the field with no uniforms or offices in command. Sometimes, battle takes place on your kitchen floor." He didn't lift his eyes to me, but he didn't need to. It was my first lesson of many.

"Penny for your thoughts?" I jump when a soft hand touches my shoulder. I turn to see Sadie, utterly naked, her eyes still drooping with sleep. When I look at her she drapes her arms across her breasts and shivers. I place my shot glass down and draw her to me.

"Did you rest?" I ask her.

"Yes," she says. "But I wondered what you were thinking of, staring out the window like that. You looked troubled."

I shrug. "I was thinking of my childhood," I tell her. "When I was taken in by Dimitri and Yana." I run my hand down her back and over the curve of her beautiful backside, pulling her flush against my chest. Lowering my mouth to her bare shoulder, I place a tender kiss there.

I smile to myself when she sighs in pleasure. "You didn't look happy, though. You were brooding. What were you thinking of?"

Lifeless eyes and pools of blood, sweet girl.

I shake my head. "Nothing." I sit and pull her onto my lap, but this time I don't fondle her beautiful breasts or play with her pussy. I just hold her to my chest and inhale her sweet, clean scent and it's there in that moment, when I'm holding her naked body to my chest and she's breathing as softly and sweetly as a baby, I know why Sadie is different for me. Her beauty comes from more than her curves and feminine beauty. There is no pretense about her. No charm or ulterior motives. Nothing but simple, unsullied beauty. She's as fresh as a field of newly-fallen snow. And though a part of her still resists me, a part of her likes this.

I lay her back on the sofa until her back hits the black leather. Pinned beneath me, her eyes widen and one small hand reaches for my shoulder. Delicate fingers rest there, not pushing me away, but anchoring herself as if she's mountain climbing and she holds the ledge.

"It isn't nothing," she whispers. "You weren't thinking of nothing. You just don't trust me enough to tell me." A note of sadness in her voice tugs at my heart.

She should hate me. Why doesn't she?

"It isn't that I don't trust you," I tell her. "But there are things I'd rather keep from you. At least for now."

When her legs part, the scent of her feminine arousal makes me grow hard. My training of her earlier was not in vain—the slightest pressure of my knee between her legs has her arching into me, her lips parted, and if I touched her pussy lips, I'd find her soaked for me.

"I want to fuck you," I growl in her ear. But no, no it isn't true. I don't want to fuck her. I want to

The Bratva's Baby: A Dark Mafia Romance

make love to her, claiming her virginity with slow, steady, firm strokes that bring her to climax on my cock. I want to plunder her virginity until she screams in pleasure and my seed fills her. I can fuck her with nothing between us, for Nikita always makes sure my girls are prepared for this.

"Do you?" she asks back, with a twinkle in her eye. No longer does she stare back at me as the shy little librarian. Now, unclothed with the pleasure I've wrought from her, a feminine beauty shines forth in her eyes as she stares back at me. "I was beginning to wonder if the pleasure would be all mine."

I can't help a little smile that tugs at my lips as I lean down and brush my lips against hers. "Part your legs," I order. She already has, but I want it clear I orchestrate this.

Her eyes meet mine in bold fearlessness as she whispers, "Yes, sir."

My cock swells with the sweetness of her compliance, but I want her fully ready. I kiss her long and hard, tasting her lips, as I grind my pelvis between her legs.

"Sadie," I groan in her ear. "Christ, *Sadie.*"

And still, she just lets her legs fall open. I release her just long enough to remove my clothes and send them toppling to the floor before I'm back between her legs.

When her arms come around me, I breathe her in,

my chest swelling when I slide my cock between the fullness of her thighs.

"Krasotka," I whisper, losing myself in my native language as I sing her praises. Her beauty and innocence slay me, and my voice is hoarse with the effort of holding back. *"Ty takaya krasivaya. Takoy nevinnyy,"* I murmur. *You're so beautiful. So innocent.* I like that she doesn't know what I'm saying. It's better if she doesn't know how much she means to me. What she symbolizes. What she does to me.

I part her legs with my knee and probe at her channel with the head of my cock. I can feel her body taut beneath mine, like a string about to snap.

When her eyes meet mine, there is no fear. "Will it hurt?" she whispers.

"Just a little," I promise. I won't lie to her. Not again.

When I push my cock between her legs, a groan emanates from deep within me. I curse in surprise at how good she feels, so tight, so perfect, everything about this moment is *right.* Our worlds collide as we become one. I lift and thrust with careful precision, so as not to harm her, but it's difficult. I want to pound into her. Impale her on my cock. Mark her with firm, savage strokes. I want her to remember this, though. The first time I claimed her.

So instead of the vicious thrusts I want, I hold myself back and glide in and out. Her legs wrap

The Bratva's Baby: A Dark Mafia Romance

around me and hold me to her, the little moans she releases making it harder and harder to hold myself back.

"So beautiful," I groan in her ear. "Relax, Sadie."

When she releases a breath, I inhale, breathing in her scent and essence. I'm vividly aware of everything about her—the soft, pliable, feminine body beneath mine, yielding to every thrust of my hips. She's molded to me, the perfect piece to the puzzle, and as her arms encircle my neck, I know. This is no mindless fucking. Our union here, in this room, with her soft moans like music to my ears, her skin flush against mine, we're joined in our mutual pain and loss.

My need to climax is building, the pressure nearly intolerable, when she screams out her orgasm. The sound of her rapture makes my chest swell with pride. Her beautiful, savage shout makes me lose all self-control, until I'm roaring in her ear, entrenched in the most powerful orgasm I've ever experienced. My seed marks her, fills her. When we're both sated, I let my body drop to hers but hold my weight above her. She's so much smaller than I am, I could crush her beneath me.

"I didn't think it would feel like that," she whispers, her eyes closing as she turns from me. Shutting me out.

I won't allow that.

Taking her chin between my fingers, I tug. When her eyes fly open, I hold her gaze with mine.

213

"What did it feel like?" I demand. I need to know.

But she shakes her head. "I don't want to talk about it."

"*Sadie.*" Warning. "Remember what I said about lying to me."

She's still beneath me, my seed leaking from between her legs, and yet she doesn't speak easily. With a sigh, she finally speaks the truth.

"It felt right, Kazimir. I'm afraid my hopeless romantic mind has conjured up some romance but there is none. You took me from my home. I'm your prisoner. And romance… real feelings and emotion… aren't forced but freely given."

I want to kiss her so hard and long for her bruised lips forget to say these lies. I want to punish her ass for destroying a moment like this. But deep down inside, I know she's right.

I don't respond at first, but pull on my jeans, then leave to get a cloth from the bathroom to clean us both. When I return, she's curled up on the couch. Not sad. Contemplative.

"On your back," I murmur. Without a word, she obeys.

"Will I get pregnant?" she asks.

"Of course not," I tell her.

"Why not? I'm not on any birth control."

The Bratva's Baby: A Dark Mafia Romance

I shake my head. I offer no further explanation. I'll let her imagination wander.

Based on her cycles and the pills Nikita gave her, contraception is an impossibility. I don't offer this information, though. All she needs to know is that she won't conceive a child.

I pour myself another shot of vodka, and when I do, she chirps up from the other room.

"What are you drinking?" she asks.

"Vodka," I tell her. "Would you like some?"

I watch as her little brow knits in consternation.

"Oh… I don't know. I've never had any before."

Tonight, she will take lifelong vows to me, in front of a ballroom filled with people. I want her to be prepared. She never drinks, so a touch of this drink might be exactly what she needs.

"It's strong," I tell her.

"Do you… dilute it with water or something?"

I scoff. "Certainly not."

"Oh boy. Alright, then. Let's have it."

With a grim smile, I take the bottle out of the freezer and pour her a tiny shot glass, half the size of the one I drank.

"Drink," I tell her and with a rueful smile, "it might help you face what we do tonight."

Chapter Sixteen

Sadie

I wish he wasn't so beautiful, standing in the fading light of the setting sun, bare-chested and magnificent. His dark brown hair falls onto his forehead, his eyes cloaked in darkness beneath stern, heavy brows. Those full lips have been all over my body. That tongue has done wicked, wonderful things to my most sensitive, private parts. When he leans against the counter, I feel like I'm in the presence of a man with the blood of the gods in his veins. Large and muscular, covered in tattoos that I want to explore every inch of. He's got one foot propped up against the wall in the kitchen when he brings the shot glass to his mouth.

"Drink, Sadie." Even his voice makes my body tingle.

I lift the shot glass and take a tentative sip. It

burns. I sputter like I've just inhaled fumes, and he bursts out laughing, the deep, booming sound so foreign to my ears I jump, startled.

"Do women in your country drink without making fools of themselves?" I mutter, my cheeks heating.

"Some," he says through laughter, taking another shot. "And you haven't made a fool of yourself. You're just a virgin in far more ways than I anticipated."

At the word *virgin,* I have to look away. He just took my virginity. Right here, in this room. I gave my virginity to my captor and I don't regret it. I close my eyes in shame. How will I ever forgive myself? My whole body is under his command. I never knew pleasure and pain could be so intimately entwined. How being indulged with utter bliss could affect me.

My heart flutters when his eyes meet mine. My hands tremble at the sound of his voice. When he speaks my name, a shiver of eager anticipation courses through me.

When he looks at me, my head feels fuzzy and light, as if it's tied to a balloon and suspended in the air.

"Wow, that's strong stuff," I slur.

"It is," he says, completely unperturbed. "Not too much, though," he admonishes. "I don't want you vomiting on me."

"Oh, ew," I protest. But when he reaches for my

shot glass, I give it to him and hope he fills it again. I want to dull this ache within my chest, ease the guilt I feel for letting him take my virginity.

I wasn't saving it for anyone. No. Years ago, I decided it didn't matter if I'd go the rest of my life never knowing what it was like to make love to someone. And now that I've experienced this... now that I've had climax after climax... I know how much pleasure it can bring.

I'm not angry with him. I'm angry at myself for letting me feel anything at all for him.

He told me I wouldn't get pregnant, so either he's fixed or Nikita gave me birth control pills, and I still haven't reconciled the fact that I took them. It's like I'm some sort of mindless animal they want to lead to slaughter. What will happen next?

"Years ago, I was trained with my brothers taking shots in an unnamed bar in the coldest part of Siberia."

"Oh, God," I say, drawing my knees up to my chest. "I thought it was inhumanly cold there?"

"It is," he says with a shrug, downing another shot. I watch him thoughtfully.

Shaking his head, he smiles sadly, but doesn't say anything. When he speaks again, he picks up his story. "It is so cold that sometimes, the vodka even freezes."

"Travesty," I say with a rueful smile.

"It was negative sixty degrees," he says. "The day I took my first sip."

"Fahrenheit?" I ask.

He shakes his head. "No, Celsius. In Fahrenheit it's much colder."

"I see. Oh, God. So did you have those huge fur coats?"

"Of course," he says. "We all did. You have to cover every inch of your skin in the frigid temperatures, or you risk frostbite."

"Ah. Wow. Even the wind will do that?"

"Even the wind. All parts of the body are covered. We would get together at the local pub with a roaring fire. When it is that cold out, drinking something that warms you to your toes is a welcome experience."

I smile. "I bet."

"And so, when we——"

But before he can talk, his phone rings and he freezes. "That's Dimitri," he says, then he puts the phone to his ear. He listens, speaks a few things, then shuts it off. There's grim determination in his eyes.

"Come with me," he says, reaching for my hand. "We will clean you up and then prepare for this evening."

I follow him when he pulls my hand. "What is the big deal about this evening, Kazimir?"

A muscle ticks in his jaw while he hangs his head, but when his eyes finally meet mine, they're earnest. "Shower first," he tells me, leading me to the bathroom. When we get there, he lays out two plush navy towels and washcloths. Stepping out of his clothes, he tosses them all in a white wicker hamper before he puts the water on.

"Talking of Siberia makes me grateful for the warm shower," he says. "I never want to experience that type of cold again." But as he speaks to me, his eyes grow distant with whatever troubles him, I know there are many forms of cold. What makes him retreat and pull into himself?

When he tests the water and it's to his liking, he takes my hand and leads me into the shower. He follows behind me, pulling my under the stream of hot water. He pulls the curtain to the side, and steps in behind me. "Head back," he says, cupping water in his large palm and letting it trickle down my scalp. I swallow and close my eyes, letting the warm water soothe me. I hear him bend to pick something up, then the next thing I know he's lathering my hair.

He cleans every inch of my body, drawing a fragrant bubbly washcloth between my legs and over my breasts. A gentle shove of his hand on my shoulder spins me toward him as he slowly, carefully lathers my entire body before he rinses me under the stream of water. Kazimir is so deliberate, he takes his time like this is a ritual of sorts, something that has to cleanse me of my past and bring me here, to my present. My future, even.

When he speaks, I can hear how much it costs him to have this conversation.

"Sadie, tonight I'll require you to do something you will not like."

"Oh?" The thought of him handing me around to his brothers… to Dimitri. I shudder and prepare myself for the worst.

"Yes," he says. "Tonight, in the presence of many world leaders and dignitaries, you will…" his voice trails off.

In front of *whom?* My breath catches at the thought of being near so many people. I can barely stand how little time I have alone as it is.

With a savage shake of his head, he plows on. "I dislike it. It's too early. But we have no choice."

"You do," I say. Even though I have no idea what he's talking about, it's a lie if he believes he has no choice in any of this.

"I don't," he says, "no more than you do."

"Are you going to tell me what I'm expected to do? What it is that you don't want to?"

Is this why he's given me hours of pleasure? Why he's given me alcohol to drink, and he's taking such good care of me right now?

JANE HENRY

His eyes meet mine, smoldering, when he finally gives me the truth. "You will marry me," he says. "We will say our vows in front of witnesses, and you will be my wife."

It's as if he's expecting me to react in horror, but I can't. I merely shrug. I'm not surprised or horrified.

"I'm already your prisoner. You already command everything. This was a natural and inevitable turn of events." His eyes register surprise as I continue. "You know, in some cultures what you've already done to me would mean we were married already."

I don't care what they put on paper. If he slides a ring that's a lie on my finger. I'm here against my will in the most barbaric way, it doesn't bother me that he or Dimitri or someone wants to make me Kazimir's legal bride. I don't really understand it, but I see no need to fight it, either. Would I even win?

"I don't understand you," he says, frowning as if he's angry, but I know by now his anger isn't directed at me. "You should be furious."

"Should I?" I ask. The hot water runs down my back, and I'm struck with the intimacy of the moment. "Because you didn't ask me? Well, you know, you could remedy that."

"What? Excuse me?"

222

The Bratva's Baby: A Dark Mafia Romance

It's the flush of water that makes my cheeks flame. It has to be. "Asking me."

I watch his whole body tense in the shower, before he reaches for my hand. "Marry me," he says, not a question, but a command. "Tonight, I slide a ring on this finger. Understand?"

"Yes, sir," I tell him. It's the least romantic proposal in the world. Honestly, it isn't even a proposal but a command. There is no actual consent here, and I wonder if the lack of outrage I'm feeling is because he's clouded my judgment with pleasure. Am I that easily swayed, that count-less orgasms makes me so compliant?

But at the same time, I'm not quite sure why my instincts still tell me to fight him. He hasn't raped me, and the punishments he's given me have been… well, not pleasurable. I can't dwell on this right now. He's leading me to a wedding for reasons I don't understand. I'm not sure what his endgame is, and at this stage I'm not even sure what mine is other than to find an eventual way to freedom.

When he shuts off the water, I blink in confusion. What is he doing? Why? Are we cleaned up already? Did he give me something to make me comply with him? Have I been hypnotized?

But the next thing I know, a plush towel's shoved in my hand before he steps out of the shower himself. He dries off, then takes me by the hand and dries me off as well.

223

"What are you going to do with me after you marry me?" I ask him.

For the first time since I've met him, he shoots me a roguish grin. "Fuck my wife."

"Kazimir," I whisper. "Really."

He leaves the bathroom with the towel wrapped around his waist, a picture of god-like perfection, and I wonder what my problem is with him. He's a dominant with a heavy sadistic streak, but he hasn't really done anything *terrible* to me… has he?

I shake my head as I exit the bathroom, decided. I've let the pleasure he's given me influence me.

But I came from a line of people who *really* abused me. Belittled me. Made me feel so unworthy of human affection, I sought to avoid all contact with humans, or as little as I could.

But Kazimir… he's not like they are.

My thoughts are interrupted when Nikita arrives. I'm getting used to this routine. But this time, she's holding a long dress covered in a bag. That's when my nerves begin to fray.

"What's in the bag?" I ask her, backpedaling toward the bathroom. Kazimir is dressed in slacks and a white t-shirt, his belt already fastened at his waist when he looks at me.

"Your wedding dress," he says. "Remember?"

"But I—I thought it would just be a simple dress," I stammer, confusing even myself as to why I'm so

The Bratva's Baby: A Dark Mafia Romance

uncomfortable with the thought of wearing a wedding gown at all. "We're not what you'd call a traditional couple," I tell him. "Why do I have to wear the traditional dress?" I groan when Nikita ignores my protest and pulls a puffy, exotic, sequined-covered gown out of a bag.

"Because tonight is about appearances," he tells me. "And you need to look the part of the Russian princess bride. If you don't, we could arouse suspicion."

His phone rings, and he answers it with his jaw tight, his eyes piercing mine. He responds in Russian, and this time I hate that I don't know what he's saying, especially when Nikita draws her lips in a thin line.

"What's he saying?" I hiss to her. I watch her eyes dart to him before she whispers back.

"He says you're ready and you won't cause any trouble."

I'm ready? How can I be ready? My belly churns with nerves and I feel like I'm going to be sick.

"No more time to discuss this, Sadie," Kazimir says. "Allow her to dress you and get you ready without any more talking back." He snaps his fingers at Nikita. "Go!"

"It would be better if you would give us some space, sir," she says. "And meet us downstairs. After all, it isn't customary for the groom to see the bride before the wedding."

225

Pursing his lips, he steps out of the room and shuts the door with a firm click behind him.

"Come," Nikita says.

I let myself go numb when she slides on my undergarments and fastens the garters. I don't even look in the mirror when she pulls the dress over my head and fastens the pearl buttons up my back. Somehow, standing in this beautiful gown, I realize it's likely worth more than *I'm* worth. I let Nikita primp and preen me until an impatient knock sounds at the door. Kazimir wants me out.

"Go down, sir!" she shouts. "There's no reason for you to be up here any longer."

The door opens and Kazimir says something in rapid-fire Russian to Nikita, likely correcting her for trying to tell him what to do, but he silences mid-sentence when his gaze comes to me.

I have a vague awareness of Nikita giggling behind me, but my focus is on Kazimir. He looks at me as if I hold magic, his eyes wide with wonder and lips slightly parted.

"Go," he says to Nikita in English. "Prepare for the ceremony."

While she leaves, he takes a step toward me. "You look beautiful."

I don't care. It's all pretend, and there's no real point to this. I don't care if he wants to doll me up and pretend I'm something I'm not. It doesn't change the reality of who I am or what I'm going to do.

"Thank you," I say, because I have nothing else to say.

"Have you even seen yourself?" he asks. It isn't until he asks the question that I realize there are no mirrors in his room, probably so his victims don't know what he's doing before he does it.

"No," I say.

"Come." He takes my hand and drags me to the bathroom. I go reluctantly, because I don't really want to see myself as a princess. It doesn't matter to me. It's all smoke and mirrors anyway, like falling in love with a mirage. A gust of wind, and the house of cards he's built will come toppling down.

When he pushes the bathroom door fully open, I see the outline of my reflection. He flicks the switch, and light floods the room. Now I can see myself fully in the mirror. I blink in surprise. I didn't quite expect to look like this.

My mousy-brown hair is tucked and pinned with loops and swirls. If I ever tried to do something like this myself, I'd end up looking like Medusa, but the way Nikita has arranged my hair, it's... stunning. The gleaming loops are dotted with luminescent pearls, swept up from my face so that my brow is pronounced, giving me an air of royalty. My eyebrows arch gracefully over dramatic eyes, enhanced with charcoal liner and thick, black eyelashes. I never knew my cheek-bones were high and aristocratic, but whatever magic she's dusted over them makes them appear so. Full lips enhanced with a light pink gloss. I look beautiful. But the dress... the sweetheart neckline dramatizes my shoulder and slender neck, dipping low in the front to reveal full cleavage enhanced with a push-up bra. The waist, bedecked with sequins and pearls, cinches then flares into swaths of silk, taffeta, and satin. I turn to the side and feel the full skirts swish. Kazimir's laugh surprises me.

"What?" I ask him. "It's a pretty dress."

"The dress is lovely," he agrees, coming up behind me and gently tipping my head to the side. "But the woman in it... she's astounding."

"Mmph," I reply, unable to respond when his lips meet my neck and send a trill through my body. "She's fine."

I yelp when he punishes me with his teeth on the tender skin. "Fine?" he growls in my ear. "If I didn't have to fight a yard of fabric I would lift these skirts to spank your pretty backside for such an understatement."

I don't reply. This means nothing to me. If he did... if I cared about him, or us, or any of this, I would enjoy this moment with him. And maybe a part of me does, a little. I like how my belly warms when he's pleased with me, and there's no denying the fact I love how it feels to have him hold me like this. But I'm mired in thoughts of capture, held hostage with no choice in this, and truly dreading being paraded around in front of a room full of dignitaries.

"Let's go," he says.

Taking me by the hand, he leads me out of the bedroom and to the exit. We go to the hallway and wait in silence for the elevator. I'm trying to quell my rising nerves with steady, deep breathing. I hate the idea of a crowd of people. Maybe even the press. I shudder. Dimitri.

"Relax," he tells me. "We'll make this brief then come back up here."

I open my mouth to reply, when my heart stops in my chest. We're not alone. My scream is frozen on my lips as I stand in terror, watching a masked man career himself at me with a knife in his hand. Kazimir must see the expression on my face, for he reacts on instinct, turning to see my assailant a split second before he shoves me to the ground and kicks his leg out to trip the man. It all passes in an instant of jumbled limbs, the hallway echoing with the sounds of blood-curdling screams I realize a split second later are mine.

"Down!" Kazimir yells at me when he pins the man to the ground. "Get on the elevator!"

I try to move but I'm frozen in fear, my arms and legs suddenly made of solid lead.

Kazimir falls to the ground on top of the man. When he rips his mask off, I don't recognize the face underneath at all. Kazimir wastes no time, but rears his fist back and snaps it across the man's face once, twice, three times. Blood spurts from his nose and bone cracks beneath the savage blows. I try not to scream, but I can't help it, sobs wracking my body at the vicious violence. I look wildly about me for something to use as a weapon, to prepare myself if anyone else comes my way, but he's the only one. I scream when the man knees Kazimir and Kazimir falls to the side. The man lunges for me, grabbing at my skirt. I kick at him to keep him away, and a vicious swipe of my foot connects with the man's nose. He howls something in Russian, but he doesn't get a chance to say another thing. Kazimir kneels on top of him, his lips set in a firm line, and without another word, takes the man's head in his hands and with one wicked, savage turn of his hands, snaps his neck.

I watch in horror as the lifeless body slumps to the floor. Kazimir is on his feet, panting, coming to me.

"Why didn't you do as I said?" he growls, yanking me toward him.

"I tried," I say, my voice wavering. He shakes his head and pulls out his phone, pushes a button, and issues commands in rapid Russian. The elevator doors close behind me. When he's done on the phone, he kicks the bleeding, lifeless body to the side and holds me close to him. Cupping my jaw in his massive hand, he brings my gaze to his.

"Are you alright?" he asks. I don't respond. I just

saw him murder someone as easily as he'd order a cup of coffee.

No. No, I'm not alright.

"I'm fine," I lie, but a full-body tremor betrays me.

"Sadie," he says, pulling me to him, but before he can say anything else, the elevator opens and four men I recognize step off, dressed in formal attire just like Kazimir. They're the other men who met with him and Dimitri earlier.

Kazimir gestures and says something to the men. One kneels and looks at the man's body. They converse, but as usual I have no idea what is said. I watch in stunned silence as one man kneels and frisks the body, wearing a thin pair of gloves. Within minutes, they're covering the man's body with a bag and Kazimir is leading me back onto the elevator. His hands are clean, and so am I. Miraculously, there's not a drop of blood on either one of us.

This is so wrong. So terribly, wickedly wrong.

We're on our way to say our vows, and a man who tried to hurt me lies dead.

"What was that about?" I ask, still trembling. Kazimir's staring away from me when he answers.

"It was a man I've known since my childhood," he says. "He cannot enter my apartment, and must've scaled the side of the building to get to the hall. Maksym will secure the hall windows more thoroughly. Demyan will review the safety footage.

The man must've seen the news of our wedding, and decided it was a good time to seek his revenge."

If the man has heard of our wedding, it suddenly dawns on me that I'm the only one who didn't know about this.

Hell, the timeframe has passed so quickly, I realize that I was likely brought here for this very purpose.

"You brought me here to marry me," I say. "You've been planning this all along."

He doesn't deny it, but when he turns to me, his gaze softens.

"Sadie, you're trembling like a frightened kitten."

I shake my head, fruitlessly trying to deny it. "I— I'm fine," I say, but my teeth chatter so badly I can hardly talk. He hasn't pushed the button on the elevator yet, and I wonder what he's waiting for. "We have to go," I tell him. "Aren't you going to take us downstairs?"

With a nod, he hits the first-floor button before he turns to me and pulls me to his chest. "Sweet girl," he says softly. "There's nothing to be afraid of."

Nothing to be afraid of? There's everything to be afraid of.

"Why would you say such a thing?" I ask. "You just murdered a man in front of my very eyes. A man who was so filled with rage at you, that he was prepared to murder your bride. It seems all of Russia knows about our wedding but me. And you say there's nothing to be afraid of?"

"Sadie," he says, shaking his head. He draws me to his chest, and despite my reluctance, I let myself be comforted by him. After all, I just witnessed an execution. When he pulls me to his chest, I close my eyes and inhale. He smells so damn good, so strong and masculine and clean. He should smell rancid, with the blood of another man on his hands like that. But it doesn't work that way.

"I'm here to keep you safe," he tells me. "I'm sorry you had to see me do that, but that man would have hurt you, and I had no choice but to do what I did. Now, prepare for what happens next."

"No need to reschedule?" I ask. "A man just ambushed us out of nowhere, and you're prepared to just go on as usual?"

"Of course." He still holds me against his chest. "There is no reason for anyone to have a thing to talk about. You were supposed to be married to me today and that's exactly what will happen."

I don't have time to respond as the elevator doors open to the large room he took me when we ate dinner with Dimitri last night.

Last night? Was it that recently? At home, my days ran into weeks and months, one much like the rest. Here, it seems as if we march to the beat of a different time. Years have passed since that dinner yesterday, eons since the dinner we ate together in America.

"Smile, Sadie," he says. "Just smile."

I paste a fake smile on my face and trot to keep up with his massive strides. When we come into the center of the room, the crowd around us erupts into cheers.

"Kazimir," I whisper, my voice trembling.

"Just smile," he says.

Chapter Seventeen

Kazimir

I don't like how she pulls away from me in this room, how even when she takes my arm she's detached and distant, as if she's retreating into herself now. I hate that. I want to bring that sweet, soft, submissive side of her out again. I can make her obey me. Hell, I can make her take vows to me and become my wife. But I can't bring out the sweet softness about her. That's something only Sadie can do.

This should be monumental. Dimitri stands as our witness, like the father I never had. I've done many things in my role. I've ended the lives of those who deserved death for what they'd done. I've trained women, broken men, coaxed powerful people to trust us when they never should have. I've stolen and plundered, ravaged and destroyed. But now

Sadie holds in front of me what I want but can't demand, coerce, or force: her adoration. Her respect. Hell, her trust.

So when we say our vows, it means nothing to me. When I slip the slim golden band around her finger and kiss her pretty mouth, I feel like an actor. This isn't who I am, and it certainly isn't who she is. These are mere roles we play.

Champagne is served amidst cheers and slaps on the back, but I quickly escort her away. I tuck her close to my side and whisk her to the elevator, denying any assistance from the servants who offer. And when I get her alone—when it's just the two of us, and we've shown our faces and played our parts like we were meant to—I really kiss her. I unpin her hair and let it cascade down her back in beautiful waves, weave my fingers through her hair, and tug her head back so her mouth parts open. Her eyes are shuttered. She's closing herself off to me. But I'm learning how to break through that exterior.

I push her up against the elevator wall and pin her there, one hand at the delicate base of her throat, the other holding her hair, and without a word I plunder her mouth with mine. My lips meet hers. At first, she's hardened to me, only going through the motions, but when I flex my hand at her neck, she moans into my mouth. I capture her lips between my teeth and push her more firmly against the wall.

When the elevator cruises to a stop at my floor, I

finally release her mouth, enjoying the look of bewilderment in her beautiful eyes.

"What was that?" she whispers.

"Our first kiss as husband and wife," I tell her. The door to the elevator opens, and she follows me silently.

Evidence of the earlier struggle is now gone, the carpet vacuumed so recently the lines still show from the machine. There is no blood, nothing at all to indicate a man was murdered here today. I can tell she's looking for evidence as well, but she won't find any. My men did their job well.

When I open the door, I notice a large bouquet of flowers beside a silver tray with a bottle of champagne and two flutes. A message in English.

To the happily married couple, here are two flutes for you to perform our tradition. We wish you many years of happiness.

Dimitri and Yana

This must have been Yana's doing. Dimitri has no such wish.

"Your tradition?" Sadie asks.

I take her flute, open the champagne, and pour her a glass. "Drink," I order.

I watch her take the flute in hand and empty her glass in one large gulp, and follow suit. The liquid is sweet and bubbly.

"Good," I tell her. "Now throw your flute at the fireplace."

I feel my lips twitch when her eyes go wide. "Throw it?" she asks.

"Throw it."

"It'll break."

"It's supposed to."

"Well that seems a terrible waste, but okay…"

Her voice trails off, but I don't let her deliberate for long. I take my empty glass and whip it at the fireplace. I watch with satisfaction as it smashes into brilliant shards. It feels good to break the glass, satisfying to watch it destroyed.

"Okay," she says warily, then with a little savage whoop, she throws her glass so hard, it practically breaks into dust.

"Hmm," she murmurs to herself. "I'd do that again."

"Once is enough," I tell her. "Come with me, Sadie. *Wife.*"

"Don't call me that," she hisses. I can't help but frown at her instruction.

"Excuse me?"

"*Wife,*" she says with disgust.

"That's what you are," I say, tugging her hair so hard tears fill her eyes, but I stop myself from

The Bratva's Baby: A Dark Mafia Romance

hurting her. I've already decided what I want from her is worth so much more than what I can get by brute force. So instead, I take another tact.

I decide not to respond. Instead, I take her to the room and stand her in front of me. I curse the row of buttons that lay between me and her, but revel in every inch of her creamy skin that's revealed when the buttons open. Finally, after I've unfastened every damn button, I lay her on the bed, so I can finish undressing her slowly. When I remove her dress, she doesn't even move, lifting her arms and legs obediently for me to slide things off when necessary. She doesn't smile when I look at her. Doesn't flinch when I pinch her nipple to prime her body. She's so passive and reserved, I lose all desire to make her mine. I pull away from her when she's undressed, and help her under the blankets.

"Get some sleep, Sadie," I instruct.

To my surprise, she blinks then. "Get some sleep?" she repeats. "Just like that? You'll strip me and send me to bed?"

"Am I supposed to do something else?"

"What about..." her cheeks flush. "*Fucking* your wife?"

I shrug. "I changed my mind. Sleep. This was a long day for you."

A flicker of the softness I long for returns to her eyes for a split second. "For both of us," she says, before her eyes shutter again. "I'd like to take my makeup off first. Please, sir?"

"Go," I say with a wave of my hand. "Come right back and get some rest."

This was just for show, and I know it, but I'm disappointed. I wanted more than her blanket compliance. So much more.

I listen as the water in the bathroom turns on and off, my gaze wandering to the beautiful dress that hangs over a chair when I freeze. Along the hem of the beautiful gown I see several dots of dried, crimson blood. For the first time in my adult life, the vision sickens me. I turn away, and after a moment I make a call on my phone, demanding a few things I need. Ten minutes later, the dress is picked up and sent away, and Sadie lays down in bed. She watches in silence but says nothing. The second request I made will take a lot longer than ten minutes.

I lay quietly next to her until she's fast asleep, then close my eyes until sleep finally comes. When it does, my dreams are filled with visions of her dress, blood-stained and torn, and her screams of pain. I run to her, my blood pounding with the need to avenge her, to save her, and I finally wake in a sweat. The sun rises out the window and Sadie sleeps soundly.

I walk quietly to the bathroom and take a shower, trying to wash off what I can't.

Chapter Eighteen

Sadie

The next few days pass in a weird blur. Kazimir is… different.

The glimmer of humor he once showed me is gone and instead, he's quiet and brooding. Sullen, even. At first, I'm thankful for the break. It's exhausting keeping up with his moods and demands, and at first, I like being left to my own devices. A few times he brings me to the library to read while he works on his computer, but he ignores me until he's done, then he has me come upstairs with him.

This goes on and on. He doesn't even feed me on his lap like he did at first, but pushes plates of food in front of me and instructs me to eat. I even decide to disobey him once, to test him, to see if I can break him from the sullenness he's descended into. When he pushes the plate of food in front of me, I shake my head and with a defiant shake of my head, tell him no. He doesn't ignore *that*. With a frown, he glares at me.

"Eat your food, or I'll spank that pretty little ass of yours."

"Would be better than your sullen silence," I mutter, then clamp my mouth shut as my cheeks heat. I didn't mean to say that out loud. He merely raises a brow and points to my food.

I don't want to push him. I eat it in silence.

I was kidnapped. I'm wedded against my will to a man I don't love. I should be happy he has almost nothing to do with me.

Why do I want to see him smile?

Why do I miss the way he would bring me pleasure and even… pain?

After two weeks of living with him in brooding misery, I decide something has to change. One morning, when he's in the shower, I think about it. I don't want to be around him when he's like this.

I want to get away from him. I'm trapped. I know if I push things, he'll punish me, but then I wonder… will he?

Do I *want* him to?

The cleaning crew will be here any minute. The bell rings, giving me a good excuse to enact my plan.

The Bratva's Baby: A Dark Mafia Romance

I open the door and Demyan stands in front of me, holding a large padded manila envelope. "Where's Kazimir?" he asks.

I shrug. "In the bedroom, I suppose. Who knows?" I wander back into the living room and pretend to slump against the couch. "He wants all packages brought to the small table in the bedroom, please."

And when Demyan goes, I run to the hallway. There's nowhere to go here, but if my plan works well enough, there won't need to be.

As if on cue, the cleaning crew exits the elevator. I greet them warmly and speak animatedly to them about utter nonsense, as none of them speak a word of English. When I hear Demyan enter the kitchen, I gesture for them to enter the apartment, and quickly grab the mop and bucket. It's industrial-size, on wheels, and big enough for me to crouch behind. I step back onto the elevator and crouch behind the bucket. Demyan comes in, clearly distracted, and gives but a cursory glance to the cleaning supplies before he punches a button. The doors close, and I feel excitement rising as we descend. I've escaped... for now. I can't truly escape, but I can get a little reprieve.

Demyan exits on the first floor, and thankfully no one else enters the elevator. When the doors close, I hit the button for the floor with the library. I wonder for a moment if it won't work for me. If somehow it only works for those who were given security access. But somehow, maybe because Demyan already unlocked it, or because security

243

measures were somehow disengaged, the elevator goes down. When the doors open to the library, I step off with a mixture of dread and glee. He'll punish me for this, but it might shake him out of whatever brooding silence he's dwelling in. And hell, I can't continue this any longer. At least if I have to answer to him, I'll get some space away from his brooding silence.

My plan goes awry the minute I walk through the doors, though. As the elevator door closes, I hear someone turning a doorknob. I'm not alone.

I drop to the floor as Dimitri and another man I don't know enter the room. They take their places, sitting by one of the fireplaces in overstuffed chairs. Because they're speaking in Russian, I can't understand what they say, but I freeze when I hear my name. I fall to the floor and hide behind a sofa, feeling like a child. I've snuck away like a little girl packing her bag and running away from mommy and daddy, and now hiding so she isn't seen.

What are they talking about? I need to work harder at my Russian. I should have picked up on more than this by now, but it's a difficult language for me to understand. This is maddening.

Their voices rise and fall. I wonder if Kazimir has realized I'm gone. I wonder what he'll do when he realizes I am.

I hope he loses his mind. I hate seeing those eyes of his dispassionate and though the brooding,

The Bratva's Baby: A Dark Mafia Romance

angry Kazimir frightens me, the complacent one terrifies me.

I crouch until my legs ache, my muscles longing to stretch. There's a tingle in my left foot as if it's fallen asleep. Ugh. This was a stupid idea. What's wrong with me?

I listen to the men carry on and on until they both stop talking. The door to the library opens, and Kazimir's deep voice resonates in the room.

Now that he's so close, my body starts to react. Heart pounding. Palms sweaty. Hope rising in my chest. Damn, I need him to pay attention to me.

He converses with the men, and to my surprise his voice takes on a more commanding tone than I've heard him use with Dimitri. I hold my breath when I hear him approaching where I crouch, his footsteps getting closer and closer, his voice right over me now. He stands right on the opposite side of this sofa, his back to me.

I hear the other men standing, and saying something to Kazimir. I feel like a lunatic, as I scramble away from where I'm crouching to avoid being seen by Dimitri.

Please, go, I think to myself. I hate Dimitri. I hate everything he stands for. His very eyes on me make me feel dirty and used.

The elevator door slides open, and I watch from where I hide as his black shoes and the shoes of

245

JANE HENRY

the other man walk onto the elevator. Just two pairs.

I swallow. Kazimir is still here.

I can almost predict what happens next when the elevator glides upward. Kazimir is no fool.

"Sadie. Come here."

Like a child caught with her hand in the cookie jar, I slowly get to my feet. I feel a little dizzy.

He's standing with his arms crossed, on the other side of the room. Between us lies a sofa and coffee table, but more. Unspoken words that hide two broken, wounded hearts.

And maybe... hope?

God, he's beautiful, with his hair still damp from the shower hanging on his forehead. Those eyes, black as the midnight sky, stare at me from beneath a furrowed brow. Those full lips, pursed and severe. Bulging biceps as he crosses his arms on his chest.

"This is how you get attention from me?" he asks, like a father chiding a child. "You couldn't just ask?"

"I didn't come down here to get attention," I protest, but a little part of me wonders if I'm telling the truth. "I came here to get away from you."

Or is *that* the lie?

I watch as he raises a brow and for one brief moment, there's understanding in his eyes before his gaze grows molten.

"And this is how you do it?" he asks, prowling closer. "Foolish girl. You can't get away from me. You're wedded to me." His tone sharpens, his eyes flashing warning at me now and something inside me ignites. I take a step back, my pulse racing.

"Sir?"

He halts a few paces away from me. I watch as he takes a breath so deep his chest expands. "Over the arm of the couch," he orders.

I blink in confusion. What?

His hands travel to the buckle of his belt when he repeats, "Bend over the arm of the couch." The jingle of a belt clasp. A tug. Leather slithers through loops, now doubled in his fist. "*Now.*"

I knew this would happen. Then why am I shaking like this? Was I not prepared for the consequences of my actions?

I lie over the armrest and close my eyes. I'm still clothed. Will he punish me like this?

"Did you want me to fear you'd escaped, Sadie?" he asks, a split second before the smack of folded leather lights up my ass. I hiss and come up on my toes. It's been weeks since he's punished me, and even over clothes, it hurts like crazy. The belt pounds across my ass, striping me with heated pain, and in the moment, when it hurts so much all I can do is cry out and hold my breath before another blow lands, I wonder crazily why I wanted this. Did I?

Do I?

"Did you think I wouldn't notice?"

"Maybe," I hiss, closing my eyes against the painful blows. He continues the spanking, the only sound in the room the *whoosh* of his belt, the smack of leather, my quiet cries as the punishment continues.

"I notice everything about you," he says between strokes. "I know when you wake and when you sleep. When you're happy and when you're sad. What delights you and what saddens you."

Tears leak from my closed eyes as he continues my punishment.

"I'm disappointed in you, Sadie." Another savage smack of the belt has me up on my toes. "You risked your safety by coming down here. But I knew this was where I'd find you." His voice hardens. "And you walked right into the lair."

The next lash is the hardest he's ever given me. I'm splitting in two, shattering into pieces. My skin throbs and burns.

"Stop," I whisper, begging. "Please, stop. It hurts. Please, Kazimir."

A pause while he stands behind me. "Have you learned your lesson, then, young lady?"

"I have," I wail. "Don't leave. Don't disobey. I get that," I choke. "Have *you?*"

It's a bold statement when I'm bent over being punished by him, but the words tumble from my mouth. I close my eyes, bracing myself for another blow from his belt, but it doesn't come. Instead, I feel warmth surround me. He's right behind me, his flank pressed against my scorched ass, caging me in against the sofa. I let the tears fall unchecked. There was a time when I questioned why he made me cry, but now I know it's useless questioning.

"Have I what, *krastoka?*" he whispers in my ear. It's the first time he's called me *krasotka* since we took our vows, and for some reason it makes my chest warm. He's spinning me around and pulling me to him. I'm drowning in his scent and heat, the feel of his arms about me almost worth the spanking I just took. My ass throbs, heated and aching, but he's lit a fire within me. A deep throb between my legs. Aching, full breasts. Anticipated pleasure.

He hasn't made me come since before we took our vows. My body hasn't forgotten.

"Forget it," I say, fearing further punishment if I continue my train of my thought. "I shouldn't have said anything."

"Speak, Sadie," he growls, fingers tangled in my hair. With a savage pull, he demands my attention. "Have I *what?*"

"Learned your lesson?" I manage to croak out. I

brace myself for his response, but it surprises me when his eyes widen.

"My lesson," he says, a trace of humor in those stern eyes. "And what might that be?"

I don't respond because I'm not quite sure what it is.

I look away, but his fingers on my chin force my gaze to return to his. "Why did you come down here?" he asks. "Let's start there. Did you want to make me afraid that I'd lost you?"

"Maybe, yes," I whisper.

"Did you want to force me to pay attention to you?" he asks.

I hesitate before I answer, but what's the point in hiding from him?

"Maybe, yes," I repeat.

He's so close now his breath makes my skin tingle and the pulsing heat between my legs intensifies. Lowering his mouth to my ear, he whispers a tortured, heated, "Sadie."

"Yes?" I whisper back.

His breath against the shell of my ear makes me shiver in fear and longing. "Did you want me to punish you?"

"Yes," I confess, before I lose my resolve. I close my eyes. The girl I was in America is gone. Here, with Kazimir, I'm someone else. It's wrong, so wrong I can't even reconcile it in my own mind, but I need him stern and angry and brooding. I long for his brutality. When I was alone and sheltered, I lived a dismal life cast in muted gray. With Kazimir, my world has become full, vivid color. It doesn't make sense to me, but does it have to?

When his mouth meets mine, I sigh into him. I let myself go right off the cliff.

Freefall. He'll catch me.

I taste the salt of my tears along with the soft but firm press of his lips on mine. Kingdoms could rise and fall in that moment, and it doesn't matter, the world ceases to exist. All that matters now is him. Me. *Us.*

He asks for forgiveness and grants pardon with that kiss, forgiveness for his sins and pardon for mine. I keen with pleasure when he yanks my shirt up and palms my breast, a reminder that he owns this body. I whimper when the pad of his thumb grazes over my hardened nipple through the fabric of my bra. The clothes I wear feel cumbersome, so when he orders me to strip, I'm happy to oblige.

"Get them off," he growls. The length of his cock presses up against my belly. My core aches to be filled with him.

With clumsy, jerky movements, I yank off my top, He fumbles at my bra clasp a second before my breasts swing free. I push down my pants and he grasps my panties, yanking them down my aching backside. Within seconds, my clothing lies in a torn, ragged heap on the floor. Shoving his pants down, his cock springs free. My mouth goes dry in anticipation. He's only fucked me once, and I fear he'll take it slow this time. I don't want him to.

Grasping my hips, he lifts me so that my legs straddle his waist, his cock at my entrance. I brace myself with my arms around him. I tuck my head against the hollow of his neck, so ready for him to claim me. Pulling down my hips, he glides into me.

"You're sopping wet," he groans in my ear. "Someone liked her whipping."

I can't respond beyond a garbled, whimpering *mphm*.

"Jesus Christ," he groans. "Fucking *hell*. You're so tight." His voice trails off in reverent, heated Russian before he speak in English again. "Jesus, Sadie. You're perfect." Thrust after thrust sends me soaring toward ecstasy, his words distant and garbled, but two words I hear with utter clarity.

"*My wife.*"

My pleasure rises and I'm going to burst apart.

"Kazimir," I groan. "I'm going to—" I gasp when a savage thrust takes my breath away.

"Come, *krasotka*," he orders. I throw my head back and give myself over to ecstasy as he roars his own release. Spasms of hopeless pleasure devour me. I hold onto him as if he's my lifeline, our sweat-slicked bodies molded together as one. When we're both spent, he slowly eases us to the carpeted floor. Panting. Exhausted.

Here in the quiet is when we should whisper our hopes and promises and vows of devotion. But we don't.

We don't need to.

After our lovemaking session in the library, things begin to change with the two of us. Kazimir is no longer distant but present, even if at times he returns to his brooding self. The days become weeks, as we fall into the most unorthodox married couple routine ever. He brings me crochet hooks and yarn, and lets me bring books up from the library. I enjoy my favorite pastimes when he doesn't have other plans for occupying my time.

"No more wearing clothes," he orders one morning, waving a hand at the clothing Nikita has left for me. "Put them away unless we're going downstairs."

Instead of fighting it, I smile to myself. I like that he wants me naked. I like that he loves my body.

I sit happily on his lap while he feeds me breakfast and gratefully take the food from his hand. He makes sweet and savage love to me in the morning and evening, until my body longs to be filled by him, and pleasured by him. He lays me out on the bed spread-eagled and secured while he anoints my body with hot wax. I trembled at first, but soon come to crave the heat and sting followed by pleasure. Every time I feel his pain, even when he punishes me, my body reacts with wanton, erotic need. Every time he brings me to ecstasy, my heart belongs to him just a little bit more.

Sometimes, in the evening, he sits in the overstuffed chair in the living room, reading. He doesn't let me near him then, and it hurts me a little at first. But when he's done reading, he tucks his book away and comes to me, his tone softer, his gaze knowing. I begin to wonder what it is he reads.

"Stay in the bedroom," he orders one morning. "No snooping around in my absence." A stern furrow of his brow makes my heart flip before I nod.

"Yes, sir. Of course, sir."

I'm dying to know what the book is that he forbids me to look at, but I know where sneaking around got me last time. Still, I fully contemplate disobeying him when he's gone, when a wave of nausea hits me so badly I double over, clutching my stomach.

How can I be sick? I'm never around anyone but Kazimir. He ate the same food I did, and he's fine.

But I can't dwell, because soon I'm hurtling myself to the bathroom and kneeling in front of the toilet. I empty the contents of my stomach, then lay my face on my sweaty-arms. My skin feels clammy and weird, and the room spins around me. I stumble back to bed and reach for the phone he left for me, programmed so that his number is the only one I can call.

I'm sick, I text, then I drop the phone and close my eyes to stop the room from spinning.

I hear the phone beep in reply but I'm too nauseous and dizzy to read it. I close my eyes and lay there until I hear the door open and his heavy footsteps entering the room.

"Sadie?" he asks. "*Krasotka.*" Quickly, he comes to my side. The edge of the bed sags under his weight.

"Need to use the bathroom." I barely get the words out when I'm kneeling again. I vomit until nothing comes up but bile.

"Kazimir," I whine, like a child. I haven't been sick like this in years, and I'm suddenly a little child again. "What's wrong with me?"

"I don't know, sweet girl," he says, in a tender tone I've heard only rarely. "Back in bed with you. I'll call the doctor."

I drift in and out of sleep while I wait. Kazimir covers me with a blanket, and I either fell asleep or the doctor came quickly, because before I know it, the young man who treated my leg injury is standing beside my bed. They converse in Russian, Kazimir's tone initially concerned but shifting to anger. He wants me better, and he wants me better *now*. But some things, you can't control. If I didn't feel so gross, I'd probably smile to myself over this. He's not a patient man.

The doctor instructs Kazimir out of the room, and Kazimir doesn't like this at all, but he complies nonetheless. The doctor takes my temperature and frowns when the reading is normal. To my surprise, he gives me a little plastic container.

"I need a urine sample," he tells me. "When is the last time you got your period?"

My cheeks flame. "Before I came here," I tell him.

"How long was that?" he asks.

I shake my head. "I'm not exactly sure." It's been weeks, though.

"And you're on birth control?" he asks. I nod. I'm supposed to be.

"I will speak with your master while you take care of what you need to," he says, heading out of the room, but I'm struck with how weird his words are.

Is Kazimir my master?

It isn't until I'm giving the doctor the sample that I really begin to process his line of questioning. Does the doctor think there could be another reason for me to be sick like this? I didn't even think about the possibility of pregnancy. Kazimir already assured me that wasn't possible.

The Bratva's Baby: A Dark Mafia Romance

I wash my hands and groan when another wave of nausea hits me. I'm sick again and again until all I want to do is curl up and sleep, even if the cold tile floor is my only respite. Someone comes in the bathroom but I don't even look up. I'm so tired and so sick, I don't protest at all when Kazimir lifts me in his arms, carries me to bed, and lays me down. He pulls the sheet up over my shoulder.

"Sleep, woman," he whispers in my ear. I sleep.

Chapter Nineteen

Kazimir

Nikita stands before me fidgeting. She's worked for me long enough to know the tone of my summons doesn't bode well for her.

"Yes, sir?" she asks in Russian.

Sadie stirs in the other room, sitting up and watching our exchange. She adores Nikita, and I'm sure she's curious why I've called her up to me.

I'm glad my exchange with her is in a language Sadie doesn't understand. I have questions for Nikita that aren't for Sadie's ears. Not yet.

"Did you give Sadie the birth control pills?" I ask her directly, cursing myself inwardly for not checking before.

The Bratva's Baby: A Dark Mafia Romance

"Sir?" she asks with wide eyes.

"You heard me," I snap, already knowing the answer to my question.

Blushing, she looks away and bites her lip without answering.

"Nikita," I say, warningly. But I already know what she's going to tell me. I hold myself back. My palm itches to strike her.

No one disobeys my instructions. If she were a man, she'd feel my wrath, but she's a woman. Instead, I'll have to fire her.

"I didn't know you wanted them, sir," she says. "You didn't order them as you've done in the past, and you said that Sadie was different. If I knew you wanted them—"

"I told you to give her the usual supplements."

"Supplements, sir. I thought you meant vitamins."

I take in a deep breath, trying to quell my rising anger. She didn't give her the birth control. Sadie is sick. Doctor Rothsky has given her a pregnancy test, and we'll soon have the results.

"You're fired," I tell Nikita. "Leave. Pack your bags and do not return."

Nikita stands, wringing her hands and pleading with me. "Sir," she cries. "Please, sir, don't." She not only works here, but has lived here for years. Dismissing her puts her on the outs with the most powerful organized crime ring in our country.

I dismiss her with a wave of her hand. She allowed Sadie to become pregnant with her negligence, and now I don't even know where I can begin to make this right.

We cannot bring a child into my world... our world. I've hurt enough innocent people already.

"Go," I order her. "You have one hour to vacate."

Her tear-filled pleas rouse Sadie, and soon, Sadie is standing in the doorway, wrapped in a sheet, looking as pale and wan as a ghost.

"Why are you crying, Nikita?" she asks, her brows furrowed in consternation. "Kazimir, what have you done?"

"I've fired her," I snap at her. "Mind your own business and go back to bed."

"Kazimir," she says reproachfully. "This *is* my business. Nikita is the one who cares for me." Taking a deep breath, she juts her chin out and meets my eyes squarely. "And if I'm pregnant, I'll need her help."

I groan out loud. "How did you know?"

"How could I not?" she asks. "He's right. I've missed my period. I didn't think much of it because I thought the birth control pills would affect my cycle, but he made me give him a sample..." her voice trails off when the doctor comes into the room.

The Bratva's Baby: A Dark Mafia Romance

In Russian, he speaks to me so that only Nikita and I understand.

"The test is confirmed, sir. She is indeed, pregnant, and her hormone levels are strong. If you'd like to terminate, I must know immediately."

I want to break something. I want to scream and tear things and gnash my teeth in fury. We can't have a baby. *No*. A baby in this life would be a disaster of epic proportions.

I look into Sadie's eyes. Though she doesn't speak the language, she knows, and yet she doesn't look away. Without a word, she glides her hand to her belly.

"Go," I tell the doctor. "Nikita, you will wait for further instruction from me." They leave quickly, Nikita whispering profusive thanks and leaving before I can change my mind.

Sadie suspects but still doesn't know the truth. I dismiss the doctor before I turn back to Sadie, who watches all of us with quiet acceptance.

I sit on a chair in my living room and beckon her to me. "Come here, please," I say. With quiet acceptance, she obeys, letting the sheet fall and sliding her naked body onto my lap.

"Yes?"

"Doctor Rothsky and Nikita confirmed my fears," I tell her. "Nikita never gave you birth control as I suspected she had. And the doctor says your test is positive."

"Was she supposed to?"

I sigh. Was she? It was part of our normal routine, but I never specified. It was an oversight with severe consequences.

"I should have specified," I tell her, shaking my head. "I assumed she'd know."

"Did you fire her?"

It should come as no surprise that the first words out of her mouth are about Nikita. She's more concerned with losing her assistance than being pregnant?

"Sadie," I chide. "You don't care about being pregnant? We'll have to terminate."

Her eyes widen in shock as she pulls away from me. "You don't want me to carry your baby?" I flinch at the pain in her question and inwardly groan. I don't want to fight her in this. I can make her do many things, but this…

"Of course that isn't it," I tell her. "It isn't you. But I can't imagine bringing a child into this world with what I do. Who we are. There will be no pink nurseries and sweet lullabies. And Dimitri…" This goes against everything we stand against. It's foolish and dangerous.

"You don't want my baby," she repeats, in a tone that breaks my heart. Shaking her head, she pushes herself off my lap. I reach for her but she steps out of my grasp, pushing my hand away.

The Bratva's Baby: A Dark Mafia Romance

"You think I'm just a pawn in this? That my own thoughts and dreams don't matter?"

"Sadie," I begin, but when she opens her mouth to continue, she pales and grips her stomach, wincing.

I watch her sprint to the bathroom just in time. When she's finished, spent and panting, I escort her to bed and give her strict orders not to get out until I tell her.

"Rest," I tell her. "We'll deal with this later. Right now, you rest."

Thankfully, I've trained her well enough in obedience that she drifts off to sleep and doesn't fight me anymore. I call Nikita on my cell phone.

"Find out whatever remedies you can for pregnancy illness," I instruct. "Then come up here. And you keep *everything* confidential."

"Yes, sir!" she says eagerly before I hang up the phone. I'll keep her. It isn't her fault Sadie's pregnant.

Christ.

It's mine.

If I force her to end the pregnancy, she will always believe I didn't want her to carry my baby.

But how can I bring a child into this violent, cruel world I live in?

263

JANE HENRY

I bury my head in my hands and wrestle with the demons I've fought for years. There are no easy answers in any of this. I stand and pace the living room, memories of my miserable childhood assaulting my mind, when I have a sudden realization so obvious I could smack myself.

A baby that Sadie carries isn't just *mine*. Its hers, too. And as I stand there, plagued by demons from my past, I envision what she'd look like. A child wrapped in a blanket, cuddled to Sadie's breast while she sang sweet lullabies. Any child of mine Sadie had would be… hers, too. Do I want to rob her of that? *Can* I?

Maybe our child would have her sweet eyes and little button nose, the pouty lips and soft-spoken voice. Maybe she'd be a bookworm like her mama, or… or maybe she will be a he.

I stand up straighter.

A son.

A lump rises in my throat at the thought of a precious child, dependent on me… a child who'd call me papa.

A daughter like my beautiful wife, or a son…

I pace the room and wrangle the thoughts from my mind that assault me. Where would we live? I wouldn't raise a family here, not in this building. We'd have to find a home. A home in the country. I could drive here to take care of business, and at the end of the day…

The Bratva's Baby: A Dark Mafia Romance

I shake my head. No. A baby is an impossibility. This can't be happening.

Maybe she'll miscarry?

The second the thought comes to me, I want to smack myself for wishing such a thing on her. Don't I wish what's best for her?

I halt in my tracks.

Do I? What am I doing here? I brought her here so that I could fulfill a simple request from Dimitri, no more or less.

I never suspected she'd come to actually mean something to me.

I pace the room until I hear Sadie moaning in the other room.

"Kazimir?" I run to her so quickly I almost trip. She's carrying my baby, and she needs to speak to me. My chest swells with an urgency I can't contain.

"Yes?" I ask her, taking her hand. And when she looks up at me with those wide brown eyes, stray hair falling across her forehead, my chest swells with emotion I can't contain. I drop to one knee beside the bed and sweep her hair off her forehead. "What is it, *krasotka?* Tell me."

When she blinks, her eyes are filled with tears. "Where will we go?" she whispers. "I don't want a baby around those men. I don't want their vicious hands anywhere near my baby. I don't want—"

265

JANE HENRY

"Hush," I tell her, putting my finger to her lips. "We don't need to worry about that right now. Right now, we need to make a plan. Keep this hidden. I don't want any of them to find out." My mind reels with possibilities, but I shake my head. "First, we take care of you. I have Nikita making sure you do what you need to. You'll need your vitamins and proper care and nutrition. Exercise when appropriate, and comfortable clothes. Plenty of rest, and I want to be sure you're monitored regularly so that—"

"Kazimir," she interrupts softly, resting her hand on mine, and it's then that I realize she looks a little green around the ears. "I just want some crackers right now. In America, we have plain ones with salt on top that some ladies say help nausea. I don't know what you have here but I need something. My stomach hurts, and I just want to ease the nausea."

I stand. "Yes, of course," I tell her, but she won't let my hand go.

"Do you have to go?" she asks, her eyes as wide as a little puppy's. My heart twists in my chest with the knowledge that things have changed between us. I've lied to myself. She isn't my prisoner. She isn't the woman I've been training to obey me, with the intent of cultivating fear and mindless subservience.

She's my victory prize for battle. The spoils of war. My most precious possession, and I'll guard and protect her with my very life.

266

"Anything," I say to her, my voice choked with emotion. This is the woman I've married, and she bears my child. "Anything, Sadie."

Chapter Twenty

Sadie

As the days pass into weeks, my body undergoes a transformation. My breasts are tender, my abdomen slowly, gently rounded already. But I'm not the only one who's changing. I watch as Kazimir does, too.

I'm ordered to bed, made to rest, and he's so smothering he treats me as if I'm a delicate, fragile creature. He's different, though. I can see it in his eyes, and the way he talks to his men when he meets with them. Though he's still their leader, there's a detachment about him that wasn't there before. And when he speaks with Dimitri, there's a distance in his eyes I wonder if only I can see. I don't ask him about what we'll do. I know without him telling me that it's the first thing he thinks about when he wakes up and the last thing he thinks about before he goes to bed. And even though our relationship began in a wildly unorthodox way, I have to admit I trust him. Plus the reality is, I'm so sick that I can't think much beyond keeping down my breakfast.

Nikita dotes on me, bringing me strong tea and candied ginger, but I'm so sick I can hold almost nothing down until the doctor gives me medication to take. I resist at first, but Kazimir doubles down and makes me. I have to reluctantly admit he's right, though. The round white pill the doctor gives me eases my nausea, and after three weeks of being nearly bedridden, I finally sit up in bed. Kazimir is in the bathroom. I hear the shower turn off, and realize he hasn't made love to me in three weeks. The awareness makes me sad.

The door to the bathroom opens, and when he emerges, all steamy and sexy, my need for him stirs low in my belly. I let my eyes roam over his strong, powerful body. I appreciate the breadth of his shoulders, and bulge of his muscles, the dangerous tattoos that grace his damp skin. He's cleaned up his beard, but it's still dark and heavy, and I can smell the masculine scent of his aftershave. Instead of making my belly flip, a deep thrum of need hits me low in the belly. I swallow hard.

"Well, hello there, handsome," I murmur appreciatively. It isn't until he steps closer to me that I notice he looks tired. Tired and weary. He's been carrying the weight of his decision on his shoulders. Responsibility to his men… to me… to our unborn child.

"Handsome?" he says playfully, his lips twitching. "Are you feeling better?"

I smile shyly. "Mmmm." Though my stomach growls in hunger, there's another appetite I want to sate. "Come over here." I pat the bed and wiggle my eyes but he doesn't come closer. Folding his arms on his chest, he gives me a stern look, though his eyes twinkle a bit.

"I may have indulged you, but in no way does that give you permission to tell me what to do, Sadie."

"Sir," I say, bowing my head, a desperate longing clawing in my chest. "Please?"

I want him to hold me. I need him to touch me. He can't stand across from me looking like sex personified with those muscles and tattoos and leave me over here for another day of ginger tea and salty crackers.

I swallow a lump in my throat. Though he's been with me, I realize I've missed him.

When he walks toward me, the towel still slung about his waist, anticipation grows in my belly. We've made love and he's brought me to pleasure so many times, my body reacts of its own accord. I know what I want, and what I want is him. Standing over me, he cups my jaw between his large, warm hands, and lifts my face to his. I look

The Bratva's Baby: A Dark Mafia Romance

up at him. He likes what he sees when my eyes meet his, and he smiles.

"It's true what they say about a glow," he says. "You always were beautiful, love. Now, you're exquisite. I could feast my eyes on you all day and never hunger for anything else."

I try to look away, bashful at the bold compliment, but he holds my gaze. "No, Sadie," he says. "Accept what I say. Know that it's true. You are my wife and the woman who bears my child. I love you."

My heart swells when he leans down and captures my lips with his. I close my eyes and sigh. I've missed this. Oh, how I've missed this. I lose myself to the kiss, a warm tingle of sensation washing over me as he lowers me to the bed and cages me in with his large, powerful body. My wrists are pinned to my side, my knees spread apart by his. He never allowed me to wear clothes to bed, but the past few weeks he's allowed me to wear a thin nightie for comfort. It takes only seconds for him to yank it off me and bare me to him.

I'm lost to feeling. Tender lips and prickly whiskers, gentle strokes and firm fingers. I moan when he parts my legs and glides his fingers between my thighs.

"I've missed this pussy," he growls in my ear, groaning when he finds me slick and swollen. "I need to feel you. Taste you. Eat you."

I nod eagerly and part my legs further, earning me

a chuckle and playful slap to the thigh. The sharp smack reminds me he hasn't spanked me since that day in the library.

I miss it. I don't understand why or how, but I do. When he puts me over his lap, my body hums with need for him. I like that when he takes control, it clears my mind and focuses me on the present.

And hell, his stern dominance turns me on.

"Yes," I groan, losing all my inhibition, I'm so desperate to feel him again. "Take me over your knee, sir. Use me."

"No, Sadie," he growls. "I will not risk your health or the health of the baby."

"Kazimir," I whine. "Don't be silly. A little spanking never hurt a pregnant woman."

Still caging me beneath him, he lifts himself up and stares at me. "You know this how? And I can't believe you're asking me to punish you."

I bite my lip. "I can't believe it either," I whisper. "But actually, that isn't true. I don't want you to *punish* me, per se, I just think a little… kinky…" my voice trails off while I flush furiously.

"I honestly… I can't… well, if you'd just… oh, forget it," I finally whisper. I'm losing myself to sensation. I'm desperate to feel the pleasure sweep through me that only he can grant.

He playfully slaps my thigh again, and my body responds with longing. "Mmm," I groan.

The Bratva's Baby: A Dark Mafia Romance

"I won't spank you until the doctor tells me I can," he says decisively.

"Kazimir," I whine. "That isn't fair."

Then he's gone. His warmth, his strength, his masculine scent. Standing over me, he mutters, "You want to be punished? No sex," he says, turning away with a twinkle in his eyes.

"No!" I yelp, sounding desperate. "Okay, okay, I'll stop begging. I'll be patient."

The towel falls the floor as he lunges back at the bed, silencing my shriek with a savage kiss, the hard length of him pressing between my thighs. "Yes," I moan. "Oh, God, yes. Please." I close my eyes when he kisses me, allowing myself to drown in sensation when he palms my breast, plays with my nipples, and his tongue slides against mine. I missed this so much, my throat feels tight and tears prick my eyes, so when the doorbell rings, I groan.

"Who's that?" I ask. "God, it's been weeks and we can't have a minute to ourselves?"

I'm muttering and groaning to myself, but he's already pulling on a pair of pants and walking bare-chested to open the door. One of the men he works with stands in the doorway. They have a brief, tense conversation in Russian, and just as Kazimir dismisses him, the doctor shows up.

Oh for crying out loud. I sigh, but then I remember I can ask the doctor about what's safe so I perk up a bit.

Kazimir greets the doctor, and escorts him into the bedroom. The doctor comes often, takes my vital signs, listens to the baby's heartbeat, and checks to see how I'm doing. I get the feeling that this isn't normal prenatal care, but something Kazimir demands above the norm.

After Dr. Rothsky's finished with his examination, I wave my hand to Kazimir. "Please don't forget to ask him what's okay for us to do," I say. "You know." I flush. Kazimir rolls his eyes but his lips twitch up, and he talks to the doctor in Russian as he leads him to do the door. A few minutes later, he returns to the room with a downcast look.

"What?" I ask, sitting up in bed.

"Seems we have to be safe and gentle during your pregnancy," he begins. "No pain, nothing dangerous, and missionary sex is likely the safest position."

"*What?*" I say. "I think the medical practices here must be outdated. There's no reason——"

But my voice trails off because he's laughing. Really *laughing.* His eyes twinkle with merriment, his shoulders shaking with it.

"I'm teasing," he says. "Unfortunately it looks like you'd better behave yourself. There will be no free card offered just because you're carrying my child."

"Oh?" I ask, excitement weaving its way through my belly.

The Bratva's Baby: A Dark Mafia Romance

"Oh," he responds with a sage nod. "I have to be sure not to constrict your air ways, so bondage is fine with limitations. Soft ropes and no loss of circulation."

"Got it," I say as he undresses and his cock springs free.

"I'm free to spank your ass," he says, a warning glint in his eyes, "though eventually over my knee will get uncomfortable and we'll have to arrange pillows. But he says a little spanking is actually good, because the hormones released afterward have a calming effect."

"I see," I whisper as he leans down and drags his tongue along my hardened nipple.

"I won't overdo it," he says. "But I know how to deliver a good, thorough spanking that will make you behave yourself."

"That you do," I agree, my voice pitching off to a groan when he clamps down on my nipple with his teeth.

"On your knees," he orders.

He's kneeling over me now, arranging my limbs so that I'm face down on my knees, with my ass in the air. "So tell me, sweet girl," he says with a growl. I feel his cock pressed hard up against my ass and I push against it, earning me a hard smack and a growl. "Have you been naughty?"

I stifle a groan while I grind against his cock. "I've been terrible," I say with a mock confession.

275

"I even touched myself when you weren't looking."

His hand crashes down on my ass, not as hard as he's spanked me in the past, but it's enough that I squeal and arch. "Did you?" he asks. "Did you make yourself come?"

I don't answer. I want a spanking. Hell, I need one. And I'm teasing him anyway. I never touched myself.

"Answer me," he says, delivering a few sharp smacks to my upper thighs and the underside of my ass. He hasn't lost his touch. My backside throbs and heats from the smacks of his palm, but I need more. I'm so swollen and ready, one swipe of his tongue or fingers would send me soaring into release.

"No," I cry out when he spanks me again. "I lied. I never touched myself. You're the only one who does."

"You lied?" he asks sternly before he delivers three more rapid, stinging smacks to my naked skin. "You know better than that, young lady."

I smile to myself. I've missed this.

"But you didn't touch yourself?" Another swat. My skin stings and burns so good. I shake my head.

"I didn't," I confess. "I want you to."

His body over mine, I'm engulfed by his heat, his

scent, his controlled dominance. I shiver in anticipation just before he fondles between my legs and strokes my clit.

"Beautiful girl," he whispers.

I arch into his back and groan when he strokes my slick folds. I need more. Harder. Faster.

"On your back," he orders, helping me flip back over onto my back. I bite my lip, smiling to myself as he arranges pillows all around me to ease my comfort.

"I'm fine, Kazimir," I protest, but his frown conveys his message, and I close my mouth.

"You're carrying my child," he says as if that explains the mountain of pillows around me. But when he buries himself between my legs and I feel his hot breath between my thighs, I shiver in delight. "Do you like that?"

"Yessss," I groan when he swipes his tongue between my folds. It feels so good I can't breathe, I can't even think. I keen with pleasure when he rocks his mouth against me, licking and sucking with such expertise I'm nearing the edge of release so quickly, I'm almost disappointed. I wanted this to last longer than half a minute.

"Wait until I tell you that you can come," he tells me.

"I'm ready," I tell him.

"Wait."

"Sir!" I'm desperate, pleading.

"Wait," he repeats, returning to the torturous assault of his tongue. I can't hold on much longer. I close my eyes with the effort and hold my breath, trying to distract myself.

"If you come, I'll take my belt to your ass," he grates, the heat of his mouth between my thighs making me moan. "You'll wait until I tell you."

"Kazimir, please," I beg, weaving my fingers through the dark head of hair between my thighs. A flick of his tongue and I see stars, I'm blinded on the edge of bliss.

"I'll whip you," he growls, with a torturously light touch of his tongue between my legs. Kissing my inner thighs, he groans. "I can taste your arousal on your legs. Christ, woman, you slay me."

"Then let me come," I beg, my voice breathy. I squeal as he nips my inner thigh.

"Is that what you want?" he lazily laps at my folds.

"Yes," I pant, desperate. "Yes yes yes yes yes. *Please.*"

One more suckle and I'm coming apart at the seams as he thrusts two fingers in my channel. "Come, Sadie," he orders.

I come so hard, I shatter into pieces. My backside lifts so high off the bed, he yanks my thighs and pulls me back down, I scream his name, bucking beneath him, climaxing so hard my muscles contract. I'm on the edge of coming down from the torrent of bliss when he slams his cock into me. I groan in pain and pleasure, the two inexplicably entwined, every thrust taking me closer and closer to a second climax.

"I love you," I breathe. He stills for a split second before he impales me again, this time harder than the last. My body is pressed against his, sweaty and heated, my arms wrapped around his strong, powerfully muscled body. He groans his own release, before he finally slows his thrusts and drops his forehead to mine.

"You're a good girl," he whispers. "And I love you. I don't deserve a girl like you, but now that you're mine, I will treasure you until the day I die."

I can't fathom how we'll make this work. I have no idea how we'll parent a child, two broken people like us with no solid place in this world. But when he sets his mind to something, he does it, and I'm no slouch. This child we have between us will have everything it needs to thrive in this world. No matter what we have to give up in the process.

Kazimir is on the phone in the living room when I get out of the shower. I smile to myself at the tousled sheets on the bed. God, I needed that.

My stomach aches with hunger when I see the large platters on the little table beside the bed. I'm starving, and this food looks amazing.

JANE HENRY

Bowls of porridge with berries and cream, platters of eggs and potatoes. Toasted crusty bread with butter and jam, and a silver pot filled with fragrant tea. I wrap the towel around me and don't even bother to change. Heaping food on a plate, I happily tuck in.

Kazmir's voice sounds harsh in the other room, angry even, but I don't really pay attention. It's not uncommon for him to conduct business like this, and I prefer to be ignorant about what he does. Especially now that we'll have a child between us. The less I know, the better.

But when I take a slice of toast to my mouth, I freeze before I take a bite. Something familiar catches my eye on his side of the room, hidden under a pile of books likely kicked loose with our crazy lovemaking, the blue binding of my journal catches the light of the room.

My journal. The one I left in America and haven't seen since the day I came here.

I rise, my hunger forgotten. I'm suddenly both too hot or too cold. I'm shivering, and I feel a strange and sudden out-of-body experience take over, as if I'm watching a stranger cross the room.

I didn't have my journal with me when we arrived here. How did it get here? Walking across the room, I look over my shoulder to be sure Kazimir is still occupied in the other room. We've just made love, and it was beautiful. I don't want to incur his anger now.

280

The Bratva's Baby: A Dark Mafia Romance

But shouldn't I be the one angry? Aren't I the one whose privacy was violated?

With trembling fingers, I pick up the book. The physical reminder of the woman I once was. The reminder of the life I once lived. I open the page and read my own writing.

Today I read the most lovely book, written during a time when it was okay for women to be feminine and demure, and acceptable for a man to ask for her hand in marriage. So traditional. I can't imagine a thing like this happening in modern day America. Courtship. Dowries. Dresses that swoop to the floor in elegance.

Women weren't allowed to vote, or work. So oppressive. So chauvinistic.

I look away and smile to myself. And yet I read the books.

Why?

I forget where I am and who I am. My body's still flush from lovemaking, my thighs damp with his seed marking me as his, while I read.

I'll never know the touch of a man, nor do I want to. I can't imagine ever allowing myself to be so vulnerable that I allow another human to hurt me the way selfish, bold men do. The adoration of a lover is for the pages of a romance novel, and that is exactly where it belongs. In a world where women still swish in romantic gowns, men still speak with civil tongues. In a fantasy world where dreams are born and die.

I close the book. I can't read on. What would the old me have thought of the present me? The marks of my husband's palm still on my backside where I begged him to spank me. I can still feel the scrape of his whiskers between my thighs, his swollen cock in my core. My eyes flutter shut as I draw my fingers across my abdomen.

His child grows within me.

Shaking so badly I can hardly move steadily, I shove the journal back where he had it and hide it. He's still talking in the other room, his voice rising and falling in that commanding way of his, but now it doesn't sound so sexy. Now it just sounds… foreign. Harsh. I should be angry at him for taking my journal, for violating my privacy, but such a thing pales in comparison to the other things he's done to me. It isn't him I'm angry with but myself.

The food I ate churns in my belly as I walk back to bed. I pull the covers over me and close my eyes. My stomach doesn't ache, but my heart does.

Chapter Twenty-One

Kazimir

I'm so preoccupied with the conversation I just had on the phone, I don't even notice at first that Sadie's back in bed until I've already made my plate of food. In my defense, she's been in bed for three weeks, so it's not all that unusual.

"Sadie?" I ask. The peace I felt after reconnecting with Sadie quickly evaporated when I had to take a phone call. Dimitri, angry and demanding, refused to tell me what he has to speak to me about on the phone and insisted I come down, alone, to see him, as soon as possible.

I wonder briefly if he knows Sadie's pregnant. Both the doctor and Nikita are bound to secrecy, and I'd hoped he wouldn't care beyond what Sadie's inheritance brought him.

283

Has he figured out she's pregnant?

We've just about come to the terms in the legal documents that specify how long she has to be married before her money becomes hers. Here in our city, I can easily have her money marked as mine, since we're a wedded couple, and after the transfer, my obligation to Dimitri will be fulfilled.

What is it that Dimitri wants to talk to me about?

He can't know that I'm trying to find a way to extricate myself from this mess. How can I keep Sadie's trust, fulfill my promise to Dimitri, and care for my unborn child, all at the same time?

I'm slathering jam on toast when my eyes fall on Sadie's plate. I take a bite, chew, and swallow, observing the large volume of food on her plate that she barely touched. She's got to be starving.

"Sadie?" I ask. I watch her shift on the bed. She isn't asleep then.

"Yes?" she asks. Her voice sounds strangely distant.

"Are you alright?"

At first she doesn't respond, but she finally just nods her head.

"Yes, sir," she says. "I'm fine." I can only see her blanketed body from where I am. I need to see her eyes.

I stand and walk to the side of the bed. At the sight of my beautiful wife, still flushed from love-

The Bratva's Baby: A Dark Mafia Romance

making, lying on her side with her hands tucked under her cheek like a child's, my heart swells with pride.

My wife. My beautiful wife.

I sit beside her and brush her hair off her forehead, but she doesn't open her eyes.

"Are you sure you're okay?" I ask her.

"I'm fine," she whispers, but when a tear escapes from the corner of her eyes, I know she's lying.

"Sadie," I say sternly. "Open your eyes and look at me."

When her gaze meets mine, I feel a stab of pain hit me in the chest. Those pretty dark lashes are framed with tears.

"What is it, sweet girl?" I ask her. I want to gather her in my arms and pull her to my chest, but something in her eyes tells me that isn't what she wants or needs right now. I'm experienced in reading facial expressions, and I see betrayal in those beautiful depths. What has happened in the brief time since our lovemaking?

"Sadie," I say, warning. She's hiding something from me, and I'll have the truth.

"What? It's astonishing to me how quickly you go from doting husband to stern task master."

"It's astonishing to *me* how quickly you go from sex-sated submissive to brat," I retort.

When her lips thin and she pulls away from me, I regret my words. I don't need to fight her to get the truth.

"Are you sick?" I ask.

She shakes her head.

"Good," I say, throwing back the covers and yanking her out of bed.

"Hey!" I ignore her protests as I lift her straight up into my arms and gently drape her over my shoulder. Even though I know the good doctor told me the baby's safe and sound, I can't help but treat her a little more gently than I normally would. When she flails, I simply hold her legs a little tighter as I walk to the corner of the room. Sliding her down my chest, I spin her around and gently but firmly push her to standing with her nose against the corner.

"What are you doing?" she asks, but she doesn't move out of the position I put her in.

"Isn't it obvious? I'm standing you in the corner. If you weren't with child, I'd extricate the truth over my knee, but because you are, we'll do it this way."

Even if I am allowed to spank her, I don't want to fear hurting her. She can learn to submit just fine this way.

"Tell me why you're angry," I demand.

"Tell me why *you* are!"

The Bratva's Baby: A Dark Mafia Romance

I smack her pretty backside, but not too hard. Just enough to get her attention.

"Sadie," I warn.

She sighs. But something catches the corner of my eye that clues me in. Her journal sticks out beneath a stack of books on the bedside table. Is she upset with me that I've fetched her journal?

"Did you find your book?" I ask her. "Were you looking through my things?"

A little nod of her head confirms her guilt, but her slumped shoulders twist my heart. I don't like to see her sad. I reach for her shoulder and turn her to me, half expecting downcast eyes. Instead, pained, tear-stained eyes meet mine.

"I'm not angry with you," she says. "I suppose I should be," she continues, swiping at her eyes, "but it isn't you that I'm upset with."

I reach for her and pull her to me, tucking her naked, trembling body against my chest.

"A normal girl would be angry at the invasion of privacy," she mutters, "but I suppose we crossed that bridge after the moment you shoved metal in my ass."

I can't help but smirk at her adorable recollection. I squeeze her ass cheek playfully, and my heart soars when it earns a little giggle. But then she sighs, and she leans more heavily into my arms. "I just—it was a reminder of who I once was, Kazimir," she says. "I didn't want this. Any of it."

She waves her little hand around the room, at the bed, at me, at her gently curving abdomen.

"I know," I tell her, a pervading sadness overcoming me at the knowledge of what I must do to keep her safe. "I know, Sadie." I think of my initial plans for her and how things have changed. "This wasn't what I planned, either." I caress her gently swollen abdomen. Neither one of us speaks for a moment.

"I have to go downstairs shortly to meet Dimitri," I tell her. "Today, you stay up here or go to the library if you'd like. We'll talk about this more later, understood?"

I wait until she nods before I take her by the hand and bring her to the table for her breakfast.

"But first, eat."

A little cluster of consternation knits her brow. There are many things on her mind, but I don't have time to really delve into her heart and mind right now.

Dimitri waits.

And then I'll make my decision.

I wait until she eats a portion that satisfies me, and Nikita comes to tend to her, before I go to Dimitri. I need to hear what he has to say before I make any decisions or plans. But when I get to the threshold of the door, I feel a tug in my gut. I turn back to Sadie and look at her, puzzled. She's on her feet, shaking her head.

The Bratva's Baby: A Dark Mafia Romance

"Don't go, Kazimir," she says, holding her belly. Begging for me to stay for both of them. "Please."

"I'm not going to be gone for long," I tell her. "Just stay here with Nikita until I return, or—"

"No!" Her eyes are wide and fearful. "You can't go."

I'm torn between anger at her defiance and real concern on her insistence. "Sadie." My deeper voice arrests her. Nikita hears the warning in my voice and reaches for Sadie's hand, whispering something in a placating whisper. Sadie shoves her away and takes a step toward me.

"Kazimir." She's only a step away from me now. I've walked toward her without even realizing I did. A sense of foreboding permeates the air between us. "I—I can't explain it. But if you walk out that door, I just know… something…" She shakes her head.

"You're overwrought," I tell her, ignoring my own reservations. I don't like leaving my pregnant wife vulnerable like this. I reason away the hesitation with logic. But there's nothing that can happen to her here, not in the safety of our home, with armed guards to protect us and her servant tending to her. When I look at the time, I make my decision. I have no more time to dawdle, and doing so could incur Dimitri's anger. "I have to go. Be a good girl."

"No," she whispers, but I pry her fingers off me and hand her to Nikita, who's standing behind her waiting, watching the exchange between the two of us with wide, fearful eyes. Sadie lets me go and hangs her head. I walk away, ignoring the tug in my gut and lump in my throat.

My decision is made. I need to get her away from here. First, I listen to Dimitri.

I step on the elevator, glaring at the buttons as if it's their fault I had to practically extricate myself from my wife to do my work. The elevator descends, but stops only one floor down. The doors open, yet no one comes on. Frowning, I push the button again, and wait until it takes me to Dimitri.

This whole day is strange. Nothing is predictable, not even me. I glance at the time and realize I'm one minute late. I curse under my breath and shake my head. I shouldn't have let her pleas delay me.

When the elevator opens, I hear shouting and the sound of glass breaking. I exit the elevator at a run.

In the dining room, the servant girl whose shoes I took kneels, weeping. Her fingers are bloodied, but she's picking up shards of broken glass anyway.

"Stop that," I order in Russian. "You're injured. Tend to your injuries first, and leave that for someone else."

She raises wild, tear-filled eyes to mine and stammers her explanation. "He won't let me, sir."

The Bratva's Baby: A Dark Mafia Romance

I know exactly who she's referring to. I look around the room until I see him, standing at the head of the table.

"Leave her and come here, Kazimir," he orders.

I look from the girl to Dimitri.

"Her hands are bloodied," I tell him. "She needs to clean them, Dimitri."

Without warning, he lifts another glass from the table and whips it across the room. It shatters into pieces against the brick fireplace. Another servant girl screams and covers her mouth.

"I said come *here*!" he thunders.

I haven't seen Dimitri in a rage like this in years. In the past, I'd obey him without question, knowing I owed him my allegiance and obedience. Now, though... now, seeing him make this poor girl weep in fear, I see him in a different light.

How could I have ever thought this was acceptable? Sadie's words come back to me.

He's a monster.

Am I? How could I have respected this man?

In silence, I walk to him, prepared to defend myself if he gets violent. I don't trust him when he's raging like this.

Do I trust him when he isn't?

I look at the man I think of as my father with new eyes. He's taught me to take what I want with ruthless precision. To raze whatever's in my path for the good of our chosen family. To exact vengeance and demand respect, take what's due to us and show no mercy.

Have I softened because my wife now bears my child?

Or have I been under his curse?

By the time I reach the table, my own anger's rising. "Why do you treat them like this?" I say in a whisper only for our ears. "What has she done to deserve this?"

Dimitri's eyes narrow as he grasps the glass in his hand so tightly his knuckles whiten.

"Sit down, Kazimir," he growls.

My gaze fixed on him, I sit. When he's satisfied I'm contained, he pulls out a chair and sits, his one seeing eye fixed angrily on me. I take a sip of water to quell my anger. If he's on the verge of losing his self-control, I'll be the one who stays calm.

But when he speaks, it isn't the wrath I expect to hear but broken resignation.

"She left me," he says. "And our plan is destroyed."

I blink, and swallow another sip of water before I respond. He's just given me two pieces of shocking news. When I speak, I keep my voice deliberately calm.

The Bratva's Baby: A Dark Mafia Romance

"Who left you, sir?"

"Who else?" he snaps. "Yana, you fool."

I ignore the insult, processing what he's just told me. Yana is like a mother to me. She's left him?

"When?" I ask.

Dimitri suddenly looks so much older. Weary. He buries his head in his hands, his shoulders sagging. "Last night," he says.

I shake my head. I don't ask why, that isn't for me to know.

"Where did she go?" I ask. "Do you know?"

When he lifts his face to mine, a chill runs down my spine. This isn't the broken, saddened man I expected to see. His cold, calculating eyes meet mine, filled with raw hatred. "Of course I know," he hisses, spittle forming in the corner of his mouth. "Do you think I'd allow her to leave me? After everything we've been through? Everything she knows. I did exactly what I had to, just as you would."

"Dimitri," I say in a low voice so no one can hear us. But I can't bring myself to ask him what he did. I don't want to know. I know too much already.

"She took her vows to me, Kazimir, and you know how I feel about allegiance. You know how I feel about betrayal."

I do. I've seen him murder men in cold blood who

293

·

betrayed him. I've seen men weep like babies in his vicious hands and come to accept they deserved their fate. But Yana...

Bracing himself on the table, he leans forward, his breath stained with the scent of alcohol. "Leaving me was not an option. I did what I had to."

"Say it," I insist, leaning toward him even though I don't want to hear it. If he's the type of man to harm his wife, I won't give him the luxury of hiding the truth.

But he won't. He holds my gaze and breathes heavily, as if he's just gotten out of a boxing ring.

"I won't allow betrayal, Kazimir."

And this time, I hear the words as if he's read my mind. As if he knows what I war with internally.

"I know."

"My wife betrayed me."

I've been a fool to think he actually cared about her.

"What did you do, Dimitri?" I demand.

"And so did Filip."

I blink. "What? Filip what?"

"He lied to me about Sadie."

I shake my head, confused. "What are you talking about?"

The Bratva's Baby: A Dark Mafia Romance

"The girl is penniless," he says with disgust. He takes a savage bite of bread and washes it down with a hefty swig of red wine. The burgundy liquid drips down his chin like blood, sickening me.

"Penniless?" For a moment I forgot why I even took her.

Christ.

I've been a hapless pawn in the game in which there are no victors.

"Worthless," he continues. "The information he gathered was incorrect. You've married the wrong girl. She's little more than a vagrant."

I grasp my wine glass to keep my hand from trembling. "You said she was worth millions. We were supposed to get her inheritance after I married her. You mean this has all been a lie?

"I'm sorry you legally wedded her before you found out the truth," Dimitri continues, holding my gaze. "But now that you know, you'll do what you have to."

Do what I have to? Like he did? Ending the life of an innocent because they failed to deliver what he expected? I never should have left Sadie alone. She's upstairs, apart from me, and if any harm comes to her—

"Sit down, Kazimir," he orders before I realize I'm on my feet.

JANE HENRY

"You've just told me the woman I consider a mother… and the woman I call wife…" my voice trails off. I don't know what to do with myself. I don't know what to think.

Dimitri finishes his wine and wipes his mouth with a white cloth napkin, staining it an ugly purple.

"And that means nothing," Dimitri says in a calm voice that belies the stormy look of fury in his eyes. "A name or title does not earn respect. It doesn't earn devotion." He scoffs. "We have jobs to do, Kazimir," he says, glaring at me. "And the only way we'll accomplish those jobs is by eliminating those that get in our way."

"Like you did with Yana?" I can't keep the bitterness out of my voice.

Unblinking, he nods. "Of course. I'm not a total savage, though, son," he says, his voice gentling. "I made sure she'll be buried by her mother."

This time, hearing him call me *son* sickens me.

"You'll have an easier job of it," he says to me. "The woman you have to bury has no family."

No family? She has a child growing within her. She has *me*.

But I have to play along. I can't reason with an insane man, and Dimitri has come unglued.

"Right," I say. "I see now, sir."

He swallows the bite of food and gives me a

piercing look. "Get rid of her, Kazimir. You have until tomorrow evening before I do it myself."

I take in a deep breath and play my part. I give him the lie he needs to hear.

"Yes, sir."

Chapter Twenty-Two

Sadie

I pace the floor near the window, wearing nothing but a pair of thin black lounge pants and a tank top. The top rides high on my waist, revealing my rounded tummy, the lounge pants slung low on my hips, and as I pace, they slip down. I yank them back up again. Distracted.

Something isn't right.

I wonder at first if it's the baby that grows in me, my hormones, or the intensity I've just gone through with Kazimir that makes me unable to focus. I can't take the vitamins Nikita has left for me, I don't want any of her ministrations today, and when she speaks to me, my mind is elsewhere.

I've just made love to my husband after weeks apart, and my heart longs to see him again. To be held by him. To hear him tell me everything's alright.

To hear him say he loves me once more.

I don't want to be here anymore, and it isn't simply because I want my freedom back. It isn't even because I dislike his brothers or Dimitri.

I want to see the haunted look in his eyes disappear. Even when he sleeps, Kazimir is tense, on guard, always prepared for a fight.

It isn't right. It isn't healthy.

And I won't raise a baby here if I have anything to do with it.

I know he's thinking of other arrangements, but I don't want to wait any longer. I want to go *now*.

Nikita's gone downstairs to fetch the tea that I drink after realizing my stock was depleted up here. So when she comes back into the room, I don't pay attention to her until she startles me by grabbing my shoulders.

"Sadie!" she hisses. Panic sweeps through my chest at the sound of her voice.

"What?" I ask, grasping at her. "What's wrong, Nikita?"

"You must go," she wails, looking over her shoulder as if someone's followed her. "You must go *now*. You and your child are not safe here." My heart races at her words.

"Kazimir," I whisper. Though we're alone I fear even the walls have ears. "Where is he?"

Her widened eyes betray my greatest fear.

"No, Sadie. He is the one who will hurt you." She closes her eyes and to my surprise, makes the sign of the cross and mutters rapidly in Russian. Though I don't understand her, I assume she's praying or something. Is this some sort of superstitious ritual?

"Nikita, tell me!" I say to her. "Tell me everything."

In broken English with tears running down her cheeks, she tells me. She was in the kitchen fetching the tea when she heard raised voices in the dining room. Sneaking to the doorway, she listened in on their conversation.

Kazimir took me because he thought I was worth millions, due an inheritance from distant relatives. I close my eyes when she says this. I never did fully understand why he took me.

He took me for money. I mean nothing to him.

Nikita continues, but I barely hear her. Dimitri has killed his wife and instructed Kazimir to do the same.

He killed his wife.

I'm not worth what they thought I was. I'm worthless.

The Bratva's Baby: A Dark Mafia Romance

Dimitri doesn't know I bear a child. But if he did... would that change anything?

It would likely put me at even more risk than I am now. If Dimitri knew I actually meant anything to Kazimir...

I swallow the lump that rises in my throat and glance around the small room. I have nothing here that matters to me. Even my old journal means nothing to me now.

I bring my hand to my belly and imagine I feel the baby stir within me.

"We have to go, Sadie," Nikita says. "I'm the only way you'll get out of here. But I can't stay any longer. He's... what is the word..." she trails off in broken English. "*Insane*. He beat Lada, our cook, and fired her after he killed his own wife."

"Yana," I whisper. Kazimir spoke of her with such tenderness. My heart aches for what he must feel.

Nikita nods, tears rolling down her cheeks. "We are not safe. We must run."

"But where will we go?" I whisper. "I do not know where I am. I have no money. No friends."

"I know," she whispers. "But first, we must leave. Quickly, put your shoes on!" I dress quickly, listening for the sound of the elevator.

"But Kazimir... Nikita, he wouldn't—"

When she turns to me, her broken voice twists my stomach into knots. "I heard him agree. I heard

301

him with my own ears. Dimitri ordered your execution, and Kazimir agreed to do it."

No.

He wouldn't. How could he? Kazimir professed his love for me and I know in my heart he meant it. I know he did.

But I have to protect my baby. And staying here, when the only chance I have at escape is presented to me, would be a mistake. So, in a jumble of tears and haste, she bundles me up, and we rush to the elevator, taking nearly nothing. I half expect men with drawn guns to come after us, but the hall remains vacant except for us. Nikita takes me by the hand when the elevator door shuts.

"We will go to the library," she whispers. "There is an exit on the ground floor I can access, and there will be fewer people there."

My heart pounds so loudly, the blood rushing in my ears nearly deafening. I'm trembling but determined. This isn't safe for me.

Kazimir agreed to murder me.

No, no, no, my heart says. But I have to stay safe.

The elevator stops at the library. I tremble, waiting for the doors to open. If Dimitri is in there... Normally on this floor, I long for the taste of freedom. I revel in the presence of the books that bring me solace, the familiar sights and smells. But today, everything seems dim and musky in here, so

The Bratva's Baby: A Dark Mafia Romance

dull and lifeless. Today, I leave the only home I've ever really known.

But when the door closes shut behind us, the elevator sweeps upward and Nikita's eyes widen. Someone's called it up.

"Hurry," she says, pulling my hand she runs for the door. I follow her, expecting someone to chase after us, but still, no one does. My vision blurs with tears when she fumbles with the lock at the door, then finally pushes it open. But the second my feet touch the concrete pavement, the first time I've left this place in months, a siren rings loud and clear.

"They know we're gone," Nikita chokes out, not bothering to modify her voice now. "*Run!*"

I don't even know where we're running to or where we're going, but I do as she says. I run until there's a stitch in my side and it feels like someone's squeezing my lungs, when my foot catches on something. I fly forward face first, bracing my fall on my hands. My head smacks concrete, the fabric on the knees of my pants tearing as they scrape on the pavement. Nikita screams, reaching for me.

"Sadie. My God, are you alright?"

A sharp pain radiates in my belly, then travels lower still. *Oh, God.*

"I… oh, no, no," I moan, grasping my belly as a spasm of pain rips through me.

"Oh, Sadie," she whispers. "Hurry. We need to go."

Nikita leads us away from the house. My stomach churns with nausea and fear, and as she pulls a phone out of her pocket, I lean against the wall and heave the contents of my stomach. I whimper, spent, and wipe the back of my mouth, just as someone answers the phone. I understand nothing as she speaks in rapid Russian. I grasp my belly, willing the baby to stay. Just to hold on. To stay with me, because I have nothing left.

Chapter Twenty-Three

Kazimir

When I see the door swinging crazily on its hinges, I know. I know before I see, I feel the loss in my very bones.

Sadie's gone. They came for her before I could get to her.

"Sadie!"

I scream her name, knowing there will be no response. "Sadie!" I bellow, needing to conjure her up, to bring her back to me. But I know before I do that it's no use.

I look about the room to see if I can piece it together. Did he send one of the men to fetch her before I could do what he ordered me to?

I wasn't going to do what I promised I would. I

could never harm her, much less kill her, and he likely knew that. Did he know she was pregnant? Or could he tell by my outrage that I hate him for killing Yana, and that I'm not a man who would murder his own wife? He thinks I'm less of a man because I can't bring myself to harm her.

In his eyes, I might be less of a man. In mine, he's barely human.

She's penniless, he said. *Worthless.*

Penniless she may be, but Sadie is anything but worthless. And she's mine.

I'll raze the city until I find her. I'll kill anyone who lays hands on her.

Fuck Dimitri and the brotherhood that forged who I am. I will not live a lonely life of violence and retribution any longer. I've seen the good in Sadie. As I've fallen in love with her, I learned to long for the simple, honest life.

But I have to find her.

I grip my hair and howl in helpless rage at whoever took her. My Sadie.

I have to keep my wits.

I look around the room and see a box of tea, still in its packaging, lying on the floor. I frown and pick it up. How unusual. I know it's the tea Nikita brings Sadie, and Sadie was just saying the other day how she was out and needed Nikita to fetch

The Bratva's Baby: A Dark Mafia Romance

her more. I pick it up, mulling over the possibilities.

I look about the room once more.

There really are no signs of a struggle. No broken furniture, items that could be used as weapons lying about. No signs of blood or broken glass.

Instead, the blankets are askew. And Sadie's shoes are gone.

Where could she have gone to?

The library.

But why is the tea on the floor?

Nikita.

Did Nikita go downstairs to get something and overhear our conversation?

I groan as the elevator door closes. If Nikita overheard anything Dimitri or I said... if she repeated any of it to Sadie... I get off the elevator, only to find the exit door swinging crazily open and the alarm we have on this door blaring like mad. I slam the door shut.

No one's come. Is that because they already have her?

"Sadie!" I shout. I need to find her. I run into the street, shouting her name. Screaming for her. Pleading.

But no one knows who she is, and my search ends in vain.

Chapter Twenty-Four

Eight months later

Kazimir

I stand in the square, dressed in simple civilian clothing. I've spent months searching for Sadie. I can't go back to my brothers. At first my life was forfeit, but since then circumstances have changed. Still, I have no wish to go back.

I've managed to discover that the day Sadie left, Nikita went missing as well.

That gives me hope.

Dimitri's fury at finding she was gone confirmed my suspicion that she escaped instead of being taken by one of his men. I've interrogated everyone I know until I found Nikita's mother. She swears she doesn't know her whereabouts, but that she always comes to visit on her birthday.

And today is Nikita's birthday.

I've plied her mother with money to keep quiet and wait for Nikita to arrive, while I lay in wait in the small barn that stands near the simple family abode. I wait until the sun sets low on the horizon, my stomach churning with hunger but hope rising in my chest. If I can find Nikita…

It's been eight months since I left the Bratva. Eight months since I betrayed Dimitri and left our ring of brotherhood in pursuit of the woman I love. Eight months since I lost Sadie.

Has she had the baby? Do I have a son or daughter in this world?

I couldn't sleep last night and haven't eaten. I'm putting everything I have into the hope of finding Sadie through Nikita.

When the sun sinks even lower, I wonder if today will be the day Nikita doesn't show. Maybe she knows if any member of the Bratva knows where she is, they'll kill her. I have almost given up on finding her, when I hear the pad of footsteps. I hide in the shadows and observe, when a young woman walks briskly past me, her head covered. I creep closer to the doorway, careful not to make a sound, until a sliver of moonlight shows her face.

Nikita.

She's come.

JANE HENRY

I look about me wildly, as if somehow Sadie followed her here, but of course she's alone, dressed all in black, as unassuming as possible. After all, she's on the run.

I wait for her visit with her mother to end, and for her to come back outside, when I see the light go off inside the house. I get to my feet. Has she left and I didn't realize it? Her mother said she never stayed the night, so I've been prepared to ambush her when she left. But no. The house is asleep, and Nikita never emerged.

I sneak up to the house, cursing myself mentally for not simply taking her by surprise when I first saw her, when something cracks me on the back of the head and I fall to the ground, crying out in pain.

I fall onto my back, and above me in the moonlight stands Nikita's shadow. In her hand she wields a large shovel above her head, prepared to bring it down in self-defense.

"Who are you?" she screams. When I don't answer at first, she lets out a wicked, heart-rending scream before she slices the shovel through the air. I roll to avoid getting struck, but she lunges. I barely escape the strike a second time, and when she's on the downswing of the heavy blow, I lunge.

Screaming, she tries to defend herself but she's no match for me. I pin her easily to the ground beneath me, my whole body vibrating with anger.

The Bratva's Baby: A Dark Mafia Romance

This is not only someone who tried to hurt me. She took my wife. She knows where she is.

I hold her down, pinning her arms above her head.

"Where is she?" I bellow. "Tell me!" I could throttle her. My hands ache with the need to hurt her, to punish her, but if I harm her, I could lose the only connection I have to Sadie.

"I'll never tell you!" she shouts. I raise my hand to strike her, and she winces in anticipation of the blow, but I stop myself mid-swing. No. I won't be that man, even when I'm enraged.

I fall back on my knees and she scrambles up, but she's cornered.

"I won't hurt you," I tell her. "But I'm not going to let you go until you tell me where she is."

Shaking her head, she turns to get away, but I've got her cornered in here.

"No, Nikita. You took something that belongs to me, and I want it back."

"Sadie belongs to no one," she seethes, thankfully confirming my suspicion that Sadie is indeed alive.

"You're wrong," I tell her. "She's mine, and if you don't tell me where she is, I'll get the information the only way I know how."

She looks at me in consternation.

JANE HENRY

"Your mother," I say simply. I'm prepared to do whatever necessary to find my woman.

"You wouldn't," Nikita whispers.

"Nikita," I growl. "I would *never* hurt Sadie. Ever. I left the day you did, and I've been combing the streets ever since, in the hope of finding her."

She blinks and nods. "This is true," she says. "I have one confidante still in the house, and they do say this is true."

I sigh as patiently as I can. "The truth, please," I say. I pull a large wad of cash out of my pocket. "Tell me, and this is yours. You can leave and start a new life for yourself." I nod to the house. "For your mother."

But the woman's loyalty runs deep. Her eye are fearful and afraid. I sigh and give her nothing but the truth.

"Nikita, I lied to Dimitri because I wanted to leave and get back to Sadie, so she'd be safe. I never had any intention at all of hurting her. Not ever." I fall to my knees in desperation. I've never needed to know anything so badly in my life. "I love her. *Please.*"

"How do I know this to be true?" she whispers.

I shake my head. "You don't. It will have to be an act of trust. But I give you my word, Nikita. I only wish to care for her. To protect her. And you already know I'm no longer in good standing with my brothers."

Nikita's eyes fill with tears. "She cries herself to sleep every night," she whispers. "And sometimes she calls your name in her sleep."

I swallow the lump in my throat. I know the pain she speaks of... I live it every day.

"Please," I plead.

Her eyes probe mine, pained but intent, when she reaches for my hand.

"You wouldn't hurt her," she whispers. "I can see your devotion in your eyes. You won't harm her, sir?"

"Never," I whisper.

Chapter Twenty-Five

Sadie

I walk along the balcony of our humble home, my eyes fixed on the mountains. Nikita secured a tiny apartment for us after we escaped. We live like peasants, but it's my favorite place I've ever lived.

A simple bone broth simmers on the stove, bread rising in the oven. We make everything from scratch with simple ingredients. We own only a few modest items of clothing and a few books. It is an unassuming life. And though I enjoy our surroundings and my home, and the freedom I wanted so badly, my heart longs for what I had.

I go into the little kitchen and stir the soup, then open the oven door and check the bread. The warm fragrance envelopes me, and hunger churns in my stomach.

The past eight months have been the hardest of my life, and I've lived through some dismal times.

When the door opens, I don't even turn to look. We're the only two here for miles, and Nikita's due for dinner. "Almost done," I tell her over my shoulder. "About five more minutes."

When she doesn't respond, I turn to the door. I open my mouth to scream but no sound comes. I stand in petrified shock when I recognize Kazimir's dark countenance, brooding eyes, his hulking form. I take a step backward. Has he come to hurt me?

But no. When his eyes come to mine, there's nothing but love in those depths.

My heart aches. I can't move. I can't speak.

"I found you," he says.

He doesn't rush me or advance on me when understanding dawns in his eyes. His mouth softens, and he drops his hands in surrender.

"I was never going to hurt you, Sadie. Not ever. I love you."

A sob rises in my throat. "But I thought—we thought—"

"It doesn't matter what you thought," he says, shaking his head. "That's behind us now."

I ran from the only man who's ever loved me. I left, but it wasn't just me I protected. I made a rash decision. The only decision.

We stand apart. In my heart, I know he tells the truth, but I can't bring myself to go to him, though. Too much has passed, too much fear and pain.

I watch his eyes gentle as he opens his arms to me, then he says the one thing that undoes me.

"Come here, *krasotka.*"

I go to him at a full run, and when I hit his chest, I break apart.

"I thought," I sob, "I ran from you but I—I thought—"

"Shh," he hushes, tucking me into his chest where I belong. "You feared the worst. Nikita was partially right, because she heard Dimitri's confession and order, but she assumed I was going to hurt you. I could never, Sadie." His voice breaks. "Never." He holds me until the weeping subsides, then rests his hand on my abdomen. "You're not pregnant. Please, Sadie. Tell me."

The baby.

Oh, God.

I push away from him and run into the small bedroom that's a little larger than a closet.

Our little boy sleeps soundly, wrapped in soft cotton blankets.

I lift him in my arms and take him to his daddy.

I watch Kazimir's eyes widen in wonder, my throat clogged. I swallow hard so I can tell him. "I thought I lost him," I whisper. "The day we ran, I fell. I thought he was gone, but I only bled." My voice drops. "He's fierce, like his daddy. He couldn't be held back. He came early, and fast, and within days I had him home with me. He's two months old." Born in a humble midwife's apartment, he came early and announced his entrance with a loud wail that made both me and Nikita laugh and cry. He's his father's son, and I'm filled with pride handing him to Kazimir.

Wordlessly, Kazimir stretches his arms toward the small bundle in my arms. My heart squeezes as his eyes rest on his son. I rest my head on his shoulder and put my arm around him.

"I lost everything when you left," he whispers. "And now, here in this room, I have my whole world."

Nikita does not return. Kazimir tells me that he paid her, and I know I can reach her through her mother. She's given everything to protect me and baby Karol.

"Karol," Kazimir murmurs. He hasn't put his son down once.

"It means strong," I tell him. "Manly. I wanted to name him Kazimir, but Nikita had a fit." We laugh together over this.

"There is always the next son," he says with a

twinkle in his eye. I lean down toward him, my heart swelling with pride seeing the man I love holding my son. His strong, deep voice makes my body vibrate with energy. Longing. It's been so long. So very long. I kiss him gently.

"It's a plan," I say.

I feed him the simple soup and bread I've made, and though he's used to dining in luxury, he declares it's the most delicious food he's ever had. He tells me how he left his brotherhood and that only last week, he got news that Dimitri took his own life.

"It may be safe for me to return," he says. "But I have no interest. Demyan has taken over as leader," he tells me. "And given our history, it's best I don't return. Demyan has always wanted to be the one in power. I do stay in touch with a few of them, though."

"We should go somewhere," I tell him. "Some place warm."

The sound of his deep, husky laugh thrills me. "We can do that," he says. "I don't much care where we go. I have what I need right here."

"Shhh," he whispers in my ear. "If you wake the baby, I'll spank your ass."

I grin against the gag in my mouth. He spent an

The Bratva's Baby: A Dark Mafia Romance

hour rocking the baby back to sleep, and he's finally peacefully at rest in the other room. I could have sat watching him hold Karol up to his chest for hours, though. My husband came for me. And now that we're back together, there is nothing that will pull us apart.

Other couples might revel in the slow, sweet love-making a reunion affords and soon, we will. But tonight? Tonight, I want him to take me the way only Kazimir can.

So when he ordered me out of my clothes and removed his t-shirt to gag me, I only spent a second staring at his powerful arms, the strength of his shoulders, my body humming with need at the sight of the tattoos snaking over his skin like patchwork, the way that patch of hair dips low on his hips.

I'm on my back on the tiny sofa and he towers over me. When he fastened the t-shirt behind my head, my eyes filled with tears.

"Are you hurt?" he whispered. I shook my head. No. I'm not hurt. I've longed for this so badly I can't contain my emotions.

There is no gentle lovemaking or lover's caress. There are no sweetly whispered words. There will be. But not tonight.

Now that he has me back, he has to stake his claim. Mark his territory. Let me know under no uncertain terms that I belong to him.

JANE HENRY

"When we move, we get better furniture," he growls in my ear, pulling me down off the rickety sofa that won't hold his massive body, and laying me gently on the little sheepskin rug on the floor. I giggle but soon my giggle morphs into a moan when he begins to ravish me.

His mouth on the tender skin at my neck. Kissing, licking, nipping, teasing. Fingers at my back, holding me against him. I close my eyes and let myself feel every blessed moment of this, from the moment his lips touch mine, to when he rocks his hips against my pelvis. His hoarse voice whispers prayers and curses and whatever else pours forth from him, some words I know now for Nikita has taught me. And somehow, in his native language, they mean more.

But he also speaks without uttering a word.

The way he holds my body to his with the touch of a gentle giant. The way he groans with pleasure and relief when he slides into me, united once more. The way he captures my wrists and pins them above my head, a reminder that he'll always be my master. The way he coaxes my body to bliss until I scream against the gag. The way he holds me on his chest after we've made love, panting and flushed but silent.

He weaves his fingers through mine and brings our hands to his lips. A soft, gentle kiss that says it all. We speak no words. We don't need to.

His kiss tells me I'm his treasure. His everything.

He came for me. He hunted me, captured me, and made me his, but in so doing, he lost himself to me.

We fought for this. We earned this.

And nothing will tear us apart.

Epilogue

Two years later
Sadie

Kazimir wakes with a start, sitting up in bed so suddenly, my heart thumps madly in my chest. The two of us breathe heavily in the darkened room, when a little voice calls out with a wail.

"Mama."

It's just Karol. It's been two years since our time in Russia, but old habits die hard.

I swing my legs over the side of the bed and reach for my robe, but Kazimir stops me.

"No, Sadie. I'll get him. You need your rest."

I don't argue with him. We might be eons away from where we began, but he still expects me to do what he says. It's just who he is. In his nature. And the truth is, I like it that way.

The Bratva's Baby: A Dark Mafia Romance

I slide back under the covers and feast my eyes on his beautiful, powerful body, as he walks out of our room wearing nothing but a pair of boxers. He's unchanged but for the tattoo he now bears on his bicep, our son's name in script.

I hear him shushing baby Karol and speaking to him in Russian, and close my eyes. The whispered nighttime comforts of a loving father are so foreign to me, I'm sometimes overwhelmed with the emotion it stirs in me.

He's so good with him. So damn good. I never knew he could be as patient as he is with our child, and though he can be firm, as it's just part of his nature, he loves our son more than life itself.

Karol's cries cease, and soon, Kazimir returns to our room.

"His little bear was stuck in the bars of his crib," he says, his accent thick when he's tired. "That boy's a strong one. Likely shoved him in there when he fell asleep."

I smile. "And you rescued him?"

"Of course." He lifts the covers and slides down next to me, tucking my body against his chest and wrapping his arm around me.

Sometimes he struggles in his sleep, wrestling demons he won't share with me. When he wakes, he anchors his arm around me as if I'm his lifeline. And maybe I am.

Sometimes his eyes grow haunted and pained. It

makes my heart sing to kiss his temple and hold him to me, to whisper into his ear how much I love him and watch as my gentle ministrations make the worry lines around his eyes disappear. I let him hold me and protect me, ever the old-fashioned husband. He opens doors for me and carries heavy things, makes me lock the door when he leaves, and when I go out I call him so he knows I've arrived. Some would find it overbearing. I love it.

I imagine that when I let him care for me, a small part of him heals. Just a little.

He tosses and turns in bed, and I can feel how restless he is.

We moved to the Pacific Northwest of America. It's beautiful here, but very different from his homeland. Though he misses Russia, and a little part of me does, too, we needed to start a new life. According to all legal documents, Sadie Warren went missing over a year ago. Sadie Romanov now lives with her son and husband in a humble home.

I teach reading to a group of local children at a small-town library within walking distance of our little home. Karol plays in the children's section while I teach. I draw a tiny salary that barely amounts to anything, but it's something. Kazimir took a job as a bouncer at a local night club. With his stature and presence, he's a natural fit. He does his job well, and it pays decently enough. His boss is an honest man, which means something to Kazimir. He asks no questions, and no one knows what the large, brooding Russian man did in his

The Bratva's Baby: A Dark Mafia Romance

former life. Kazimir likes that when his shift is done, he leaves his work at the door.

Kazimir has a significant sum of money put away, and we can access it easily if we need to. We both enjoy the security it affords us, but for now, the simple life appeals to us both.

When he left his brothers, Demyan surprised us both by giving him an ample severance of sorts. I didn't expect anything like that, but Kazimir feels in some way, Demyan is paying him off to never return. He wants to command his men the way he sees fit without dealing with the allegiance the other men show Kazimir. It works for me. Our little home is paid for.

Kazimir suspected he was no longer considered in good standing with his brothers, but after Dimitri's death, things changed. Though most of the men are happy to consider Kazimir long gone, Filip and Maksym both sent us little Christmas gifts for Karol, like doting, long-distance uncles. It was sweet, and I think it meant more to Kazimir than he lets on.

"Why can't you sleep, Kazimir?" My eyes are so heavy, I close them, but I wiggle my ass against his crotch. He gives me a playful spank and chuckles.

"Maybe because I have the most beautiful woman in my bed," he says. "My eyes are tired, but my cock doesn't want to rest, *krasotka*."

I reach to his crotch and palm his erection behind me. "Down, boy," I order. "I need to sleep."

325

But when his mouth comes to my neck and kisses me in that tender spot, butterflies dance in my belly. When he lifts his hand to my breast and cups it, then lets his thumb carelessly drag over my nipple, I moan and roll over on my back.

"I thought you were tired," he growls in my ear, taking my lobe between his teeth.

"I was," I whisper. "I am. If people can sleep walk, I can sleep sex."

He lifts my leg and drapes it against him, chuckling.

"Sleep sex," he tells me. "As if I've hypnotized you."

I smile at him. "Haven't you?"

"I don't see you on your knees sucking my cock, so apparently I didn't do a good job of it."

I giggle, then moan as his mouth comes to mine. I sigh, losing myself to sensation, as he eases me out of my panties and slowly, with torturously languid strokes, takes me until I'm panting my release while he groans in my ear. When we're done and clean, I yawn.

"Now, will you sleep?" I ask him.

But he's already softly dozing beside me.

Kazimir

The Bratva's Baby: A Dark Mafia Romance

. . .

When I pull up to the house, she's swinging her legs off the side of 'the porch swing. I groaned when I saw her eyes go wide at this house. It needed so much work, and I'm tired. But I saw how badly she wanted it before she ever told me, and I have to give my girl what she wants.

We worked together, though. Sanding the wooden floors, polishing the built-in shelves of the tiny room no bigger than a pantry that she calls "the library." Painting and priming, and making it ours. And now, when I come home, and see her swinging on the swing and Karol pushing trucks up the steps, my heart aches with emotion I can't name.

I love my family more than anything in the world. I don't deserve such perfect beauty in my life, and it's my mission to make amends for what I've done by devoting myself to them.

When the past haunts me, she sees it in my eyes, and soothes what plagues me with her gentle voice, her tender touch, her little arms about my neck. She hands me rope to bind her and bends to my will, begging me to paint her naked skin with my belt or mark her with my hand. There's no hiding how aroused she gets when I dominate her. But I know there's more to it than that. She knows I grapple the past when I master her body.In giving me her trust, she makes me whole.

When I get out of the car, Karol runs to me. I pick

him up and toss him high in the air, catching my boy when he squeals and laughs. Sadie gasps, but she's learned to let it go. I would never hurt him.

I right him and send him on his way to play with his trucks, then greet her with a kiss.

"I have news for you," she says. "Come. Sit with me?"

Today she went to the doctor without me since I had a meeting at work I had to attend. She said the appointment was routine, but now I wonder.

I sit on the porch swing, draw her on my lap, and rest my hand on her swollen abdomen. She smiles and pulls a little paper out of her pocket.

I blink. It's an ultrasound picture.

"The doctor wanted to be sure I was as far along as we thought," she says with a smile. "Turns out, I'm *three* months pregnant, not two. And so…" she holds the paper up. "*Look.*" Beaming at me, she whispers. "A baby girl."

A girl. I blink and swallow the lump in my throat. "A girl," I finally manage to say. "Are you sure?"

"Very."

I think about what it means to have a girl. "She'll grow up and look like you," I say, tweaking her nose. "If I'm lucky."

"Well, our boy has your eyes, so maybe my genes will win out on this one."

The Bratva's Baby: A Dark Mafia Romance

"Maybe. And if they don't, we'll try again."

She laughs out loud and lets her head fall on my chest.

"Again? I thought two was enough."

"Well," I say with a shrug. "We have five seats in our car."

Her laughter and sigh of contentment soothe me in a way nothing else does. I watch the sunset while Karol plays with his truck, a soft wind rustling Sadie's hair against my cheek. The same sun sets just as it did in Russia. Tomorrow it will rise again, dawning on a new day.

A new life. A second chance.

THE END

Island Captive preview

Chapter one

Heat rises from the sunbaked earth as I pretend to be a normal civilian who isn't seeking the blood of an escaped convict. I lift a pile of limp green vegetables in my hand at the market and raise a brow to the man standing on the other side of the table. His beady-little eyes watch me touch his wares. He's charging twice what they're worth because I'm a white woman, so fuck that. My mission's left me edgy and irritable and I don't have patience for this bullshit.

There's no way he's going to negotiate with me. And I don't need this anyway, so I'm out of here. I place the greens back down on the pile and turn on my heel. "Have a good fucking day," I mutter under my breath, ignoring the way he pleads for me to come back and negotiate, loud enough we catch the attention of a few women and children nearby who watch me with wide eyes.

I catch the eye of my partner four tables out. With his dark complexion and eyes, he blends in better than I do with my pasty white skin. I could pass for a tourist. He, however, melds with the locals perfectly. Convenient when we need to ask questions, and hell do we have questions. Carlos shoots me a chin lift, a sign that we proceed as usual and meet in our rented apartment above the marketplace. He's gotten no more information than I have. I smirk. At least he's got an armful of vegetables.

If I hadn't trained myself to never let my guard down, to never truly relax even in my sleep, I might have missed him. But I know him as soon as he comes into my peripheral vision, because I've studied him with careful, mesmerizing precision.

I've spent countless, sleepless hours memorizing every inch of this man's physical appearance before I got on a plane to hunt him down. I've tracked him now for months, putting him back behind bars my primary life focus until all I could do was hone in on finding him.

I know that silvery scar that runs along his neck better than the back of my hand. I know that that black tribal tattoo peeking out from beneath his shirt is actually a full tat that covers every inch of his broad, muscled back and wraps around the front to his torso.

I know his name is Adrian Barone, though he'll be going by another name here. I know he grew up on the wrong side of the Bronx thirty-seven years ago, the oldest of six children raised in abject poverty until his father solidified mafia connections. I know he served three years of his life sentence before he escaped. I know his eyes are so dark they're nearly black, he has scarring on his neck, back, and legs, and that he has perfect vision. His blood type is A negative, and he still has all his wisdom teeth.

Before I'm done with him, I'll know the pitch of his voice, the way he smells, and the sounds he makes when he screams.

But first I have to capture him.

I don't let on that I've seen him. There's no way he expects me here, but it's best I keep my cool until Carlos is here for back-up. If I fuck this up, I'll never forgive myself.

I try to catch Carlos' eye, but Carlos is chatting it up with a beautiful, scantily-clad native sitting on a nearby bench. I'll fucking kick his ass. He makes a move, steps closer to her and nods, encouraging for her to continue her story. His back's to me. He might be making plans to meet her tonight for all I know, since the signal a minute ago meant he effectively dismissed me. I should be up in the apartment by now.

I pull out my phone to shoot him a text, walking as quickly as I can so I don't lose our man, but not fast enough that I arouse suspicion. I have to play this safe. He's walking in the opposite direction of

Carlos, so there's no way I can grab my partner and get his attention.

I glance at my phone and watch the text stay suspended. Of course. Just when I actually need the damn thing to work, it's uncooperative. I shove my phone in my pocket and pick up my pace. Beyond the marketplace lies a cluster of buildings strewn with women and children, and soon when the men return from work, finding one person will become impossible.

I shoot one final glance in Carlos' direction. He's completely oblivious to me, the lovely little native practically sitting on his lap. Son of a bitch. I'll kick his balls when I get my hands on him.

I'm going in alone.

A small passel of children skips rope to my left. I skirt around them, but as I quicken my pace, one of them trips and goes sprawling. I yank the kid up by his armpits and steady him on his feet. "You okay?" I ask in English, nodding my head. *Yes, yes, you're okay, now get out of my fucking way.*

I practically shove the kid aside, and when I look up I see no trace of him.

Shit.

I break into a trot. I drop the fruit I bought at the stand, the sounds of the children squealing as they pick it up quickly fading. My pulse quickens, my lungs contracting as I inhale the humid air and try to run faster. I take a left at a building, then come to a screeching halt when I realize I'm at the top of a long, winding, spiral staircase that's dimly lit with one bare bulb. I catch a glimpse of him below, the light catching the silver of the scar on his neck and reflecting. He's below me now, still oblivious that he's being followed, but three staircases below the main marketplace, descending into the darkness of a staircase that leads underground.

No fucking way.

The spiral staircase ends in a courtyard ten feet or so below. Once he disappears down the cave-like stairs that lead to countless dank rooms and doorways, I'll never find him.

It takes me a split second to make my decision. With a surge of adrenaline that nearly makes me nauseous, I grasp the rail, heave myself over the edge, and jump, the screams of those who saw me drowning in the rush of air that surrounds me as I fall. I hold my arms and legs tight as I plummet, landing on my feet like a cat. Pain shoots through my heels and calves, but my mark was accurate: I'm within arm's reach of Adrian.

I use the momentary shock that registers in his eyes to my advantage and grab my taser. Just as he turns to run, I line up my target and pull the trigger. He freezes, jerks, and drops to the ground. I've trained for a full decade, and even though he outweighs me by a hundred pounds or more, I'm thin and lithe and vicious, *petite belette* my mama called me, little weasel. Even though he's on the ground and paralyzed, I kneel above him, not really caring that his head cracks on the stone hard enough to hurt but not injure.

The pictures I received in my file on Adrian arrived with the pictures of Lori Arsenault, the woman he murdered. They were vivid reminders of her mutilated, brutalized body that suffered torment before her life was taken from her. Those pictures haunted me in my sleep and followed me into the waking hours. Day and night, there was no escape from those images. The rope burns where he tied her wrists and ankles. Bruises along her thighs, back, and ass where he beat her. This is the son of a bitch who hurt her.

This man violated a woman who trusted him, brutalized her and then ended her life.

I don't always take jobs so personally, but the image of Lori Arsenault's brutalized body affected me harder than I anticipated. She came to America as a foreign exchange student. Like my mother. She hailed from Saint Paul de Vence, a little town south of Paris. My mother's hometown.

She isn't your mother, I tell myself. I mean, the girl was younger than I am. But I can't reason with the anger that fuels my need to hurt him.

This is not just a job to me.

I want to hurt him like he hurt her.

But I'm no bounty hunter. I work for the American government.

That isn't what makes me let him go, though. I

could get away with murdering him and still, even now, be lauded as a hero. But no.

Death like that would be far too merciful. He needs to suffer before he dies.

So with a twist of my arm, I let him live, but take pleasure in watching him pass out, limp on the ground beneath me. Once I'm confident he's out, I reach for the pair of cuffs I keep on me, and quickly snap them on his wrists. Heaving with the effort of the takedown, I get my phone and squint at it, needing a signal. One bar flashes, then disappears. Fuck it. I hit *dial* and breathe a sigh of relief when the crackle of a ringer sounds.

"Nadine?"

"Meet me in the courtyard, ground floor," I breathe into the phone. "I've got him cuffed and unconscious." Stunned silence. Did I lose the connection?

"Carlos?"

"I'm here. Say that again?"

I repeat my command, but this time don't bother with formalities. "Fucking *move.*"

Our prisoner hasn't said a word to me since Carlos found us and helped me haul his huge body up. It was no easy task, but between the two of us, we

The Bratva's Baby: A Dark Mafia Romance

managed to get him to the holding cell we'd prepared. The local police have several they've given us for our disposal. If we'd come to arrest a native, they'd have other things to say, but apprehending an American criminal is another story. They give us everything we need and send us on our way with reporters asking questions we wouldn't answer.

Though Adrian hasn't said anything, he doesn't need to. Carlos ran his specs and confirmed I'd apprehended the correct man. I knew I had, but you play it safe when you work for the government. So now that our criminal is safe and secured, we bring him back to the states for prosecution.

There are exactly five of us on this private jet: Me and Carlos, with Adrian between us, and the two pilots up front navigating us home.

I hate that I have to follow protocol. He's still subject to due process and shit like that, and I can't beat his ass when I bring him back. I wish I'd hurt him more when I brought him down. The bruising along his chin and forehead do little to sate my need for blood.

Here, while we're airborne, however, I'm subject to no such laws. Things happen in transport.

"We have five hours," I say calmly to Carlos.

Carlos blinks at me and raises a brow in silence.

"Five hours before we're responsible for the way

we treat this piece of shit." Our prisoner doesn't react.

"Oh?" Carlos asks.

"We arrive in America and we can't punish him." When we get to Hawaii, there's a cell and a court waiting for him.

Carlos nods sagely. "True. But the pilots could know what we've done and report us."

"For doing what? Self-defense when in mid-air would hold up in court."

"I don't know," Carlos begins. "Jesus, no wonder your mom called—""

The jet plane lurches suddenly downward in a sharp descent that makes my stomach clench. I grip the armrests so hard my knuckles turn white. I blink, getting a grip, then breathe in through my nose.

Just a little turbulence, I tell myself, but the thought barely forms in my mind before we begin to plummet. It lasts just a few seconds but enough to terrify the fuck out of me. My skin is on fire, my breathing tormented like someone has a plastic bag over my head. I open my mouth to breathe but can't. I'm dizzy, I'm going to pass out, but no, I'm way too pissed off to lose my shit like this. With a vicious swipe, I unfasten my buckle and lunge toward the cockpit.

"Nadine. Get your ass back here," Carlos growls. I shoot him a glare for daring to use my name in front of a prisoner. I don't like prisoners to know my name. He ignores my anger, though. "Sit your ass down and buckle up," he says. "We've hit turbulence."

"No shit, Einstein," I retort. For fuck's sake. Who does he think I am?

I go to open the cockpit, forgetting for a moment that it's always locked from the inside once we take off. I can't get in there if I tried. I growl and turn back to the seats, my eyes momentarily meeting our prisoner's. I've avoided eye contact with him until now but it's as if I'm drawn to him by a some magnetic pull force I can't control.

His eyes are narrowed on me, and when I look at him, he allows his gaze to roam slowly down the length of my body. I try to ignore the way it makes me feel. I hate him. I fucking hate him. He undresses me with his eyes, a lewd twist of his lips making me feel suddenly naked and exposed. He meets my gaze once more, cocks his head the side and raises his brows as if to say, "What now?"

Son of a bitch.

I won't let him fuck with me.

I spin around at the sound of the door to the cockpit opening. The pilot's eyes look at me, widened, and clears his throat. He's a short, portly guy with balding blond hair and large, watery blue eyes. "We have a rapid fuel leak," he says. "It seems the inspector missed something before we left. There's no other explanation for why we've lost fuel so rapidly."

It seems for a minute we're suspended in some sort of alternate reality. I can't quite comprehend what he's saying.

Losing fuel? We've lost fuel. *Fuck.* That means we don't get back to American soil at 3 a.m. as we'd planned.

Jesus.

"Do we have enough to get back?" I ask, knowing the answer already.

"No, officer," he says, shaking his head. "Nowhere near enough to get back to our take-off, and nowhere near enough to get to our destination. In fact, our only chances of survival are an emergency landing."

Carlos swears behind me. Our prisoner, however, begins to chuckle. He fucking *laughs.* I blink, trying to process this, and ignore his sadistic laughter, and for one ludicrous minute suspect he's done this.

I turn an accusatory glance at him, but he only laughs. There's no way. There's no fucking way he could have caused this.

"Emergency landing where?" I ask.

"We're figuring it out now," he says, turning back to the cockpit. I follow.

"*Christ,*" I swear under my breath.

The Bratva's Baby: A Dark Mafia Romance

"The nearest island is far too small and forested to land on, so our best option is to land as close to the shore as possible."

Fuck. That means we're landing *in the fucking water.* Someone's put a rubber band around my lungs, as they're suddenly constricted, and I can't get enough air. The pilots don't even notice I'm there, as they begin emergency protocol. Gerry, or whatever the blond guy's name is, grabs his remote and pushes a button.

Gerry speaks into the radio, "Oakland Oceanic, Gulf Stream 563, Emergency."

A raspy response comes on the other end. For a brief moment I'm hopeful. He reached someone. Maybe they can reach us? Then I remember we're flying over endless blue in the Pacific, and nothing short of a miracle would get anyone to us now.

A response comes in a crackly voice. "Gulf Stream 563, state nature of emergency, souls on board, fuel on board, location and intentions."

"Gulf Stream 563 is 06 33 decimal 01 north, 162 36 decimal 05 west. We have five souls on board, one hour of fuel remaining and a rapid fuel leak. We are proceeding direct 08 39 decimal 14 north, 162 32 decimal 30 west. We will attempt a water landing on the south side of the island."

I wait for the response. We all do. But nothing comes.

Did they hear us? Has anyone heard our plea

341

for help?

"Sit back down, please, officer," Gerry says.

"Did they hear you?"

His jaw tightens. "I have no idea."

For twenty minutes I sit and worry my fingers together, ignoring the stoic way our prisoner sits erect. Carlos mutters prayers in Spanish.

We don't talk. There's nothing to say. This plane is going down, and whether or not we survive is out of our control.

"Is there anything we can do to prevent injury on impact?" Carlos shouts to the cockpit but the door swings shut.

I stare at the door, my hands on my hips.

"Sit down," Carlos growls. "For fuck's sake."

"Sit down? Have you completely forgotten your head?" I ask him. I don't wait for a response as I'm making sure we all have life vests. We won't need oxygen masks unless the cabin pressure drops, but they're supposed to deploy if that happens.

"Put this on him," Carlos says, shaking it at Adrian.

I glare at him, the image of the brutalized woman coming to mind. I'm supposed to help him? But then I remember. If I don't help him, he could die. And how will I see him punished if he's dead?

The Bratva's Baby: A Dark Mafia Romance

Carlos doesn't respond, so without a word, I pull a vest over my head, stark orange that lights up the inside of the cabin of blues and blacks. It looks so flimsy, way too flimsy to save anyone's life. There's a place where I pull to inflate it, but I'm not supposed to pull that until we hit water. I hand Carlos a life vest, but can't give our prisoner his, because he's cuffed.

I lean in, and ignore the way my hands shake, and my palms grow clammy when I draw close to him. He's bigger, stronger, and more muscled than I remembered from the brief time I touched him. He's fucking huge, so big he could pick me up with one hand and snap me in two.

I'd like to see him try.

"Uncuff me," Adrian growls. It's the first time he's spoken. His voice is dark and gritty like gravel and pitch, carrying with it a scary, commanding vibe. "When we land, you'll need my assistance and if I'm the only other survivor and you can't find that key, you'll wish you had."

"Nice try."

I glare at him, bend down, and go to put his vest on, but as I do, he quickly turns his head. I jump, gasping, expecting him to bite me, and just about drop the vest when his tongue hits my wrist, lazily lapping at the tender skin. I curse, drawing back is if his mouth is fire, the wetness of his saliva on my skin making nausea roll in my stomach.

"You son of a bitch," I growl, and without

thinking about it, smack my hand straight across his cheek.

"Nadine!" Carlos reprimands, looking at me sharply. Like I give a fuck? We're crash-landing a jet with a wanted murderer. It isn't time to be politically correct.

Adrian only shoots me a lewd grin, revealing perfectly straight white teeth. I shiver involuntarily and toss the vest to Carlos.

"You lick *me*, I'll knee your nuts," Carlos mutters, turning to face Adrian. He puts the vest on, but Adrian only sits there meekly.

Son of a bitch.

The plane pitches down, and I stumble forward, smacking my head on the wall. I blink, trying to clear my star-filled vision, Carlos's voice coming from too far away as if he's in a tunnel.

"For Christ's sake, Nadine. Sit your ass down," he says. I make my way back but I'm falling, stumbling about the cabin like tumbleweed on a prairie, wild and reckless. Our prisoner's body lunges as far as he can go, as if he wants to reach out and catch me or something, but he's buckled in and cuffed, so there's no way for him to help me. I tell myself it's the fear making my brain irrational, imagining things that can't be. Finally, I fall into my seat and snap the buckle in place, craning my head to look out the tiny window. We're so close to the ocean now I can see the foamy flecks and the angry rocks below.

You're gonna die. This is it, I think to myself, closing my eyes and bracing for impact. I try to let the cadence of Carlos' jumbled prayers soothe me into a sort of acceptance of my fate, but our prisoner's lewd, raucous laugh makes it impossible.

This isn't the landing they planned. This isn't what we were supposed to do. We hit the water, the sound of wrenching metal and screams the last thing I hear before I lose all consciousness.

So much pain.

So much darkness, and so much pain. My head throbs as if I've been whacked with a baseball bat. One knee radiates pain so badly I wonder briefly if I've lost a limb. The thought makes my stomach clench, as I slowly, painfully, reluctantly regain consciousness.

My first thought is *I survived.*

The second thought is, *how badly am I hurt?*

And the third, *did anyone else make it?*

I try to open my eyes, but my lids are so heavy, it's as if they're pinned in place with super glue. I can't open them. My head throbs with a dull ache, and something warm and wet trickles down my face. The metallic smell warns me that it's blood. Mine, or someone else's?

I take stock of the pain I'm in. My head is killing,

JANE HENRY

both internally and externally. Hot pain flares along my forehead, confirming that I have a head wound, but I can breathe. I focus on taking deep, cleansing breaths, welcoming the familiar rise and fall of my chest and shoulders with the effort of breathing. This is something I can still do. I may not be able to open my eyes, or speak, or walk, but I can breathe.

It's a start.

I try to grasp the threads of memory but it's hard when my head is throbbing and thoughts saunter in and out like wisps of clouds. Wet. Something is wet. Am I? Panic floods my gut as I remember we were crash landing in water. But no, I can still breathe. If I can still breathe, then I'm either not underwater or I'm dead.

Death shouldn't be this painful, though.

Should it?

My clothes are soaked, clinging to my body like cling wrap, my head heavy with damp hair.

I have to open my eyes. I must open my eyes.

With considerable effort, I open one of them. I'm on shore, and the wreckage of the plane is about ten yards from where I'm lying. Torn metal, smoke and small licks of flames litter the beach. The sun has almost set, the horizon a dark blue, and I realize with a shock that when that sun sets, I'll be plunged into darkness.

Then what?

I push myself up to sitting, taking inventory of my wrecked body. My left leg feels miraculously fine, but pain radiates near my knee on my right leg, and I realize there's something sticking out of my leg. It's a piece of metal, like shrapnel, wedged into my leg below my knee. If it's deep enough and I pull it, I could bleed out. Then what? Is anyone else here? With my stomach clenched in nausea and shaking hands, I reach for the metal that's torn right through my pants, crimson blood staining the torn fabric. A dry sob catches in my throat. I have to get to safety.

Is there safety here?

That's when my gaze falls on the unthinkable. It takes me a minute to make sense of what I'm seeing.

Plane wreckage isn't covered in blood-soaked fabric.

A body ripped asunder in the crash is strewn on the sandy beach in front of me, arms and limbs torn brutally apart as if ripped by cruel hands. I roll to my side and retch onto the ground, emptying the contents of my stomach until nothing but bile remains. I swipe the back of my hand across my mouth and fall to my back, wrecked. I can't look again. I recognized white, though, which means that body was a pilot's, and not Carlos or Adrian. Carlos was wearing regulation navy and Adrian in the clothes we found him in.

Something else caught my attention, though. I need to see again, so I open my eyes and look to the sandy beach, pretending the body parts washed on shore are part of the beach. I can't look again.

Out in front of me, stretching all the way to the waves crashing on the shore, lies a path where my body was dragged. I didn't land here, where I am now. Someone found me and hauled me out of the water while I was still unconscious, so I wouldn't drown. That would explain my soaking wet clothes and the fact that I'm here, on dry land, and breathing.

Someone else survived, then, or there are natives in hiding. Where did they go? Did they have to leave me here so they could rescue the others?

I push myself up to sitting again, ignoring the pain that flares in my leg, and scan the coast with gritted teeth. The task ahead of me makes nausea swirl in my recently emptied stomach.

I need to identify bodies. I need to know who I'm here with. I didn't become who I am by nursing my wounds and hiding in fear.

I push myself to my feet, but the pain in my leg is unbearable. I look down. The piece of metal sticking out is smaller than I thought at first, but it has to come out. When I pull it out, I'll bleed, which should cleanse the wound, but if I make a tourniquet, or even a bandage tight enough, I could staunch the flow of blood. I quickly undo the buttons on my top, take it off, and wrap it around my leg to form a loose loop above the wound. I'll leave it there to grab when the time comes. My hands shaking so hard I almost lose my balance, I grab the piece of metal and pull. My screams echo in my ears, the pain so intense my vision blurs. I throw the blood-soaked metal away, then quickly wrap my leg in the shirt. I watch as the bleeding slows. Temporarily I'm okay, but I won't be able to bear much weight on it. I'll need to rest it to heal.

In the dim light of the fading sun, I scan the coast.

Then my eyes fall on navy.

Carlos.

I whimper and drag my hand across my eyes, wanting to push this vision away. How do soldiers at battle deal with sudden, violent loss and devastation?

Get up, I tell myself. *See if you can help him.*

His legs lie at odd angles, broken beyond repair, white bone shining clear through one stretch of torn fabric. I kneel beside him, lifting his limp body in my arms. His eyes are open, staring vacantly to a place beyond. I know he's dead, but I need to prove it to myself. Gently, I place his body back on the sand where it falls with a soft thump, then pick up his arm and place my fingers where his pulse ought to be, where lifeblood should be flowing through his veins. No pulse. I turn away, the confirmation my partner's gone making sudden tears spring to my eyes.

But I don't cry. And I won't now.

I close my eyes tightly and give myself a moment to deal with the pain of loss, before I stand and look across the sandy beach once more. I don't have time to spare.

The plane lies in a heap of twisted metal on the shore, half in the water. I can see how one wing is completely blown away, and reason the wingtip must've hit a wave or rock, causing us to impact the water harder than we were supposed to. That wasn't the landing our pilots had planned. Ignoring the waves of pain that make me want to vomit, I stumble on unsteady feet toward the plane. And then I see it. One final body slumped against the window in the cockpit filled with water. Dead on impact? Drowned, pinned in the cockpit? I'll never know.

I fall to my knees as the memory of the pilot's last words come back to me.

We have five souls on board.

Including myself, the two dead bodies of the pilot and Carlos, I now have four.

I still haven't found our prisoner.

READ MORE

About the Author

USA Today bestselling author Jane Henry pens stern but loving alpha heroes, feisty heroines, and emotion-driven happily-ever-afters. She writes what she loves to read: kink with a tender touch. Jane is a hopeless romantic who lives on the East Coast with a houseful of children and her very own Prince Charming.

What to read next? Here are some other titles by Jane you may enjoy.

Want to be notified when I have a new release? Get access to free books, giveaways, and exclusive content? Sign up to my newsletter!

Contemporary fiction

Dark romance

Island Captive: A Dark Romance

Criminal by Jane Henry and Loki Renard

Hard Time by Jane Henry and Loki Renard

NYC Doms stand-alones

Deliverance

Safeguard

Conviction

mybook.to/NYCDoms

Masters of Manhattan

Knave

Hustler

The Billionaire Daddies

Beauty's Daddy: A Beauty and the Beast Adult Fairy Tale

Mafia Daddy: A Cinderella Adult Fairy Tale

Dungeon Daddy: A Rapunzel Adult Fairy Tale

The Billionaire Daddies boxset

The Boston Doms

My Dom (Boston Doms Book 1)

His Submissive (Boston Doms Book 2)

Her Protector (Boston Doms Book 3)

His Babygirl (Boston Doms Book 4)

His Lady (Boston Doms Book 5)

Her Hero (Boston Doms Book 6)

My Redemption (Boston Doms Book 7)

And more! Check out my Amazon author page.

Stay in touch!

The Club (reader group on FB)

Jane Henry Romance

Made in the USA
Columbia, SC
15 November 2019

83424934R00196